Siberian Lessons on Life, Love and Death

Hans Wissema

Siberian Lessons on Life, Love and Death

Uitgeverij Aspekt

Siberian Lessons on Live, Love and Death
© Hans Wissema
© 2013 Uitgeverij ASPEKT
Amersfoortsestraat 27, 3769 AD Soesterberg, Nederland
info@uitgeverijaspekt.nl – http://www.uitgeverijaspekt.nl
Omslagontwerp: Mark Heuveling
Photograph for the cover page by Feyona van der Molen Photography, Amsterdam
Binnenwerk: Paul Timmerman, Amersfoort

ISBN: 978-94-6153-358-6
NUR: 730

All rights reserved. No reproduction copy or transmission of this publication may be made without written permission.

To Alex

In memoriam Jan Willem Wissema (1969-2001)

Contents

Introduction	11
Basics	17
1. Moscow – On the way	19
2. Vladimir – Happiness	23
3. Vladimir – The Inner Guide	27
The outer cylinder	27
The inner cylinder and the talent of love	28
How talents are prioritised	28
The middle cylinder	29
4. Vladimir – Barriers to development	33
Overcoming inhibitions and false ambitions	33
Generation transfer	36
Projection	38
Problems of the outer cylinder	39
Problems of the inner cylinder	41
5. Nizhny Novgorod – Know yourself	45
Introspection	47
Listening to weak signals	48
The subconscious	49
Reason and emotion	51
The will	52
6. Kirov – Personality archetypes	55
The dimensions of the archetypes	56
The pioneer	56
The conqueror	57

The balanced ruler	57
The administrator	58
The defender	58
Archetypes and relationships	59

7. Perm – The stages of life ... 63
    Birth ... 66
    The apprentice stage ... 66
    The stage of opportunity ... 67
    The production stage ... 69
    The stage of recycling ... 71
    The stage of digestion ... 71
    Our host and I ... 73

8. Perm – Matrioshka ... 79
    Parallel stages ... 80
    The circle of confidence ... 81

Love ... 83

9. Yekatarinburg – Universal love ... 85
    Forms of love ... 89
    The meaning of love ... 90
    Hate ... 93

10. Yekatarinburg – Friendship ... 95
    Deep friendship ... 95
    Acquaintances ... 96
    Sex ... 98
    Friendship between men and women ... 98
    Brotherly love ... 100
    The girl and I ... 100

11. Verkhoturye – Total love ... 103
    Phase of total immersion ... 104
    Development phase ... 105
    Mature phase ... 106
    Young love and intimacy ... 107
    Unbalanced growth ... 109
    The school of love ... 110

12. Verkhoturye – Enduring love — 111
Four dimensions — 111
Homosexual love — 113

13. Tyumen – Partial love — 117
A second love — 119
Impossible love — 123
Sin — 124

Life — 127

14. Omsk – Family life — 129
Bringing up a child — 131
The larger family and the basic human deficit — 133
Growing up in a family — 134

15. Novosibirsk – Professional life — 137
Finding physical security — 139
Social skills — 139
Professional development — 140
Building the cathedral — 141
Leadership — 142
Choosing a profession — 142
Shared interest – the dimension of enduring love — 143

16. Krasnoyarsk – Cultural life — 145
Three levels of art — 146
The aesthetic level — 146
The emotional level — 147
The religious level — 148
Art and the three cylinders — 152

17. Yeniseysk – Religious life — 153
Mysticism — 154
The early Christians and the rising dogmatism — 156
Gnosticism – the first movement — 157
Constantine and the establishment of the Church – the counter movement — 158
Rituals and sacraments — 160
Baptism — 161

Consolation	162
Following Jesus	163
The Bible	164
Jesus	164

Death — 167

18. Irkutsk – Fear, impasse, depression — 169
The abbot and the Church — 169
Fear — 173
Impasse — 175
Depression and suicide — 176

19. Chita – The meaning of life — 179
Material and spiritual development — 180
Memento mori — 181
God — 182

20. Khabarovsk – Death of a loved one — 187
Sin and death — 191
Guilt — 192
Resurrection and ascension — 193
After parting — 194

21. Vladivostok – Your own death and the balance of life — 197
The nature of death — 199
How to prepare your legacy — 200
The moment of your own death — 200
How to prepare yourself – the balance of life — 202
Bidding farewell — 203

Epilogue and the School of Love — 205

Itinerary and prayers — 211

Notes — 213

Introduction

It was near Novosibirsk, in the boundless wilderness of the Siberian plains, that I met Yevgeni Nikolayevich Rostov, abbot of one of those Russian monasteries that over the centuries have been guardians of Christian culture. His cloister was located in the middle of endless birch tree forests, far away from the city with which it was linked by a small, winding road, icy in the severe Siberian winters, dusty in the intemperate summers, muddy in the rainy seasons in-between. Although it was well-known, the monastery was so isolated that only few people knew the way. They rather found it on the Internet when seeking answers to poignant questions about life, love and death. Naturally, like many others, I had heard of the abbot but had it not been for a colleague at the university, where I was working temporarily, I would never have met him.

I felt deeply honoured to meet this famous and high-ranking priest of the Russian Orthodox Church. I was happy he would receive me and we would have a chance to talk although I was not sure about what. I am not religious but what I had read about him had convinced me that he had to be a most interesting person.

It was already getting dark when I was led to his office where I was told to wait. He came in almost immediately and showed me to a seat. He would have been my father's age, hardly wrinkled and wearing gold-rimmed glasses, looking over them with warm, inquisitive eyes. A monk came in and asked what we wanted to drink. I chose tea and so did he. 'One could call it our national beverage', he said, 'At least we have that much in common with you Brits' and he laughed at his own joke. 'Actually we also enjoy a glass of vodka', I offered. 'Well, I am not very Russian in that respect', he said, 'The Church provides me with enough spirit', and he laughed again. I did not know how to react so I expressed my surprise he had agreed to see me. Instead of offering an explanation he responded with a question. 'I was going to ask you the same thing. What brought you to Siberia in the first place?'

I told him that I studied theoretical physics in Cambridge, UK, that I had just completed my PhD and that I was now working at CERN in Geneva. While the Large Hadron Collider was being reconstructed, I was offered a temporary job on the magnetic spectrometer of the University of Novosibirsk to gain some experience with this new technology.

'Well, besides, I guess I wanted to travel. I have always been intrigued by Siberia. Imagine the Trans Siberia Express and all the different cities it calls at'.

He nodded, pensive, but did not say anything.

'As a matter of fact, I also wanted to practice my Russian', I added.

'Now that you mention it', he reacted, 'your Russian is excellent. How did you learn it?'

I told him that ever since I read *Dr Zhivago* I had always been intrigued by Russia, especially its vastness, that has so much influence on its culture, more than anything else. When I noticed there were courses in Russian at the university where I did my PhD, I took my chance to learn the language as a diversion from my research. I started to explain how large-scale accelerators work, but he waved me away:

'Listen, I am just a simple chemical engineer and all this is too complex for me. But why did you study Russian as a diversion, didn't you want to go out, have fun, meet girls?'

I was a little surprised by this worldly comment. I didn't want to tell him the sad stories of my encounters with women and that I never seemed to understand them, so I said that ever since my student years mathematics and a well-structured language like Russian had been much more comprehensible to me. Although I did not mention Clara, certain sadness overtook me. He noticed it and I saw he wanted to explore the subject further but, on the other hand, he didn't want to push it and asked instead:

'In addition to being intelligent, you must be pretty well organised to do your PhD and learn Russian in such a short period of time'.

'I guess I am', I answered, 'I was very motivated. To tell you the truth, I am just as proud to be able to read Tolstoy and Dostoyevsky in the original as I am of my cum laude degree in physics. Russian is such a beautiful language'.

Again, he nodded absent-mindedly, his thoughts being elsewhere. Was he checking me out? I gathered my courage and asked him how a chemical engineer like him had ended up in a monastery. It turned out that after completing his studies he got a job at an international company, visited many countries and was completely absorbed in his work until he met his wife.

'It was a happy marriage', he said, 'The sad thing was, it ended prematurely. My wife delivered a stillborn child, a boy. It was a difficult birth and then, there were complications. She outlived the baby by only a few days. It was a nightmare, we were ready to welcome the child and then, having just turned forty, I lost everything. I gave up my profession and gradually found consolation in religion. After some years of travelling and wandering around, I decided to become a monk, which I have now been for over thirty years. Later, I was ordained as a priest and still later the Patriarch made me abbot of this monastery. I love the monastery, it is a sanctuary for me and my office provides a good platform for helping people and conveying my views'.

I did not know what to say and took a sip from my bottle of water.

'Steve, you are an alcoholic', he exclaimed.

'No, father, this is just water', I hastened to say.

'Ha! That's what I always tell my monks', he laughed.

The afternoon passed quickly and the abbot urged me to join him for dinner. In the refectory we sat at a separate table and continued our conversation. It went smoothly in spite of all our differences, it was as if we had known each other for years.

Despite his advancing age, Yevgeni Nikolayevich impressed me as a powerful, yet tolerant man. He was not one of those Church prelates who just preserved ancient traditions and beliefs. Rather, he sought to find answers to contemporary issues in which he was led more by the original messages of Jesus than the elaborate works of the Church fathers. This had often brought him into conflict with the Church leaders, but as monasteries are relatively independent and he himself was widely popular throughout the country, nobody dared challenge his position. He only mentioned it casually. For all I knew, the Church did not exactly welcome divergent opinions, but it did not seem to bother him so I paid no further attention to it.

We continued talking, he served excellent wine. He confided his worries about his country and indeed, the world, the confusion on what is right and wrong. As a good shepherd, he tried to bring light by providing insights and answered to those who sought his advice, but he felt this was too incidental and he should do more.

'The clichés don't work anymore. It seems that the traditional reference points that people could use as an anchor have evaporated', he said.

The clichés, did he hint at the teachings of the Church?

The problem was not resolved, we went to bed, rose early and after Prime we shared a quiet breakfast. Then I left.

The first snow was already falling when he called me, a few months later, to invite me to the monastery again. The four by four was ploughing through the mud – at one point the car got stuck and we had to use the winch to pull it out – but once I was there, I was again taken in by the warm atmosphere and we continued our talks where we had left off. He was deeply troubled by the general uncertainty about fundamental issues of life and he told me he considered travelling by train from Moscow to Vladivostok, calling on the major cities, to deliver sermons for those who would desire to hear him. This sounded like a good idea but I was worried about his age, could he make it all right? He waved my concern away, after all, at seventy a person is hardly old and at the same time wise enough not to take unnecessary risks.

It was a fascinating plan although it was quite an enterprise. He started discussing the itinerary, with maps and timetables of the Trans Siberian Express on the table. I got quite excited and it suddenly occurred to me:
'Instead of giving sermons prepared in advance, wouldn't it be better to answer questions from the congregation? That way, your Lessons will be more spontaneous and more in tune with the needs of your audience'.
'H'm', he pondered, 'You have a point but I don't want to say the same things over and over again'.
'Then why don't you have it broadcast. Thus people can hear the previous Lessons and come up with new questions. You could also upload the texts on the Internet, and reach out even further'.
'Yes, but then someone has to come with me to take notes and make a transcript of the sermons on a computer', he reacted. 'And I don't think any of my monks would be up to the task'.
Then, looking at me, he continued:
'Actually, why don't *you* come with me? It would be good for a person with your background to hear something about the real issues of this world. You could write out the texts, post them on the Internet and you could organise the publicity'.

Well, that was quite something. Ever since I went to Novosibirsk, I had wanted to see more of Siberia and a trip on the legendary train, with the longest track in the world, was quite tempting. I started to raise objections, I did not know the first thing about religion, I was not familiar with the Russian media, others would do a far better job, etcetera, but he had already made up his mind:

'No, Stephen, we have a lot in common and I feel we could very well work together. We shall start in the spring when the snow begins to melt. I will let you know where and when'.

Although I was thrilled, I had to think about it. It had become pitch-dark in the monastery – the abbot's room was only lit up by a candle. I looked around and saw he had a skull as well as a sandglass on his table. It reminded me that time was passing and that I should take this opportunity as there would never be another. There was some bread left and with it some salt – the abbot was a modest man. Away from his desk was a lectern and on it a book, obviously the Bible. I brought the candle to take a closer look and saw it was open on the first chapter of St John's gospel.

'I always leave it open at the first chapter of St John', the abbot said, serious now. 'It tells us there is always light even when you don't see it and that darkness cannot extinguish it. There is always hope'.

Sudden warmth engulfed me and I did not know what to say. Then I thought that if we could leave in the spring when it would still be dark, it would get lighter during our trip and we would arrive in Vladivostok before the heat of the summer.

And so we did. We took to the road. The abbot answered questions in sessions that were often penetrating, I took notes on my laptop and we discussed them in the train, heading for the next stop. Eventually, the Lessons were published on the monastery's web site and now they come to you in print.

Moscow, summer 2011,

Stephen Winderoy

BASICS

1. Moscow – On the way

In Moscow, the bell tower of the cathedral of the Andronikov Monastery, the oldest building in the city, rose up against the blue April sky when I rode up the escalator out of the Iljitsa Square metro station. I was told that the abbot was studying the frescos of Andrei Rublev, the famous painter, or rather, what was left of them. 'Look, Steve', the abbot said, when I found him at last. 'It makes you think. Once these murals were the most beautiful in our part of the world and now there is hardly anything left. *Sic transit gloria mundi* – thus passes the glory of the world'. I couldn't help thinking of the skull and sandglass in the abbot's office and shivers went down my spine. We walked to the river Yauza, then turned back, walking past the monastery towers and along the walls that were once built to protect the Kremlin from the hordes invading from the East. Now we have to defend our culture from other enemies: intolerance, ignorance, superstition, absence of values. Suddenly it was time to go.

We boarded the motorcade that was to bring us to the Yaroslavska railway station taking the main route via Zemlyanoy Val and Kalanchevskaya and Krasnoprud Streets to Komsomolskaya Square. At the station, there was quite a crowd and the major radio networks were all there – my telephone calls had worked! It was obvious that the abbot should make a statement. This is what he had to say:

'Every day I am confronted with much confusion: parents who do not understand their children, couples who do not understand each other, students who do not understand themselves. Some have lost a loved one and wonder what happened to him, others expect a child but are not sure how to raise it, old people who are satiated with life and want to step out but don't know how and whether they may.

Our world is rapidly modernising, changing from simple, traditional structures to complex and confusing ones. Some people seek security in dogmas and in trying to revive an ancient world, seemingly well structured. This, however, is an illusion that only leads to intolerance, violence, terrorism. Others surrender to consumerism, which may give quick satisfaction but does not alleviate the emptiness. Still others try to be in peace with themselves and seek advice.

I myself live extremely frugally amidst rich and varied nature. For many decades I have studied the old books and traditions, contemplating the lives of Jesus and the saints, at the same time answering questions about life, love and death from those who sought and seek my advice or just my ear and whom I call my pupils. These pupils I have tried to help as a remote and modest follower of our Lord, contemplating with my brothers how I should listen and teach, learning from their reactions. Do not expect me to preach the way you have heard priests do. I want to help people, in direct ways and simple words, by divorcing Jesus' humanistic message from the deadweight put on by our Church'.

There was some movement in the crowd when the abbot mentioned the 'deadweight of the Church' but order was soon restored and the abbot continued:

'I am a practical man. I was trained as an engineer and I worked as such for several decades, living a full life as a scientist, friend, councillor. Then I followed my calling, became a monk, later a priest, still later an abbot. Like Freud, I am a student of my own life. I took many initiatives that brought me into different worlds and it is my nature to contemplate what I experience. Much of what I saw defied logic and created strong emotions in me. In order to live in peace with the world and myself I was inspired to reconsider my experiences, let my logic penetrate my emotions, then summarise the fruits of my reflections into models and theories. These have become my Lessons and I hope to talk about them on this trip. I offer no ready-made solutions but I try to give insights, hoping these will be 'good fruits' that give my pupils new directions to explore'.

The abbot had hardly finished as one of the reporters nearly stuck a microphone into his mouth, asking:
    'Father Yevgeni, could you say something about the core of your Teachings, the central truths?'
    The abbot's face took a pensive expression, then it cleared up as he answered:
    'Over the years, I have learned that living consciously is a precondition for happiness and fulfilment. And in my opinion it is based on some simple principles.
        Know yourself, contemplate your life, let the rational part of you access the emotional part. *It is you who it comes down to,* who is responsible for your

life and it is you who will be the ultimate judge of it. Do not blame others for what goes wrong in your life, even if people are destructive. It is you who has to resolve every situation, taking new directions when needed. In doing so you fulfil the main objective of your life: *to become who you are.*
In all your dealings, consider the position of the other. Live your life consciously. Give and receive love because that is what life is all about.
Respect your origin – which also is your destination. Be ready and saturated with life when you have to go'.

The abbot's three commandments, I thought. The reporters wanted to ask more questions but the train was already half an hour late. I cleared my throat discretely and when the abbot looked my way, I pointed at my watch. The abbot understood and started making his way through the crowd, taking his time to bless the gathering. Finally, we settled down in our compartment and as the enormous train was gaining speed, he said: 'At last we are off. Let us see what this journey brings. Steve, be nice and ask the provodnitsa (lady guard) to bring us a samovar and tea'.

When the guard entered our compartment the abbot got up to greet her. This embarrassed her and – blushing – she crossed herself. He thanked her and after she had left, I asked him why he got up. 'It is always good to be courteous', he said, 'and we should honour those who take care of us'.

I wondered whether I could ask him another question, then plucked up my courage:

'When you said that you divorce Jesus' humanistic message from the deadweight of the Church, what did you mean?'

The abbot made himself comfortable which gave him time to contemplate the answer.

'As early as the first century, there has been controversy in the Christian world about what should come first: conscience or doctrine. The Church maintains that the doctrine is always to be followed and has prosecuted those who deviated: the Gnostics, the Cathari, the Bogomils of Bulgaria, the Lutherans, Calvinists, Mennonites and so many others. I want to stay loyal to the Church because it has done much good but sometimes I have my doubts'.

'Of course we should follow the doctrine', I reacted. 'What is the Church for, otherwise?'

'It is not as simple as that. When Jesus said: 'Whoever is without sins, let him cast the first stone', he followed conscience and neglected the doctrine. That is why I call him the first humanist'.

'What do you think yourself?' I wondered.

'I don't know, it's a tricky subject. As a servant of the Church I have to follow the doctrine but it often brings me into conflict with myself'.

I decided to change the subject. 'When you said events caused strong emotions in you, what did you mean? Or is that too personal a question?'

'Not at all, go ahead, ask me anything, that's what I am here for. Well, I hear many stories from members of our congregation and also from people who send me e-mails. I try to step into their shoes and understand them. This can be very emotional. But also small things, like a sunrise over our wilderness, can evoke strong emotions'.

I did not quite understand what he was talking about.

'I don't have that', I said. 'And I hope this will never happen to me. I prefer to work on my computer and solve problems in physics'.

'Come on Stephen, you have more emotions than you think', the abbot replied mysteriously, and I could see he now wanted to take a rest. We finished our tea and took a nap before we approached the next station.

2. Vladimir – Happiness

It took the train only three hours to get to Vladimir, the first stop. Vladimir is an old, now very much industrial city, founded by and named after the revered Knyaz (Count) Vladimir who brought Christianity to large parts of Russia. There was an unexpected April drizzle, which was more a problem for me than for the abbot who was protected by his thick woollen habit. I wondered whether the abbot was bringing a new version of Christianity to the Russians, following in the footsteps of Knyaz Vladimir, but I discarded the thought as rather pretentious.

The trip had been widely announced in the media – I had taken care that the radio reporters would install their equipment in order to have also this Lesson broadcast – and there was a crowd waiting for the abbot. He wanted to address the gathering but our host, the elderly abbot of the Bogoroditze-Rozhdestvenski Monastery (Monastery of the Nativity), took him immediately to his car saying that lunch was waiting and there was no time to lose. We drove down Bolshaya Nizhnegorodskaya (Broad Lower Town Street) to Bogolyubovo, a suburb of Vladimir, which took not more than ten minutes as the monk at the wheel clearly enjoyed speeding. At the entrance there were more people but the host-abbot had no respite ('People have to wait their turn') and before we knew, we were in the refectory where an excellent meal was served. I saw that our abbot was irritated by our host's assertiveness. He felt obviously sorry for all those who had been waiting all this time in the rain. After lunch, Yevgeni Nikolayevitsch asked to be brought to the grave of Alexander Nevski, the legendary warrior who fought the Swedes in 1242. We descended to the river Klyazma and, after having prayed at the grave, the abbot paid tribute to the hero's icon which accompanied him in his battles and that he later donated to the monastery.

'Remember Alexander Nevski', the abbot said. 'He is the founder of Russia and he has become a symbol of all that is Russian'.

'Are your Teachings Russian?' I took the courage to ask.

'They are Christian through and through yet I dare hope they are truly universal', he responded.

We returned to the monastery with its beautiful blue domes and were surprised to see that the refectory was turned into a meeting hall seating a large number of people. 'You see', the host smiled, 'It has all been planned'. Apparently, he liked to do things his way but the abbot looked at me with a disapproving twinkle in his eye, he did not say anything however. There was hardly time for that as the host-abbot had already started introducing Yevgeni Nikolayevitsch and inviting questions. After an initial silence and some hesitation, an old man got up. He was bold with a thin beard and he had a wrinkled face with deep-lying eyes. He had to clear his throat several times before he could speak:

'Father Rostov, perhaps I may turn to you about the following. During my life, I have known periods of happiness and sadness. My childhood was tough with my parents beating me up frequently. Still, I have happy memories of that period. Later on, when times were better, I felt less happy. It seems there is no correlation between happy circumstances and one feeling happy. This makes me very uncertain as I do not know what I should do to feel good'.

The abbot responded as if he had been waiting for this question, it probably had been asked before. Turning to the old man, he said:

'Let us first discuss happiness. Happiness has two parents. Security is the mother of happiness. Knowing that you have enough food on the table and a roof over your head gives you some security and this makes you happy. This is why everybody likes to have a home and enjoys returning to it. Security has a material side but there is also an emotional side to it, a side of love. In love we feel secure, without it – we do not, even if we have all the money in the world.

If security is the mother of happiness, the possibility to develop our talents is its father. At birth, the good Lord gives each of us talents, some many, others only a few. You can have artistic or intellectual talents, talents in sport or rhetoric, visionary or religious talents and many others. These talents want to be developed, they are crying out for it. They compete with each other, they all demand attention just as children do when the mother comes home after work. Developing our talents gives us great joy and deep satisfaction, independent of how successful we are in the eyes of the world. On the other hand, if for some reason we are unable to develop our talents, we shall never be happy, even if we have all the security we need'.

The old man got up again and said, collecting his thoughts as he was formulating his question:

'So what you say is that happiness is security plus development'.

He paused. The abbot nodded approvingly which made him go on:

'How do I know what to do at a certain moment if I want to be happy, should I work on security or development? And if on development, which talent to choose?'

The abbot prepared to answer but before he could do so, a young woman got up and asked:

'I work at the university but my career does not make much headway. My husband wants me to stay at home and take care of our little daughter. Recently, a young professor was appointed to the university and we were immediately attracted to each other. He offered me all kinds of assistance to put my career in higher gear and although that is tempting, I do not want to jeopardise my marriage. I just want a simple life'.

She was very charming and a strange feeling overtook me. The abbot looked sideways and noticed my confusion, but he could not talk to me, as he had to answer her:

'Yours is a problem of choice between security and development. You are afraid to lose your security by getting into conflict with your husband if you decide to spend more time at your work. On the other hand, meeting this young professor awoke your desire to develop. Perhaps your husband does not realise how important your work is for you and you should have a stiff talk with him. You will find this difficult to do but it might clear the air, just as the sky becomes crisp after a thunderstorm'.

Addressing the old man and the audience in general, the abbot continued:

'During the course of our life, the emphasis shifts between developing security and talents. At certain stages we feel that we must develop ourselves, even if it means we have no time to eat or sleep. Look at the lives of some of our great writers and composers who were deeply into development, not caring about even the most basic forms of security. At other stages we feel we just have to extend our base of security, perhaps by doing work that is not necessarily interesting but brings in a good income. Now, to answer your question: you don't need to decide which side to work on, you just follow your Inner Guide. This guide will also tell you which talent should come to the fore at a certain stage. But you must try to understand what your Inner Guide is saying and why'.

Now lots of people got up and raised their hands. Many were asking about the Inner Guide. Others were saying that the abbot actually made a stand against Maslow's theory of the hierarchy of needs – to which the abbot agreed. It all became rather messy and we had to rush out to attend Vespers. The abbot promised to resume after the prayers and that concluded the meeting.

While we were walking out, the abbot asked me:
'Were you attracted to that young lecturer, Steve?'
Now I was even more confused, she had reminded me of Clara.
'I guess I was', I reacted, and quickly added, 'but only for an instant'.
The abbot could not hide a smile.
'She is not your type, Steve. Someone who wants a 'simple life' is not for you. But you will always be attracted to this kind of woman. Never give in'.

3. Vladimir – The Inner Guide

After Vespers, there were a couple of hours left before dinner. On the way to and from the Chapel we heard a muffled but lively discussion about the Inner Guide. Some older and serious-looking men were arguing that: 'Your soul always knows what is best for you'. Some others even invented an Outer Guide, representing the circumstances we live in, saying this was more important than the Inner Guide as people's choices depend on what the world around them has to offer.

The abbot watched them smilingly. To end the confusion he took the floor, saying:

'Let me tell you how I look at people. You can regard a person as comprised of three concentric cylinders: an outer, inner and middle cylinder. Together they form the Inner Guide. The Inner Guide is, therefore, a complex system and that is why we often don't understand what it is trying to tell us. Allow me to explain the cylinders to you'.

The outer cylinder

After sipping some water that was put in front of him, the abbot continued:

'The outer cylinder is our interface with the world. It is like a hull around our more private self, it stands between our inner self and the world around us. The outer cylinder filters the information we receive from our environment. Only a small part will go to the conscious part of our brain and the rest will go elsewhere. For instance, we see a dreadful event which is too much for us to handle. We ignore or suppress the images and, later, we cannot remember the event, it has been stored in our subconscious.

The outer cylinder also shields our inner self from prying eyes, others only see our hull, our appearance, not our inner self. We can manipulate our appearance to a certain extent, which allows us to adjust the way in which other people perceive us. The gentlemen in the back, for instance, look quite respectful but they might look different on a summer wedding party'.

The group of women split their sides with laughter at this comment. The men just smiled, a bit dryly.

'Sometimes you can take a glimpse through someone's outer cylinder, when that person makes a Freudian slip, a spontaneous utterance, often out of place, that reveals something she really means. Or her body or facial expression betray her true intentions'.

Now it was the men who had a good laugh. The women did not say anything but their body language spoke volumes!

The inner cylinder and the talent of love
When calm returned, the abbot continued:
'Let us now look at our inner cylinder, our treasury, our soul. It houses our talents, positive and negative – as we can also have destructive talents. Each human being is unique in the sense that at conception the good Lord gives him a number of talents, each with specific intensity. 'Talent' is to be understood as not only intellectual, artistic and physical talents, like sports, but also emotional, social and religious talents. The gift to see into the other world is a talent and so is our intuition. Many fairy tales describe how witches or spirits bestow positive or negative talents on a newborn baby: a capacity, a curse, love, hate.

The most important talent is the talent to love and to be loved. The talent to love and the talent to be loved go hand in hand – you can only absorb love if you can give it and if you can't give love, you can receive only attention, not love proper.

Talents can be strong or weak. This applies to the central talent, the talent to love and to be loved, as well as the other talents'.

How talents are prioritised
By now, the audience was as confused as it was intrigued and since no one raised their hand, the abbot went on:
'The purpose of our life is to develop our talents – in doing so we serve God. We have no choice here: the talents demand to be developed and we have to follow their call. Now only a few talents can be developed simultaneously and the question is: which comes first and which comes next? In your own life you will have observed that at some point you become obsessed with a certain subject, sports for instance. Some time later you lose interest and you develop another talent. Or you become so totally absorbed in a love relationship that

you skip your music lessons. In these cases the first talent has been satiated for the time being, making space for another. Or, alternatively, another talent becomes so anxious to be developed that it pushes the first one aside.

Certain talents re-enter our lives several times, others make only one appearance. The talent to love and to be loved is always present – with varying intensity – as it is our central talent'.

I observed that a mood of peacefulness descended over the audience when the Lesson turned to love and I wondered why. I tried to find examples. Wasn't Jesus talking about love when he gathered huge audiences? I did not remember exactly but then it occurred to me that whenever there were large audiences, at rock concerts for instance, the subject would always be love. Could this be taken as confirmation of the abbot's thesis that love is our central talent, one that everyone develops all the time, more or less?

The middle cylinder
As I was nurturing this thought a stout women got up:
'Father, I like the way you speak about love. Perhaps we should be pursuing this talent more intensively but there are so many other things to do. How could we possibly put love at the top of the agenda?'

The abbot did not have to think about this:
'The order in which and the intensity with which we develop our talents depends on two things: the strength of the talents in the inner cylinder and the opportunities in the world around us. So, a match has to be made and this is where the middle cylinder comes in. Sandwiched between our most sacred self and our interface with the outside world, this layer sets the priorities for our development. It matches the urgencies of talent development as manifested in the inner cylinder with the external opportunities as perceived by the outer one'.

The woman responded immediately. It turned out she had an agile mind:
'That would mean, father, that we always take perfect decisions. Speaking for myself, I must admit that I often make the wrong choice'.

Her friends started laughing again, perhaps they knew something we did not. But the abbot was unperturbed:
'So do I! The thing is, the middle cylinder is not just an objective traffic policeman. It also plays its own game as it may harbour false ambitions and emotional inhibitions'.

The abbot noticed that the audience was rather puzzled by this statement and, realising the need to give an explanation, he went on:

'Let us first look at the false ambitions. In general, there is nothing wrong with ambitions. The fact that our talents want to be developed is just another expression for 'ambition', but we can easily be misguided. False ambitions can make us desire achievements that do not correspond to our talents: we want to be like this, we want to achieve that, we want to be better than so and so. False ambitions arise from identification, ego and pride. Ego and pride can be powerful forces for the good but they can also be bad advisors. When people pursue false ambitions, they head for disaster. Often, they cannot be warned; the more they fail in reaching their illusionary goals, the more obdurate they become in pursuing them. In hindsight, they wonder how everything could have happened, how they ignored or misjudged warning signals, how they vigorously persisted in what later turned out to be no more than an illusion.

Emotional inhibitions are the opposite of false ambitions. It is as if there is a voice, a judge, in our middle cylinder telling us: 'You cannot do this' – while it is obvious for others that we perfectly well can. Or the 'judge' says: 'You are not allowed to do this' – while others wonder what the problem is. When we grow up new opportunities open up but we may be afraid to explore them. Sex is a good example. Young people are often afraid to explore it. Usually these inhibitions evaporate when they grow up and sexuality becomes just another talent that is to be developed. Unfortunately, our culture is very ambivalent about sexuality. We may internalise an external demand for 'decent behaviour', which then becomes an inhibition in the middle cylinder. Unless it dissolves, it may harden there into a permanent taboo that blocks our interaction with the opposite sex, impeding our normal development. Such a taboo becomes so much a part of ourselves that we don't recognise it as something abnormal. When for some reason we get rid of our inhibitions, we discover new worlds'.

I wondered whether he had me in mind. But I would never dare ask him. Then I noticed that he began to look tired. Although it was obvious that there were many more questions, I thought I had to protect him – and myself – and I raised my hand. When he nodded in my direction, I suggested resuming after dinner. He first seemed to protest, then agreed. We all got up and went to the refectory, not a moment too soon, as the meal had been served already.

We were sitting next to our practical host. He did not seem to be very impressed with the abbot's Lesson.

'You pretend to bring something new but fortunately you stick to the doctrine', he challenged him in his straightforward way.

'As a good man of the Church, I always stay close to Jesus', the abbot retorted and I thought of the teachings of Jesus about the development of talents.

'But why do you say 'fortunately'?'

'I am happy that our East-Orthodox Church stays so close to the roots of Christianity. We are investigating some hymns which we believe date back to the first century. If we can prove that, we shall restore them to their original state and include them in our hymnal'.

'Wonderful', congratulated the abbot. 'I myself am trying to help people see the place of Jesus' true message – which was somewhat lost during the centuries – in their own lives'.

4. Vladimir – Barriers to development

It was already getting late when we resumed our session after enjoying the hospitality of the Bogoroditze-Rozhdestvenski Monastery. The abbot was visibly refreshed and carefully listened to the next question, which came from an old, wise-looking, slowly-speaking woman:

'Father. The way I understand it is that the soul, the inner cylinder, if healthy, gives us vitality and the power to develop our talents as well as our security. The outer cylinder, whether it perceives the world rightly or wrongly, recognises opportunities and constraints. The middle cylinder mediates between the two but it can play a foul game of its own'.

And, after some hesitation:

'My question is: How do we recognise false from healthy ambitions and emotional inhibitions from real constraints?'

Overcoming inhibitions and false ambitions

Well, she had put that down neatly. As ever so often, the summary cleared it up for me. I must have looked relieved but only for a moment as the abbot's face became serious when he was formulating his answer:

'We learn and develop by trial and error. A child admires a tightrope walker and sets out to imitate his act. After having fallen a number of times, it will decide that its ambition was a false one and it will give up on it. Or it may be afraid of a spider, only to learn that spiders are friendly and harmless creatures and that it is safe to overcome this inhibition. We can also learn from other peoples' experience and since time immemorial, people have been creating myths and legends to that end. Reading such stories as well as fairy tales and novels can help us recognise the tricks of the middle cylinder. Culture helps to align the middle cylinder. Distinguishing false from true ambitions and emotional inhibitions from real constraints is part of learning to know ourselves. Learning to know ourselves is a lifelong process that takes different forms as we proceed, but it never stops'.

An older man, a bit funny, apparently a bon vivant, took the floor, smoothing his beard and smiling broadly, as he set out, taking his time:

'Perhaps I may relate a kind of humorous story in this context. When he was about fourteen years old, the son of our neighbours decided he wanted to become a film actor. Although he had no acting experience to speak of, he was convinced that he would be a star because he thought he was a natural talent. His parents took his wish seriously as they realised that simply pointing out that this was not for him would make him only more obstinate and might alienate him. They took him to see drama schools but all was in vain. Later, the desire evaporated by itself and now he is a successful banker'.

'Alas, this happens often', the abbot replied, 'In puberty, children can develop these unrealistic ambitions, often harbouring them for a long time. Girls want to be fashion designers or ballerinas, boys – pilots or computer specialists. As they grow up, these ambitions fade away. Sometimes, they are not completely unrealistic and the ambition may come back at a later stage in life, as a hobby for instance. I would not be surprised if your neighbour's son would at some point take part in amateur theatre'.

The man clearly enjoyed getting so much attention so he had another story to relate:

'Another boy in our part of town was very good with people. Even when he was small he helped his friends resolve their problems. He is a likable boy and when the moment came to enrol at university, psychology was the logical choice. But his studies did not go anywhere and he had to give up on them. We all wondered what he would do next. Much to our surprise, he picked information technology. Like all boys at the time, he was fascinated with computers but we never thought he would make it his profession'.

'What happened', the abbot wondered.

The man loved it.

'He joined an international computer firm where he is now in charge of relations with distributors. This requires good insight in people so I guess he is back to square one albeit in a different setting'.

At this a smile went through the audience, there was even a light applause.

The abbot concluded: 'Young people all have dreams. Some dreams will become lifetime passions, others will vanish. You can tell the difference between a dream and a passion by the *actions* a person takes. If a person starts working on the dream, stumbling and getting up again, it will be his destiny. If, however, he just keeps dreaming while doing other things, it has been just a childhood illusion. The touchstone is action'.

The woman who had asked the first question had not been listening. Broodingly, she said:

'And what if we don't overcome false ambitions or emotional inhibitions?'

The abbot:

'Inhibitions and false ambitions become dangerous when they are persistent and grow like a cancer in our middle cylinder. This blocks the energy flow from our inner cylinder. Our vitality cannot come out, we have a passion but are unable to do anything with it. We become frustrated, depressed and ultimately sick. The talent to love and to be loved also becomes locked and in this case the person is lonely beyond bounds yet looks happy and lively. A person in such a state can suddenly kill himself, with everyone wondering how it could happen. The health of the inner cylinder determines our vitality, the health of the middle cylinder determines how much access we have to this vitality'.

The woman nodded slightly, then asked:

'If the middle cylinder is dented as you say, how does a person cope with it?'

The abbot more or less continued his answer:

'If the middle layer is blocked, a person will try to compensate and build some kind of 'satisfactory life', often by developing intellectual talents and neglecting emotional exchange. He would move and talk like a robot without showing or sharing emotions. One would say: 'He has a good brain, but it is more a liability than an asset'.

The woman jumped in for the fourth time:

'What can you do about it?'

The abbot answered:

'Sometimes an obstruction goes away because of some event that makes the person think. Or it just disappears. More often, it is friends who heal the middle cylinder. Friends give us feedback, they knead the middle cylinder and patiently create awareness of the falsehood of our inhibition or ambition. Only when the falsehood is exposed, can it be removed'.

A sensitive man, in his late thirties, with curly hair, unusual in this part of the world, got up and said:

'All my life I was afraid to follow my passion for art. What you describe is exactly what I have experienced: friends encouraged me to overcome my fear and show my paintings at an exhibition. It was such a relief when I did it although the exhibition was not a success'.

The abbot reacted immediatey:

'Talents often come with fear. The stronger the talent – the greater the urge to develop it but also the greater the fear to explore it. And we are very clever in covering up our fears. Many people are driven by fear which they compensate through acquiring power and money. But this does not take the fear away, it would take an inner process to replace fear with confidence. This is what Jesus meant when he said: 'Look at the birds, they do not worry and yet our heavenly Father nourishes them'.

Generation transfer
A middle-aged, rational looking man stood up and worded the following comment:

'You said earlier that a blocked middle cylinder can also block the flow of love. I was brought up in a rather rational family. My parents took good care of us but they considered manifestations of love something inferior, *obyezyanya lyubov* – monkey-love – they would call it. I only learned to give and take love at a later age, just in time to pass it on to my children. When I see how they love their partners and children, I wonder whether this was made possible by what I call my 'conversion''.

The abbot responded immediately:

'You prevented what we call generation transfer, that is when parents or teachers transfer their norms, values or life style to the next generation. Of course, many good things are transferred this way. But also bad things or shortcomings are passed from generation to generation. In your case, you may have internalised the lack of love – though not of care – you experienced in your childhood. This may have blocked the middle cylinder, or rather, it may have prevented its normal development. This can be remedied later in life by love. If it isn't, no love will flow to that person's children and this will result in their middle cylinder being underdeveloped and blocked in turn. This way, the 'disease' with its symptoms – lack of direction, inability to love, lack of self-confidence, depression – moves from generation to generation. This is the meaning of the saying: 'the curse will be passed on to future generations'. It is difficult to break the chain of generation transfer and whoever so manages does it to the benefit of the generations to follow. Your children will probably never know how grateful they should be to you'.

Another man got up, remarking:

'My case is exactly the opposite: my parents wanted me to pursue the career of a doctor. I obliged but I found no pleasure in that profession'.

The abbot:

'This is another form of generation transfer. In your case your parents created a false ambition. Our middle cylinder is sensitive to external influences, especially at a young age when the outer cylinder is still being developed. Parents and other people we trust can be very destructive, for instance if they want the child to fulfil an ambition they failed to achieve themselves or want the child to continue their own career or lifestyle. 'Look here, the new director of our family enterprise', says the grandfather at the cradle of his grandson. This is almost incestuous because it will be very difficult for the child and later the adult, to find out whether to be a director is really what he wants for himself. The culprit is often a victim of the ambitions of the previous generation and therefore cannot offer guidance. Sorting out the middle cylinder occupies at least the first part of our life. Distortions of the middle cylinder, either self-generated, caused by the generation transfer or by people and events later on in life can be overcome, albeit not easily, by friendship and focussed development'.

A woman in the audience did not agree:

'The generation transfer can be very rewarding, giving satisfaction to the parent as well as opportunities to the child. I play in an orchestra and our conductor is a young and very talented musician. His father played the violin in a gypsy band. He never got a proper education, couldn't even read music. He spotted his son's talent when the boy was still very young, gave him lessons and, later, found professional teachers for him. The poor boy had to practice six hours a day and he hated his father for it. He became a child prodigy and played Tchaikovsky's violin concerto with our orchestra when he was just seven years old. I can't tell you what a marvellous experience it was. His father was proud that his son had the opportunities that he never had. In the end, the son was very grateful because another father might not have recognised his talent and he could have missed a fulfilling career as a musician'.

'Alas, these are the exceptions to the rule', the abbot reacted.

'I don't agree', the woman insisted, 'Our talents are ingrained in our DNA which we pass on to our children. It is logical then that children inherit talents from their parents. The parents will be the first to recognise such talents, as they are familiar to them. They may have to put pressure on the child to develop the talent but in the end the children will be grateful'.

'Unfortunately, more often than not, talents are not transferred to the next generation', the abbot continued. 'If they are, a dream, that probably all parents have, comes true. It is a great disappointment to parents that they cannot transfer their experience and, eventually, wisdom, to their children as they often have different interests. This can be a great source of sadness in people's lives. But we have to accept it out of respect for the child'.

Projection
A middle-aged woman got up and said:
'All my life I wanted to study but my parents were against it and wanted me to help with the farm. Using your terminology, they were manipulating my middle cylinder'.

The abbot responded:
'I wonder whether you can say that your parents manipulated your middle cylinder as I would hardly call 'helping with the farm' the planting of a false ambition. If you had been really eager to study, you would have convinced your parents or eventually run away from home and found the means to do it. Instead, you keep saying: 'I wanted to study but my parents did not want this and now I am unhappy and frustrated and this is because of them'. It seems your middle cylinder plays a trick on you that we call projection. You project your inability to get organised on your parents and when you do so, you fool yourself. Either there is an inhibition in you that prevents you from studying – and then you fool yourself by blaming your parents – or you have a false ambition to study, and you fool yourself with a dream. In the latter case, you do not really wish to study, you only imagine so and you are all too happy to find an external reason not to do it'.

The amateur painter, who had spoken earlier, was hesitating to ask another question. It soon became clear why:
'When I started painting, I met a woman who was already an established artist and she saw great talent in me. We became lovers and I moved in with her, we shared a studio. She would advise me and I learned a great deal from her but to no avail, I simply did not have it in me, not enough. She became disappointed and after some years we broke up'.
'Why did you break up if you were in love?' the abbot enquired.
Again the man hesitated. It was difficult for him to speak but the audience was patient and so was the abbot.
'When it became obvious I was not the talent she thought I was, she started becoming aggressive, calling me names I wouldn't like to repeat. It hurt me deeply but when I mentioned this, it only got worse. At one point she got so worked up that she threw things at me – paint, brushes, anything, and then I decided to leave her despite the fact that I still loved her'.
'You did well'. The abbot's reaction was kind and warm. 'When a relationship

becomes destructive, one should end it. It is the same with men who beat up their wives and be nice to them the next moment. Women in this case hope that things will get better until it is usually their friends who convince them it cannot go on'.

'I still feel bad about it', the man said. 'Having disagreements is not a reason to end a good relationship'.

'I subscribe to that', the abbot responded, 'But in this case there was much more than disagreement. If there are disagreements, let us say about practicalities, it can be a temporary situation that love will resolve eventually. In your case, it seems your girl friend projected something of herself in you and when you failed in her eyes, she may have feared she had failed herself, all at the subconscious level. I think this might have been the case because otherwise she would have simply suggested you try something else while she would carry on with her own career. Disagreements are not a reason to end a love relationship but destruction is and if that is the case you have to end it immediately in order to protect yourself'.

'But wouldn't that be selfish?' the man asked.

'Not if you have tried to solve the problems. If you fail, you have to realise you are not God and that everyone bears the responsibility for his or her own life. If there is no lasting respect, there can be no love'.

Problems of the outer cylinder

The abbot then looked at the middle-aged woman who had wanted to study. She was puzzled but did not know what to say, so the abbot continued talking to her:

'It is also possible that you read your parents wrongly. Perhaps they were not really against your studying and you perceived a stronger resistance than there really was. Recognising and overcoming inhibitions and false ambitions starts with the training of the outer cylinder, as our perception is often subjective and therefore inaccurate. We see what we want to see even if it may not be there, while we fail to see what we do not wish to see although it is pretty obvious. Or, in the words of St John Chrysostom: 'We see one thing and believe another'. In this way, the outer cylinder also plays a trick but it does so with good intentions, which is, to protect us from impressions that may be too strong to handle. Children instinctively bury their face in their mother's lap when they see something frightening. All teaching, therefore, must start with perception: 'What is it that you really see?' The observation and subsequent description of nature as it really is, is the key to modern science. Art can only be enjoyed if we first learn to be aware of what we see or hear'.

Now the woman came back and asked:
'Can perception be learned?' to which the abbot reacted:
'You can train your outer cylinder by developing awareness of what really happens in the world around you. What does the body language of the person you meet, say? Is it consistent with what he tells you? If someone remarks that the weather has gone foul, is that true or is he simply grumpy and projects it on the weather? Comparing your observations with those of others can be of great help so, in important meetings, you should always be accompanied by a friend who will take notes and can supplement your comments with his. In very threatening situations, for instance when a loved one is struck by a life-threatening illness or when you have to face a serious legal dispute, your perception of what has been communicated cannot always be trusted'.

Here an older man joined in saying:
'I am so glad you say this. About ten years ago my wife was diagnosed with cancer. I always told the family that it was a benign tumour with nothing to worry about until one day she objected: 'You were there in the hospital when the doctor told you it was malignant'. I could swear I had never set foot in that hospital but when I checked my diary it was there, the appointment, and the memory came back'.

The abbot looked sad as he replied:
'That must have been a terrible experience. What we can learn from this is that it helps to take notes of whatever the doctor – or lawyer in a legal case – tells you and put it into a diary. Later, you may find out that your memories of what has been said are completely contradicted by your notes'.

Then an apparent friend of the woman who had spoken earlier, another young woman, slowly got up and asked:
'I don't go to work with pleasure because I am fat and ugly and people don't take me seriously'.
The abbot looked at her, smiled and responded:
'You don't look ugly to me! You may be a bit plump but that is a matter of taste. You have a warm smile and you display vitality, which is why people will find you attractive. Your problem lies in yourself, there is something wrong with your own perception of yourself. This is a damage of the outer cylinder. This may sound bad, but do not worry: repairing the damage of the outer cylinder is much easier than healing the middle cylinder. Outer cylinder damage can be stubborn however, as we tend to stick to our misconceptions and reinforce them by misinterpreting other people's reactions. Listen to people who tell

you that you look fine, let this sink in as an antidote to your delusions. Outer cylinder damage is very common, hence it has become big business as all kinds of products are advertised to take care of it: the soap that makes you attractive to the opposite sex and the likes'.

Problems of the inner cylinder
It was now really getting late but before closing the session, our host had a question disguised as a hint:

'Brother Rostov, you have discussed damage of the middle and outer cylinders. I fear what you are going to say about the damage of the inner cylinder'.

At once, the abbot's smile disappeared and he answered:

'The damages to the inner cylinder are wounds that lie deep in the soul. They are caused by violence or exposure to violence, especially when experienced at a young age and by people one trusts. This can happen at war, in concentration camps, but also at home, on the street, in a taxi – anywhere. Bearing heavy responsibilities at a young age, for instance taking care of siblings when the parents have died, or betrayal by people you thought you can trust, can cause deep wounds. Being forced to do evil damages the inner cylinder of the wrong-doer as much as the victim.

The wounds are covered up by shame, guilt and fear of discovery. This triggers a self-perpetuating circle: when covered up, the feeling of shame only increases, like capital in the bank. The victims live in a 'self-inflicted prison of fear and seclusion' as one of them put it. They think they must be strong enough to withstand the fear as giving in to fear would lead to weakness and hence the risk of losing everything: friendship, a job. In this artificial world a victim's first priority is to preserve himself – his deepest self.

It takes incredible energy from the victim to get out of this situation, rediscover himself and return to, or enter, some form of 'normal life'. Even then the demons keep coming back: as nightmares or sudden fears during the day. When the victims manage to have a career and become financially independent, they may push the memories back until they eventually retire and the bills are presented at the end of the day.

Only love – unselfish and patient – can help a victim to find a secure place in the world: a home, a job. Then, when there is enough security, love can help get the stories out. Talking about what happened – again and again – may chase the demons away but the pain will never be washed out completely. You cannot heal the wounds of the inner cylinder but you can learn to live with them'.

'What then should our attitude be?' our host asked.

'Extreme experiences alienate the listener. The victim fears judgment and subsequently expulsion so the understanding, warmth, security and respect the listener gives to the victim should be unconditional. Once a relationship of trust and respect has been established, the stories of what happened have to come out – a wound can only heal when the pus is out. The events will only surface up in bits and pieces. Compassion from the listener will encourage the victim to take more risk and share more. That is good but the listener should never be prying. Helping people with wounds in the inner cylinder requires patience and experience but one should leave the treatment to professionals'.

This was – at last – a good moment to stop. On the way out, the plump girl who had asked a question approached the abbot for an autograph. He was obviously pleased and asked her:
'Are you married? Are you a student?'
She told him she was reading geography and lived with her parents.
'Are they nasty to you, do they beat you up?', he asked.
'No, of course not', the girl exclaimed. 'They are very nice to me'.
'What a pity', the abbot retorted.
'Why, what do you say, why is it a pity?' she froze in her tracks.
'If they would have done that, I would wrap you up and take you with me. You are so charming', the abbot replied with a smile.

I went to bed but could not sleep. I kept thinking about the long day and how it had changed my perception of the abbot. I knew he was a wise man, that was nothing new. What intrigued me was this strange mixture of his intuitive approach and the way he displayed his models, almost in an engineering way. I was surprised that he could be quite a charmer. I puzzled over his comments and only got a few hours of sleep.

The next morning the rain had stopped and when we approached the train, there were radio reporters waiting for the abbot – I had arranged it well in advance. They wanted to know all about the three cylinders because, as they said: 'This model is so intriguing'. I asked them for which networks they were working and they told me the talks would be broadcast all over Russia. 'There is a lot of interest in the abbot's lectures', they said. 'We get reactions from all over the country, especially places where the abbot still has to go as they want to understand the context of what he is going to say in their city'.

A sharp whistle reminded us that we were holding up the departure of the train. We hurried past the long line of carriages until we found ours. The train started gaining speed and we stared out of the window to watch the landscape passing by.

5. Nizhny Novgorod – Know yourself

It was another three hours to Gorki-Mosk Vokzal, as the railway station of Nizhny Novgorod (Lower New Town) is still called after the former name of the city – Gorki. We were by now so used to crowds, escorts and hosts waiting for us that we were rather surprised to find that nobody met us at the station. I felt a bit embarrassed for the abbot but he seemed to think it was actually quite nice. 'Let us go and enjoy an anonymous cup of tea in a restaurant I know on the bank of the river', he suggested. We walked around the enormous red Nizhny Novgorod Kremlin (castle) that was built around 1510 to withstand attacks from the Tartars – Russia has always been the protector of Western civilisation against Eastern invasions. We then climbed up to the restaurant, on the high Western bank of the river Oka. We chose a table by the window and from there we had a magnificent view of the vast waters where the Oka, going north, flows into the Volga, running from west to east. 'Now you see why I did not mind they forgot us', the abbot said solemnly, 'This view is one of the most beautiful in Russia. If you look north, you can see the monastery huddled in the hills on the left bank of the Volga'. And indeed, the blue domes, the white churches and living quarters of the Pechersky Uzpenski Monastery (Ascension Monastery of the cave) stood out against the green hills. I called our host. He sounded surprised as he said he had expected us a day later. He would send a car but it would take a while as there is only one bridge crossing the Volga and there are always traffic jams at that point.

The question of orthodoxy kept bothering me. After our tea had been brought I asked the abbot whether he was not afraid of introducing new doctrines, while he had fought so forcefully to remove the layer of Christian orthodoxy from Jesus' message, which he had called 'humanistic'. He listened to me and said:

'I see your point but I do not consider my Lessons the absolute truth and the last thing I would do is to impose my ideas on people. When I present them, it is like saying: 'This is how I see it, compare it with your own insights and come to your own conclusions'. Religious zealots would force their followers to accept their views as the unquestionable truth and burn at the stake those who would not accept them. I present what I see as the truth in my Lessons leaving it to my pupils to decide for themselves.'

'What you say sounds so logical that I start to wonder why there are doctrines in the first place. There must be a need for them otherwise they wouldn't be there'.

'It is an interplay between those who think they are right and who like to impose their convictions on others, and weaker souls who are unsecure. They want to do the right thing and become followers. One gets a great feeling of comfort in belonging to a group where people think alike and have a common mission'.

'But surely that is an illusion. Aren't people able to make their own decisions?' 'Of course they are but some are weak. The ancient Gnostics, later the Cathari and still later the Mennonites, favoured and created a world free of doctrine. But they were prosecuted in the most cruel ways by the Church, which wanted to defend the doctrine, and worldly forces that saw advantages in doing so'.

'Why does doctrine always win?' I was very emotional about this for some reason.

'You are angry because you don't want to be told what to think. But fundamentalism does not always win. It is rather the effect of the pendulum. In times of uncertainty – politically or economically – doctrine takes the upper hand. In the affluent society of Western Europe doctrine is on the decline, even the Irish prime minister dares criticise the Roman Catholic Church in no uncertain terms, politically a brave act but reflecting the increased self confidence of the Irish electorate'.

'So, if the times become more uncertain, fundamentalism might get the upper hand again?' I ventured.

'You see that in the United States, Israel and in parts of the Arabic world', the abbot agreed.

'But that is frightening', I exclaimed, thinking of the vast arsenals of weaponry in these countries.

'Remember the pendulum', the abbot answered, 'But you have to realise that it is us who have to make it work'.

'How do we do that?' I asked.

'By trying to create a world in which everyone has some basic security and is free to develop his talents. The values of the Enlightenment are universal. Fundamentalism offers solace but not solutions'.

I thought that was easier said than done but wanted to ask something else.

'Father, you are not only a teacher. From what you say you have been counselling people a lot'.

'Depending on the situation, I am more a councillor than a teacher. I will listen to my pupils, trying to help them understand their emotions and define their problems. Then I will try to offer suggestions'.

'If you are both a teacher and a councillor, what then is the common denominator?' I asked.

'You can only be a good teacher and a good councillor if you love your pupils', he said.

Meanwhile, the arrival of the abbot had not passed unnoticed and soon people started coming in, taking off their caps and crossing themselves as the abbot invited them to join us at our table. They had heard the broadcasts from the abbot's departure in Moscow and his visit to Vladimir and many had questions on what the abbot had said about 'Know yourself'.

'Let us make that the theme of this afternoon', the abbot whispered to me.

At last, the abbot of the Pechersky Monastery arrived, an elderly man, hairs and habit rather untidy. He apologised, gesticulating profusely – they simply got the date wrong. In order to make time for people to come to the gathering, he suggested we visit the famous art gallery with not only romantic paintings by Shishkin, Repin, Lewitan and the inevitable Ayvazovski, but also Malevich, Kandinski, Goncharova and other avant-garde artists. Our host turned out to be quite knowledgeable about art and I asked him why he called Ayvazovski 'inevitable'.

'Oh, Ivan painted so much that his works can be seen in any Russian museum', he said, as if he was talking about a close friend.

The sun had already started to go down when we arrived at the monastery. Upon arrival, the abbot bowed to the monastery, in reference to Count Salahub, who wrote: 'When in Nizhny Novgorod, one should bow to the Pechersky Monastery because it contains the entire history of Russia'.

Introspection

At the refectory the crowd was surprisingly large, as word had got around quickly. We recognised the people who were with us in the restaurant. The abbot opened the meeting, saying:

'I understand that many of you have questions about what I call *know yourself*'.

Some people nodded and the abbot continued:

'Knowing ourselves is perhaps the most difficult task in our life, indeed, the process of getting to know ourselves continues all our life. When brother Vasili was entrusted to us, I gave him the same instruction I gave you when we left Yaroslavska Station: *Live your life consciously*. In the beginning, he did not know how to respond to this. Then one morning, he came to me and said: 'I am starting to understand the meaning of what you said. Yesterday evening, after Vespers, I was overwhelmed by an inexplicable feeling of great happiness. Nothing special had happened that day and I kept asking myself why I was so elated. Then I realised, I had been chopping wood most of the day and it subconsciously brought me back to the time when I helped my father in the forest. I was so very happy then. When I became aware of this, a feeling of nostalgia overcame me and I started to weep'.

Several months later, I asked him again about his efforts to live consciously. He then told me: 'I have made a habit of analysing myself every evening after Compline. I analyse my feelings and the reasons for my good or bad mood. I would remember, for instance, that one of the brothers had said something nasty to me that I had forgotten, but the bad feeling would persist until I had found the cause. After that the feeling subsided'.

I wondered whether Vasili would confront the monk who had said something nasty. Vasili said sometimes he would do this while at other times he would not bother. When he confronted the wrongdoer, it would often turn out he was not aware of the feelings he had aroused or he simply wouldn't care'.

Listening to weak signals
A young man was eager to take the floor. He was good-looking, wearing a shirt and tie, most likely a young professional and it turned out that he was also quite smart:

'Father, if I may interrupt, it seems to me that introspection only works when you pick up signals in the first place, external signals, in the case you mentioned, signals of anxiety when Vasili's colleagues made an unpleasant remark'.

The abbot responded:

'You are absolutely right. You have to be aware of the weak signals that come to you all the time. They need not necessarily come from outside. In the first example Vasili got this feeling of happiness from inside and, at first, did not know how to place it.

But I agree that external signals are vital for getting to know yourself. Friends comment on your behaviour, like 'This remark is just like you', or: 'I was surprised you can do this'. This gives us food for thought but without introspection, it leads nowhere. We learn from other people'.

The subconscious

There was a murmur in the congregation. It came from a group of women who apparently had arrived together. They were all wearing *platki* – head shawls, the way rural women do. They had their arms around one of them who had become quite agitated. The entire congregation started to look at her, which made it even worse. The abbot opened his arms, inviting her to speak, but she was only crying. Her friends tried to soothe her and as she calmed down a little, she managed to say:

'Father, you don't understand'.

The abbot looked puzzled but kept his warm, enticing gaze on her.

'I do get these moods but when I try to understand where they come from, it only gets worse'.

Again, she started sobbing, then calmed down and looked at him expectantly. She was really upset, that much was clear. I found it disturbing and I wondered how the abbot would cope with this. He took an unexpected turn:

'When you bought your *platok*', he asked her, 'How did you make your choice?'

She was so surprised that she forgot to sob.

'Oh, there were a lot of colours, I just fancied this one'.

'Were they all the same quality? the abbot continued.

'Well, there were some cheap ones but I don't want to look cheap'. It came out a bit caustically.

'Then your choice of quality was a rational one'.

'Of course'. It sounded even more acidly.

'But then, your choice of colour was not rational'.

'How can such a choice be rational?' By now she was getting curious where he was heading.

'Many of our choices are made subconsciously', the abbot continued, 'The conscious is but the top of an iceberg, it is what you see but there is a much vaster quantity of ice under the water. Likewise, the subconscious holds much more information than the conscious part of our brain. You could say that brother Vasili had 'stored' images in childhood of how he helped his father chop wood and how he felt about it. In a similar situation the feeling came back and after a while the subconscious memory surfaced up'.

Obviously, the woman had no idea what this had to do with her. But she was brave and kept listening.

'Your subconscious not only has a much larger memory than the conscious, it can simultaneously process different tracks of information – the conscious part can only do one thing at the time. When you make a subconscious decision, you say: 'I fancied it', or: 'I feel good about it'. This means that your subconscious has been working hard – not noticed by you – and the outcome is that you feel good about the decision. When you say: 'My intuition tells me that this person cannot be trusted', it is also the result of a subconscious process. You stored experiences in the past and your subconscious made a quick search through them with the result that you identify this new person as unreliable, even though you are not aware of the earlier encounters that led to this outcome. The subconscious needs time to process information and come to a conclusion. Especially when you have to make decisions that have many aspects, it is good 'to sleep on it', as the saying goes, and the next morning, the solution may come up. When you are stuck in some creative activity, you might as well go to sleep and a good idea may dawn on you the following morning'.

Well, the abbot certainly took his time. He had still not responded to the poor woman and this was too much for her. She burst into another bout of sobbing and we were back where we started. It was also too much for one of her friends, a buxom woman with a blue apron and apparently a good heart, who took up her cause:
'Look Father, what you have done! The poor girl is even worse off than when she came here. Can't you tell her at least where all her emotions come from?'

The abbot took a sip of water and looked at both women. He paused for a second – perhaps to let his subconscious work – then continued, looking at the woman who had started sobbing:
'When you have these emotions, your intuition is trying to tell you something. When you have a feeling of discomfort, and you cannot relate it to something that happened recently, the subconscious tries to warn you. So, listen to your subconscious, the voice inside you, your intuition. Introspection is linking conscious experiences with the subconscious'.

She came back acidly:
'And how am I supposed to 'listen to my subconscious'?'
'Perhaps you have to learn how to meditate. In meditation, we close ourselves to the world and we gain access to our subconscious. This yields unexpected

insight and you get a feeling of relief, peace, happiness. Meditation is an age-old process that has a place in all religions of the world. Having quick access to the subconscious is a talent that some people have more than others. It can be learned, at least to a certain extent. Artists, authors, scientists, clairvoyants, all of them have such a talent. A writer can say: 'I had an inspiration, the book wrote itself'. That means he was guided by his subconscious, what he wrote came right from the bottom of his soul. Mozart is a perfect example, he never corrected what he wrote down. There was no need for it, it came right from his inner self'.

Reason and emotion
The young professional had been trying to speak for some time.

'Father', he said when he finally got the chance, 'My problem will sound superficial, I am afraid, but I hope you can help me as it has bothered me for some time. It concerns the conflict between what I know is good for me versus how I feel about it. Let me give you just a simple example to cast light on the problem. Imagine I am looking for a new suit. I like some of the latest designs but I know they won't do down well in my line of business. What should I do, follow my gut feeling or use my brains?'

The answer was not so simple:

'We have to talk about emotion and reason. Emotion is the spontaneous feeling that springs up in us at every contact we make with another person or something we take in through our senses. Our young brother Ilya said a feeling of happiness overwhelmed him when he saw the high peaks of the Urals for the first time. His head filled with music and he completely forgot everything else around him. Brother Sergei is not such an emotional person. 'Yes', he says, 'I very well remember the first time I saw the mountains and I was immediately intrigued by their geological structure'. It is good to have someone like Sergei in the monastery. The other week we had a leaking roof. Sergei climbed up in the middle of a thunderstorm and fixed it. In the beginning, he was not very popular because he just went on and on explaining everything to everyone. Ilya was quite his opposite when he joined us. If one of the brothers was ill or in trouble he would be overwhelmed by emotions, often stronger than those of the person affected. Initially, Sergei and Ilya did not get along well. Sergei used to scold Ilya: 'Stop it! All that lamenting leads to nothing'. 'Yes, but you do not know how I feel', Ilya would reply. I tried to let them get to know each other.

Now, here is my point: there is an Ilya and a Sergei in each of us. In some of us, the rational side is more strongly developed at the expense of the emotional side, in others, it is the other way around. Just as Ilya and Sergei have to learn to work together, we have to learn to let reason and emotion interact. If our rational side does not relate to our emotional side, we do not learn from our emotions, they simply overtake us. If a strongly developed rationality does not leave room for feelings, we shall never fully understand people and we shall be forever lonely. It is like the Oka flowing into the upper Volga: together they become the stronger lower Volga'.

Then, addressing the young professional:
'So what you have to do is to keep searching until you find a suit that you like and that you know will meet your requirements'.

The man had been nodding while the abbot spoke, he thanked him politely and sat down. But I was very much puzzled by this intervention. I felt I was more like Sergei than Ilya. After all, even the abbot had said: 'Stephen, you are a smart guy', something my father never did. My emotions always revolved around Clara: why had she not wanted me. But I could not see the connection between my smartness, whatever, and my love for her. I only knew that if I studied hard enough those thoughts remained in the background. I wanted to ask a question about this but I didn't know whether it was appropriate for me to do so and, anyway, I couldn't formulate a question so quickly.

The will
While I was still puzzling, the woman in the blue apron took the floor. Her otherwise friendly face looked worried when she tried:
'I understand what you say about the two rivers flowing together. But isn't it sometimes more advisable to control one's emotions?'
The abbot replied:
'Absolutely. When you see the weather going foul, you feel bad about it but at the same time you know you have to pull yourself together and get your laundry inside. When someone is wounded in an accident, you know you must not give in to your emotions but help. The emotions are then pushed into the background, they are overruled by the will'.

He paused to take a sip of water, then continued:

'Emotions are the driving force in life, we need the will to guide this energy. People with little emotion tend to be rather passive. But passionate people are easily led astray. The inner cylinder gives us signals in the 'language' of intuition. The outer cylinder transmits your observations. The signals meet in the middle cylinder where the decisions are being made. The middle cylinder is the seat of the will. From that position it tries to match the emotions that bubble up from inside with the realities of the world as observed by the outer cylinder. When a child grows up, it has to learn how to balance intuition and reason. If it wants to advance in the world, it has to develop its will'.

As we walked out, I was wondering whether it was my weak will that prevented me from forgetting Clara. I must have looked awful when the woman in the blue apron suddenly pulled me against her, kissed me on the forehead and said: 'I can see you have a problem son, but trust me, all will be well. You have a good heart'. I felt tears welling up and I buried my head in her shoulder. She calmly stroked my back. Then she gently pushed me away 'Come on lad, we have to attend Compline', and as we mixed with the crowd going out, I felt warm, a bit embarrassed and extremely confused.

After Compline it was time to leave, we had to catch the 3.39 a.m. to Kirov and it would take us at least half an hour to get to the railway station. We had a sleeper to ourselves and we ordered a light supper. I wanted to talk about the Lesson but didn't know how to start.

'Father, I think this was a very good Lesson', I finally ventured.

He looked at me over his glasses with a questioning smile:

'So, what did you like about it?' his reaction did not come as a surprise.

'You get to know yourself by introspection and introspection is the link between the conscious and the subconscious. And you achieve this link through meditation. Is that right?'

He nodded vaguely and I could see this was not the full answer. I suddenly had a flash of inspiration and I spoke before I knew it:

'But you use prayer to get to yourself? Is prayer the same thing as meditation?'

He sighed and shifted his legs into a more comfortable position.

'When I lost my wife, there was this old priest who was conducting the funeral service. He invited me to see him afterwards and made me tell my story step by step. He was compassionate, he did not say much, he only listened. I started visiting him more often and one day he said: 'Let us pray'. I thought that was ridiculous. I had never prayed in my life. But he was insistent. He would almost hit me: 'Pray boy, pray!' Then he would be silent again and gradually it came: I learned how to pray and be at peace with myself. It was this experience that made me decide to go to a monastery and become a religious man'.

There was nothing more to say. We tried to get some sleep, we only had six hours to Kirov.

But again, sleep did not come. I went over everything that had happened this week. It had been only a week! I had the impression that the abbot had by now communicated the core of his philosophy. I had learned a lot about myself. It was as if a veil had been lifted from my eyes but only partly, as I realised there was so much more to learn.

6. Kirov – Personality archetypes

We had only had a little sleep but when we arrived at 9.43 a.m. at Kirov's Passagirski Station the abbot of the Uspenski Trifonov Monastery (The Monastery of the Ascension of Trifon Vyatsky) had a plan. He suggested Yevgeni Nikolayevich started with his lecture right away and took a nap in the afternoon. For the evening he invited us to see Alexander Ostrovsky's play Snegurochka (Snow White) featuring Miss Beljajeva in the leading role.

'I wouldn't miss Vera Stepanovna for the world. It has been a long time since she played here. Didn't she emigrate?' the abbot asked.

'She did', our diplomatic host replied, 'but it so happens that she is visiting the city for a few weeks and we persuaded her to take up her old role again. I thought you would like it and we have bought the tickets already'.

Well, that settled it.

Thanks to the enterprising abbot, at 10.30 a.m. we were seated with a lively congregation. Our host put a note in front of the abbot.

'Here you are', he said, 'this comes from a young man who is too shy to speak'. He pointed him out to us – he was seated in the very last row.

The abbot put his glasses, read the note, and after collecting his thoughts, addressed the audience.

'I got a note from a young brother here and I will try to respond to him. What I understand from your note is that you are in conflict with your father. He says he gives you freedom to make your own decisions but at the same time, you feel strong indirect pressure to follow where he leads. His presence in your life is like on/off: sometimes he is there, very much present, teaching you useful things. At other times, he is out of reach, immersed in one of his many interests. He is nervous and chaotic, you feel you cannot rely on him, you always come second. Yet you know he loves you and that he cares for you in his own way. You want to know how to handle the situation as you also care very much for your father. Is that right?'

The young man nodded.

The abbot continued:

'It seems your predicament results from the combination of the personality of your father and the problem of the generation transfer. I discussed generation transfer in Vladimir and let me give you the highlights. Parents tend to have dreams and desires about their child's future, often these include the ambitions or achievements the parents did not accomplish themselves and now want the child to accomplish for them. The dream can also be for the child to continue the family tradition, take up family norms and values, a religion, perhaps a family enterprise. The 'strong, indirect pressure' you experienced from your father, may be caused by the generation transfer. It is indirect because your father does not deliberately try to manipulate you, it happens semi-consciously'.

The dimensions of the archetypes
The abbot looked at the young man to see whether his message had come across, and when he felt it had, he continued:

'Often frictions between people stem from the fact that they have different personalities. Over the years, I have come to outline five personality archetypes, they follow a logical order. It seems your father has the characteristics of what I call the pioneer. Understanding other people's archetype can help you accept their peculiarities and appreciate their strong points. Understanding your own archetype is a great help in knowing yourself. Perhaps I should say 'archetypes' because nobody matches the descriptions exactly, we all have elements of different types but usually one type is dominant'.

He was waiting for some reaction but it didn't come. Our host abbot decided to step in:

'Brother Rostov, I think this is very interesting. Please go ahead' and he looked at the audience that answered with a murmur of assent.

The pioneer
The abbot looked at the audience and continued:

'The first archetype, the *pioneer*, is driven by challenges, by achieving something unique: the first to reach the top of the Mount Everest. Pioneers are emotionally driven without thinking of the consequences. Napoléon (*'On 's engage et puis on voit'* – You go and then you see) and many artists, entrepreneurs, scientists and discoverers have much of the pioneer. They are daredevils, hyperactive, anticipatory, driven by circumstances; they are casual lovers. They elude you and are difficult to love but they need your love most of all people. Their thinking is divergent, strictly original, disconnected, and intuitive-irrational. Pioneers inspire others, they rarely achieve much on their own, they depend on others to put their idea or discovery to use'.

While the abbot was speaking, I tried to make up my mind whether I belonged to this archetype. I was certainly creative – I had many original ideas. But then, I was not a 'casual lover', on the contrary, there had been and would be only one woman in my life to whom I would forever be faithful.

The conqueror
Everybody was probably wondering about the same thing, whether this type applied to him. There were no questions and the host abbot stepped in once again:
   'You make us curious about the other types'.

The abbot hardly needed further encouragement and went on:
   'The second archetype, the *conqueror*, is also creative but more in the sense that he takes the original ideas from the pioneers and then forges them into something logical, something practical that makes sense to other people. Conquerors are often passionate people and passionate people can inspire others, they can create a vision. Conquerors are motivated by expanding their sphere of influence. They get inspiration from starting something new and they will go to great lengths to get it going. However, they lack the ambition for fine-tuning, for finishing off a job, let alone being in charge of a going concern. They subscribe to William Congreve's line: 'Uncertainty and expectation are the joys of life'. Conquerors are energetic, nervous but with some self-control. They are sensitive to 'weak signals', they can see the value and the possibilities in the employment of new ideas. Socially, they tend to form small groups of chosen trusted friends like our Lord with his twelve disciples. By their nature, they are serial lovers, lovers with great intensity. Conquerors get the recognition for the innovations they push through but they stand on the shoulders of the pioneers.

The abbot took a sip of water – winking at me, unnoticeably to others – looked at the audience, but as no one reacted, he continued:

The balanced ruler
'The third archetype is open to new ideas but he will not invent them on his own, he lacks the imagination for it. He is a practical person with the word 'balanced' as his key characteristic: balanced in his work and judgment, balanced as a husband and father. He is creative in finding solutions to get

a given job done. This *balanced ruler* is motivated by stable growth with a minimum of risks. He gets satisfaction from, and strives for, control over the situation. His attitude is stable, 'according to agreement', focused on achieving objectives. He is well organised and the perfect team player: loyal, trustworthy, amiable, the dream son-in-law. As a husband, he is the faithful partner, not the type for adventures. He lacks the vision and energy to create and rather completes an initiative of the conqueror. The balanced ruler thus stands on the shoulders of the conqueror while he looks for inspiration to the pioneer.'

Fortunately, I took notes automatically – on 'autopilot'. This was helpful as I was rather distracted while the abbot was speaking. What did he mean with his wink? Was he implying he was a conqueror? Or was I? Or our host? The latter seemed more a balanced ruler to me but the abbot had already moved on.

The administrator
'If the balanced ruler is an archetype that thrives on stable growth, the *administrator*, the fourth archetype, is the perfect person for keeping a going concern on a steady course. He is driven by maintaining the status quo, the situation as it is. He will fiercely defend his territory when attacked. The administrator functions stable-static, wait-and-see, yes, but…. He thinks in terms of procedure and precedent. He is often a specialist in his field – his thinking is deep and conformist. He is introvert and trains people by explaining the rules rather than listening to them. He is a loyal but demanding husband and a father who has clear ideas about everything. He does not accept divergence from his principles. In love he will not take many initiatives. The administrator can be a powerful 'keeper of an empire', avoiding new ideas and influences. He will pass on the traditions and culture to the next generations'.

Many of my teachers had been of the administrator type. They were able to explain difficult issues – administrators often make good teachers. They were not inspiring, like the flamboyant young doctor, who would simply read from his PhD thesis, leaving it to us to make sense of it. Still, I owed a lot to all of them. I would not be where I had managed to come without administrators.

The defender
Meanwhile, the abbot had already continued:
    'More conservative than the administrator is the *defender*, the last archetype. He is driven by the desire to bring back the times when life was still good, standing up against new developments that will in his view disrupt the social order and bring the world to an end. His role in society is to warn against ill-

conceived ideas. His level of activity is lethargic, he will do what needs to be done but nothing more. His way of thinking is legalistic, ideological, rigid, orthodox, he knows what is right. He lives according to the rules of the forefathers that he goes to great lengths to explore. He is the *Blut und Boden* (traditional values) type that considers the place he was born his point of reference for the world'.

While the abbot paused, it occurred to me that some politicians seemed to be of this type. Turning their back to the future they try to bring back a world that has long gone. Then a shiver went down my spine. Had not the Church overwhelmingly been governed by fundamentalists and was there not a large proportion of 'defenders' in its higher ranks? If they would consider their role to be to 'warn against ill-conceived ideas', would they put the abbot's Lessons in this category? If so, was he heading for trouble, like so many liberal preachers before him?

Archetypes and relationships
Suddenly I broke out of my reverie, I had to pay attention. A woman got up and asked:
'Does our archetype, or, I should say, set of archetypes, change when we get older or does it remain the same?'
The abbot:
'I think a person's archetypes-mix does not change with age but circumstances further certain elements and suppress the development of others. The mix in old age can therefore be slightly different from the one in childhood. I use the word 'slightly' because basically the archetypes do not change that much, just as our DNA, they remain the same over time'.

'Are the archetypes a good indicator for relationships?'

That was a legitimate question and I was curious what the abbot would say:
'People of different archetypes, if not too distant on the scale, can form very synergetic and stable relationships while people of the same archetype do not. Usually people choose a partner who is only one or at most two archetypes away from their own leading archetype. The first archetypes provide inspiration to the later types while the latter tend to give security to the former'.

It had been a long session and the congregation became restless. The abbot smiled and said that he admired his listeners' patience, then asked for one more minute:

'I would like to respond to the young man who started today's conversation. Your father, my child, seems to have many of the characteristics of the pioneer-archetype and that has made him seem unreliable to you. Sometimes he was close to you, at other times he was very distant and his life was elsewhere. That is why he did not give you the security you needed. At the same time, you do not want to blame him, as you are grateful for the inspiration and the experience he did give you. It explains why you are in such a confused state when you think about your father. His dual attitude towards you is reflected in the way he deals with the problem of generation transfer: he wants you to make your own decisions yet he forces his life style on you all the time. You must come to a conclusion about your father and I hope your judgement will be lenient, he has given you what he can and what he can not give you is as much his problem as it is yours'.

We all got up and, actually, I was quite relieved as we had had little sleep and the abbot should have been exhausted after this long session. I also had a lot to think about as I was asking myself the question that probably everyone in the audience was now confronted with: What type am I? The abbot had been right: when you hear about the archetypes, you wonder where you belong. I also wondered how the abbot would see himself. Could I ask him or would it be too impertinent?

We had a light lunch, then took our nap. Fortunately, the abbot woke up well before we had to get ready for the theatre and I asked him the questions that had been bothering me. He took it lightly and was quite willing to discuss my concern:

'Of course you can ask me, but I can only speak for myself', he started. 'I am mainly a conqueror, sometimes a pioneer, a balanced ruler if I have to, like our host. My studies of the old books have inspired me to take the Message further rather than to defend the orthodoxy of our religion. I believe my monastery should be thoroughly modern, maintaining the status quo would make us a relic rather than an active instrument of God. As a good shepherd, I look after the well-being of my flock. This is a difficult task as it is not I but God who calls his own and I have to accept whoever is called upon and give him a place in our group. I have to distribute the tasks and match them with the characters of the brothers. This is the essence of leadership'.

'But you are not only a balanced ruler, you are also a renewer of the faith', I ventured.

'That would be too much of an honour for I am not the first one and I rely on others', he replied, 'but I certainly have my own ideas and as they are rather systematic, I guess that makes me a conqueror most of all. So what about you?'

'I don't know', I answered honestly, 'I always thought I was highly original, a typical pioneer so to say. But I am a very systematic worker and I realise I take a lot of ideas from others, sometimes from the strangest of sources. That would make me a conqueror. Right now, I am in a supporting role and it comes natural to me to behave as a balanced ruler. I guess it depends who I am with. I really have to think about it.'

'Steve, you are still young', he laughed. 'Wait and it will all come around'.

Here we were interrupted by our host who took us to the Na Spasskoi Theatre on the corner of Vorobskogo and Drelevskoi, all perfectly organised and we got there in time. We enjoyed the play in which Vera Stepanovna showed she had not lost anything of her talent to entertain the audience. 'I wish I could do that', said the abbot as we turned in for the night.

7. Perm – The stages of life

We settled comfortably in the train as it would take most of the day to reach Perm, one of the coldest cities of Russia, although not as cold as Oymyakon, where temperatures can reach 70C below zero. Twilight set in as we, for the first time, had to adjust our watches – we were now two hours ahead of Moscow. The train slowed down to enter the tunnel under the river Kama, then made a sharp turn to the left to pull up at 5.22 p.m. at Perm II station. Our host, the abbot of the Svyato-Troytzkiy Stefanov Monastery (Monastery of the Holy Trinity of Stefanov) used the short ride to the Visimskaya Street to tell us as much as possible about the city. He seemed a warm person, he had intelligent eyes but was a bit nervous and quite excited. He rattled off the tourist information. Perm is an old Christian city. The bishopric of St. Stephen of Perm was founded as early as the fourteenth century. It is the gateway to Siberia. Nature is incredible and it is the only city to have given its name to a geological period, a phase in the development of the earth. Boris Pasternak wrote *Dr Zhivago* in Perm, my beloved novel about the life of Yuri Zhivago during and after the Revolution, a landmark in the history of Russia. He went on and on and I could see that the abbot was relieved when at last we arrived at the monastery. It had a beautiful church with five gilded domes – a large one in the middle and four smaller ones on the corners – and a separate belfry, all sparkling white. The chapel was also white with golden icons, a relief after all the smoke and soot-blackened churches we had seen so far.

It was about dinnertime, and our host invited us to his private quarters where he offered some of the local vodka. He was still nervous, but I immediately felt at home with him. He told us he had listened to all the talks on the radio and also liked the interviews the abbot had given in Vladimir about the three cylinders. This flattered the abbot and he too felt at ease. Later on dinner was served in his room, just for the three of us. It soon became clear why our host had chosen this unusual arrangement: he wanted to ask a question himself. He started by talking about his own life and what it came down to was that he was no longer satisfied with the work he had enjoyed so much over the past twenty years: leading a monastery in a period that witnessed many changes. He said he felt exhausted, his mind was tired. When the abbot asked whether he wanted to resign, he said that he would rather not do so as it would give him little pleasure 'to just water the flowers'. He was in an impasse, even I could see that. I could also see that raising the issue relieved him, his nervousness was gone. I was wondering how the abbot would deal with the situation but he only asked about our host's age. He had just turned sixty and wondered why that was relevant. The answer made it clear:

'You know I teach that we spend a good deal of time getting to know ourselves. It is a never-ending process as in the course of our lives new prospects open up. One reason for that is that at different stages of our life, we have different objectives. What is desirable for the youth is no longer of interest to the mature man. Knowing oneself, therefore, implies that we must have a good understanding of the stages of life. There have been many attempts to characterise the stages of life, from ancient times onwards. I prefer to think in terms of five stages of growth with periods of transition in-between, each lasting about twenty years although you cannot set your clock by it – it depends on the individual. When people die before they become a hundred years old the later stages are compressed but the principle remains the same.

Each stage of growth has its own objectives and characteristics. At the start of a stage, growth is driven by passion: you suddenly see through the intricacies of that stage and you are filled with urgency to explore it. This brings success and success breeds more success and self-confidence. However, at some point the speed of development slows down. Experiences become repetitive and dull and the passion dries up. Eventually this leads to an impasse – there is always a crisis between two stages. Stages of growth are of an extravert nature – the energy is directed outwards. This is the time for action, external accomplishment. Crises are a time for reflection and contemplation, internal growth – the energy is directed inwards. It is like the day and the night. During the day, the golden sun warms the earth and when you are in a stage of growth, you are like it – you shine and warm up your surroundings. At night, the cold, silvery moon makes the world look mysterious – a time for meditation.

The crises are a period of transition marked by uncertainty, even fear. You have to round off the previous stage and prepare for the next. A crisis is a process of search and as long as the search has not yet yielded a new purpose, you have the feeling: I am not doing what I want because I don't know what I want. Each crisis is made up of two elements – threat and opportunity, farewell and hello –

and this also applies to the last crisis, the crisis of death – the most penetrating of all'.

Our host was listening attentively and so was I. Therefore the abbot continued:
'Having passed through a crisis successfully means that you have completed the previous stage, that you are satisfied with all that belongs to it and that you do not wish to go back to it, rather, you look forward to the next stage. If you remain hovering over the previous stage although it has nothing more to offer, you have not managed to overcome the crisis and your behaviour will look immature. When you have lived each stage to the full you will die satisfied with your life and in harmony with the universe. People, however, who missed part of a stage will search for compensation all their life and will not feel satisfied, however rewarding the other stages in their life may be'.

He paused and we tried to give him a chance to eat something before his dinner got cold. Our host asked me whether I had known such periods – more for the sake of the abbot than out of real interest, I thought. I answered that I had a period of lethargy after I finished school, as I did not know what to do. All the alternatives seemed equally interesting while none was interesting enough. 'How did it end?' he asked. I told him that by coincidence I met two elder sisters of my father's and they mentioned a cousin of theirs, working at Cambridge University. The cousin and her husband invited me, showed me around and infected me with their enthusiasm. Before I knew it, I was immersed in the study of physics and the longer I worked on it, the more involved I became. I love solving puzzles and that is basically what maths and physics is all about.

He looked surprised but I could not help saying: 'Thinking of it, what is science but putting the pieces together and solving a problem? You can admire the view until new pieces are placed on the table, they don't fit and then you have a new riddle to solve'.
'Interesting', he commented and, looking at me, he added: 'Would you say science is your destiny?'
Before I could answer, the abbot intervened, muttering something with his mouth full, like: 'Much too young to answer that, and, besides, he talks too much like a pure scientist, not like an engineer', the rest being inaudible. His mind was on the Lesson and he resumed:

'To sum it up, the key to happiness is to understand the stages and crises of life and do what you need to in each of them. It seems you are at one of the turning points, leaving a stage behind you and entering a new and unfamiliar one. You feel uncomfortable and you wonder what is going to happen. Do you want me to talk about those stages?'

'Oh yes, I have always admired your views, Yevgeni Nikolayevich', his expression showed eagerness, 'I have my own views on many subjects but I can't come to a conclusion about my restlessness'.

Birth

While he and I continued our meal, the abbot began his explanation.

'Life starts with a crisis. Birth is a crisis as you come from a different world and you enter one that is completely unfamiliar, threatening and challenging to you. The objective at birth is to be welcome. Many people are not. If parents and other grown-ups do not demonstrate it explicitly, the baby will anyway feel it. One of our most important duties in life is to be very sure we only bring life into this world that is truly welcome. Not only should your baby be welcome, you should communicate this to the baby and later to the child, even to the grownup child, yes even into old age. When a baby is born, we usually send the parents a card with congratulations and good wishes. It would be better to address the card to the baby, saying: 'Welcome to this world' and hoping that one day he will read it.

The apprentice stage

The apprentice stage is a stage of learning, finding your place in this world. At about the age of twenty you should be able to sustain yourself, to be independent, self-supporting. 'Independence' requires physical and emotional freedom. Emotional independence means becoming free from generation transfer and carry-over. *Carry-over* is the unfinished business from your previous life. If you die suddenly in the midst of a conflict, you will take it to your next life where you will be plagued by anxieties that you cannot place. If, on the other hand, you manage to 'digest' your life before you go, you will not have such anxieties in the next life. A person at the age of twenty will perhaps not be completely free from generation transfer and carry-over but progress is important for his emotional freedom'.

I did not know much about the doctrines of religion, but I was surprised that the abbot mentioned 'previous lives' and 'the next life'. Did he believe in reincarnation? Our host was also quite surprised by the abbot's statement. I noticed he stared at the abbot with wide-open eyes, but, like me, he did not want to interrupt the discourse and, anyway, the abbot was already carrying on:

'Physical independence means knowing your way in the world, having had education or training which allows you to support yourself, being able to establish relationships with friends and superiors. If, as a student, you are still relying on your parents, you can consider yourself independent anyway, as you could be on your own if you would so choose.

Toddlers have not yet developed their outer and middle cylinder. You can see right through them, while signals from the environment go to their inner cylinder unchecked. Then the outer cylinder is gradually formed, protecting the inner cylinder. Later, the middle cylinder comes into being and the child starts to make friends. Still later, sexuality develops and with it comes a deep need for connecting, a need that the child cannot yet satisfy but that eventually leads to glorious intimacies with a partner.

You leave the apprentice stage when your objective – to be independent – has been fulfilled: you are no longer a child. You dare show yourself as you are, you state 'I am who I am'. You stand up for your opinion and you are no longer afraid of conflict. When you leave this stage your development continues, in a sense you will forever be an apprentice'.

He paused to finish his meal and I reflected on my childhood, puberty, adolescence. How vividly I remembered my 'deep desire to connect' that indeed, I had not been able to satisfy as Clara had always remained so distant. I felt sad that I had missed something essential and that this need of belonging was still with me. However, it made me curious about what was to follow.

The stage of opportunity
I did not have to wait long because, as he wiped his mouth, the abbot was again in full swing:
'At about the age of twenty, you are ready to enter the world on your own and begin the development stage of your life. This is the *Stage of Opportunity*. Everything seems possible, there are no limits to what you can achieve. You dream of becoming a famous artist or scientist, an Olympic champion, a powerful business leader or the president of your country. You explore and undertake many things, the stage of opportunity is first of all a stage of exploration. As you explore things and people that cross your path, you develop many aspects of yourself. If you do so, you will greatly benefit later in life. During your apprentice years you remain in the safe environment of the home of your parents and masters. Now it is time to move out – the stage of opportunity is a time for travelling. You learn from different cultures like the

medieval fellows who learned their craft from different masters, you become a *Wandergeselle* – a travelling fellow. You get to know many people, you make new friends while losing your friends from school, unless you manage to give these friendships new impulse. You pick up interests and friends spontaneously, you do not worry how they would look on your cv. Enjoy these years, this springtime of life. There is no need to get serious too soon, use it to explore all things and all people, see much of the world and get a full understanding of human life.

In this 'stage of the fellow', emotion and reason start developing independently. They become increasingly distanced and uncontrollable and this makes life most difficult. You feel madly in love and deeply hurt when your love is not reciprocated or when your ideas are not understood and appreciated. The twenties are the years of *Sturm und Drang* – tempestuous passions. To quote Goethe again, you feel alternatively *himmelhoch jauchzend* and *zum Tode betrübt* – jubilant in heaven and distressed to death.

Your task is clear but you do not see it: you have to develop your will and re-integrate reason and emotion, this is the meaning of Adam and Eve's longing to return to paradise. While you follow your many interests, you gradually discover your strengths and you create more focus in your life. At a certain stage, you commit yourself to your loved one to start a family. Your large and wild circle of friends shrinks to a circle of intimates. You rediscover your family, you find a passion in a profession.

At about the age of forty you will experience a summit: the moment when you have found your destination: your profession, your family, your peers, vital social contacts. You have established a reputation, people know who you are. You have reached the objective of this stage of your life: *to have found your place in the world*. Now you realise that playtime is over and that you have to take seriously the responsibilities that you have all the time longed to bear. When you get them, you rejoice because of the recognition you receive but in your heart you are scared. During the day you are jubilant but at night you worry. This is known as the midlife crisis – threats and opportunities again. Now you have to accept masterhood, overcome and deal with the midlife crisis – death and resurrection – and start the next stage of your life, the *Production Stage*'.

Well, I did not in the least have a feeling of a 'midlife crisis'. I was enjoying my life intensely – travelling, exploring and meeting people, just as the abbot had said. Perhaps I was not doing so badly after all?

'Ah, yes, those were the days', our host exclaimed, taken by memories. 'I was very adventurous but it was also a time of uncertainties. I always had a sense for the religious but I pushed that aside, exploring rather the early computers. We had a machine the size of ten large refrigerators with a memory of six kilobytes, programming it in machine language, literally bit by bit. At the same time I did a lot of Bible reading, it was like living in two worlds'.

'What happened?' the abbot asked.

'I guess I succumbed to my destiny. My two worlds increasingly clashed and when autocode was introduced, my interest in programming dwindled. One day I saw light – you might say it was my Damascus moment – and I presented myself to this monastery. In hindsight, I often wonder what took me so long'.

'How old were you then?' the abbot enquired.

'I remember it as if it was yesterday, I had just turned forty-two', came the answer.

There was no need to comment.

'See what you think of the rest of the story', the abbot said smilingly, as he continued.

The production stage
'Having reached masterhood, you take full responsibility of an enterprise or other fulfilment. It is the stage of production, fulfilling your destination, advancing your career, living a full family life if you have it. These are the years in which you will earn most money and in which you have your greatest expenses: for the education of your children, perhaps the care of your parents and other family members, and in forming holdings that will support you in old age. During this stage, your responsibilities increase. Life is harder, you encounter not only loyalty but also betrayal, triumph and deception follow in rapid succession. You realise that at this stage there is no escape, you cannot afford to make mistakes. You know what you want to achieve and you are willing to fight for it. You may change jobs, perhaps even frequently, but the changes follow a well-recognisable pattern, a line of upward mobility. You remain in the pursuit of your destination.

It is a busy life where you have to be economic in the use of your time and talents. Your work demands much of you and so does your family. There is hardly time for hobbies or contemplation and you regret you cannot attend cultural events the way you used to. It is a time of prioritising, especially after fifty when you will find that your energy level decreases. Initially, you do not mind very much because by now you have enormous experience that more than offsets your diminishing energy. But you have to admit that your children and their friends do certain things better than you. You are no longer the mommy or daddy superstar, you have to earn your position of a parent, they no longer need you. At a certain moment, you meet your children's partners – and their parents and eventually grandchildren – who will play an important role in your life but it is not you who chooses them, you can only hope to establish happy relationships.

People have a deep desire to round off their production stage with a masterpiece, an effort in which they can use all their talents and experience, an effort that will make history. Literature provides many examples: the older artist who produces his masterwork, the scientist who writes his ultimate book, the manager who completes his most difficult project, the sheriff who arrests the most vicious killer.

The objective of the production stage is *to become satisfied with your professional performance* and provide sufficient security for old age. When you have reached this point, you hand over your responsibilities and you retire. Retirement is a crisis, you feel useless while you still have lots of energy and you do not know what to do with it. For women this crisis is less acute as, at the age of sixty, they have overcome the perils of middle age and are full of new energy. Not all women are like this. Garbo never got over her retirement as an actress and Callas kept listening to her records in her Paris apartment behind drawn curtains. Men often feel they have no role to play anymore. They join clubs of peers where they brag about how important they still are – the word 'still' creeps up increasingly. Some men cannot resist the temptation to leave everything behind and marry a young woman in an attempt to start all over again. This, of course, is a dead end. Men who pursue this course have to face the disappointment of their new partner as well as the anger of their former family. Wise couples make a new start together, picking up new or revived interests and getting used to their role of grandparents. Young people – grandchildren and young professionals – need their love and support, experience and wisdom in judgement. It matters no longer what you do, it matters what you are. Once a person has accepted this new role, sees the benefits of it and enjoys the absence of pressing responsibilities, he has passed successfully the crisis of retirement and a period of new vitality begins, the *Stage of Recycling*.

Our host had become increasingly distressed as we had gradually come to the stage his life was at. He leaned forward in his chair and his eyes widened as the abbot continued:

The stage of recycling

'During this fourth stage, roughly from sixty to eighty, you take the role of the 'elder statesman'. A farmer in our neighbourhood said that instead of pulling the cart, he helped to push it while his son was now doing the pulling and steering. You will give back what you have learned, you will coach or teach younger people and you will be satisfied to sit in the back and let others take the driver's seat. This is especially true in your role vis-à-vis your grandchildren: you are not responsible for them yet you play an essential role in their lives. During these years, you can still carry on working but you have to reinvent yourself, in the words of Bob Dylan's song 'That he not busy being born is busy dying'. Rather than take pride in your own success, you find fulfilment in the achievements of others. Neither should you give in to the excitement of passive consumerism, to 'enjoy a well-deserved rest in retirement' as the saying goes. We were created to develop ourselves and love our neighbour, not to sit idle, and having obtained your security does not change this. You have to give back to society what it gave you, like the trees that in the fall return their leaves to the soil whence they extracted the leaves' building blocks in the spring. You discover pleasant new interests for which at last you have the time: life begins at sixty! You will have gained wisdom and you want to use it to help others. Much time will be devoted to judging and guiding younger people, refereeing competitions or professional contributions, writing surveys or guidebooks. The objective of the Recycling Stage is *to pass on your knowledge and experience to the next generation*. In doing so, you will gain a better understanding of what you have experienced – by recycling you ruminate your life. Thus, you prepare for the time when your energies diminish, you prepare for winter. Young people 'are immortal', death feels distant, something theoretical, even when they have been confronted with it. But at the stage of recycling, death becomes much of a reality as friends your age pass away. The frightening *Oh Mensch, gibt Acht!* – Oh man, beware – in Mahler's Third, drives this awareness home. Get your affairs and relationships in order and prepare for the last stage'.

The stage of digestion

While the abbot was speaking, memories of my father came back to me. As a family doctor he had developed an interest in the psychological state of his patients. At the time, this was something new, he had to invent everything himself. He got frustrated, there simply was no time for analysis in a busy GP's practice. Before he could take a turn and follow this new mission, he passed away, deprived of what no doubt would have been a fulfilling recycling stage. If only I could make up for this.

The abbot saw my distress but chose to continue his Lesson. After all, he was talking to our host and had reached the stage of life our host wanted to hear about.

'Gradually your physical strength diminishes and you may develop physical ailments. These, however, should not be a reason to become inactive. At about eighty, you will find that your energy will not be sufficient to carry on at even lower pace. Your contributions become less effective, you are too distant from the realities of the world as it has moved on, you have to give up your driving license and you may need help which is a strange experience for those who have never been seriously ill or disabled. As far as sex is concerned, it is like Picasso said 'There may be little action but it is always on your mind, perhaps more so than ever'.

This is where you enter the last stage of your life, the *Stage of Digestion*. This stage will start at about the age of eighty and it will continue until the moment you have to pack your bags and make the transition to the next life. The objective of the last stage is to prepare for this transfer: to clean up the bits and pieces left behind after an active existence, to digest your experiences in order to start again on a clean slate. You will spend much time reconsidering all you have been through, going over it for the second, third, umpteenth time, contemplating what you did and why, coming to terms with all the things you did wrong or did not finish. You become introvert, you have clear memories of your early childhood and you relive your life, digesting it as it were. You become focussed on the past instead of the future. You have had enough of the daily hassle, you want rest. In the previous stage, there was an urgency to rectify or complete developments that you did not attend to earlier. After eighty, you no longer feel this desire, you live more in your own world.

In the stage of recycling the outer cylinder becomes thinner and you reveal your inner self more explicitly than before. You are past embarrassment. Some people become ever friendlier, others – ever more bitter. Your true nature surfaces up.

When I am in Moscow, I visit an old friend who is now ninety-four and lives with his granddaughter who, together with her children, takes care of him. I buy him some chocolate at Tverskaya and ask whether he has time for me. He has nothing to do yet he seems very busy. He tells me he does not read the papers anymore, he sometimes watches television for a while but there is usually too much violence for his taste. His radio is next to him but he rarely switches it on. He says it is difficult to explain what he is doing. He spends a lot of time in bed but he does not sleep. He thinks about events of the past, his childhood, his parents, his wife, his children when they were young. These are not contemplations but images that run like episodes of a movie, he passes no judgement on them, they just happen and he is satisfied with the way it goes. Images of his early childhood that he never remembered before come through quite clearly. He says his great-grandchildren are afraid he is bored but that is not the case, he is beyond boredom. He does not think much of death – what to think of it? – but he has made arrangements for his funeral, a mass in our church, like his parents and his wife before him. He hopes it will not be painful and if it is, he will get medication against the pain. He says he is lucky that his granddaughter and her children respect him because many people use babytalk to old people – they no longer take them seriously. That is hell, he says.

Gradually your energies dry up, the light of your candle fades away and you start longing for the moment God calls you. Death is the last crisis with severe threats and unseen opportunities and I will discuss it later'.

Our host and I
The abbot waited a moment, then continued:
'Back to your problem: it seems that you have trouble making the passage that corresponds to one of the six watersheds of your life. The one at sixty is the most difficult as it is the transition from expansion to contraction. Rather than be sad that the production stage is over, you should be proud to have delivered good successors and hope they will do even better than you. And if they look independent, do not forget they still need you, not your physical strength, but your wisdom, your mental support and your love'.

The words of the abbot sounded prophetic as the candles in the room were burning down.

'To step back will be very difficult for me', our host whispered. 'Perhaps I have reached my level of incompetence. What should I do about it?'
'Only a good coach, or, better still, a number of unselfish peers can help you out. Being a man, you are at a disadvantage as it is women who are more likely to listen to others and take their advice. Men want to be in charge, they want to do everything themselves. Or they get bad advisors, loyal perhaps, but not up to the task. We should never forget that everyone needs a coach, or coaches. If we listen to what they say while following our own instincts, we shall overcome the hurdle and rise up to the job, do what needs to be done, and come out successfully'.

Our host repeated in his own words what the abbot had said and it seemed that the advice was exactly what he needed: to step down from his responsibilities and take the back seat but he didn't seem quite ready to accept it yet.

'It seems to me that the passage from one stage to the next is very difficult if you feel that you haven't accomplished the things that have been most important to you', he said.

At this moment it was Clara who suddenly came to my mind. I realised that the stage in which she could have played the leading role had irrevocably passed. My eyes were filled with tears. Both abbots sensed immediately that something was wrong and their faces straightened while they sat up in their chairs.

I tried to pluck my courage. Finally I stumbled:

'When I was eight, a new girl came into our class'.

And, looking at the abbot:

'I am sorry, I never told you this'.

He nodded encouragingly. Our host was silent, he sensed the tension.

'I was head over heals in love with her the moment I saw her. I know that sounds peculiar for an eight years' old, but that's how it was. I tried to be in her company as much as I could but I did not make much progress, boys and girls don't play together at that age, at least, not in England. We moved to grammar school together. It was a conservative small town, there was not much choice'.

I could not help it, my voice had become shaky. The abbot sat close to me and put his arm around my shoulder. That made it even worse. I felt so ashamed.

'You must go on Steve, don't stop now', the abbot whispered.

I composed myself and went on:

'At grammar school my infatuation was so obvious that I became the butt of jokes. I was paralysed. When another boy took her out, I didn't know what to do, even tough it probably did not amount to much. Finally, in the exam year, we established a relationship. It was a hot spring and we would go for a swim in the river nearby. I would wait for her at the crossroads and we would bike there together. I was in heaven. Gradually we started doing our homework together. In my room I had a radio-amplifier and I had saved up for a CD-player. It was a beautiful afternoon, very peaceful. When we finished work, I put on Dvorak's Ninth, such powerful piece, a blend of classical music and jazz. Something must have happened and we started kissing, it went all by itself. It felt like a holy moment, after ten years of torture. I asked her whether she would now be my girl-friend and she said yes. We started behaving like a couple. She was my source of inspiration, I passed my exams with flying colours. But we could not spend the summer together, our parents took care of that'.

Our host got up to put in new candles. They didn't fit. 'They always buy the wrong ones and now I have to trim them', he grumbled. He got a pocketknife from a drawer and started working on the candles above a wastepaper basket. He made a wrong move and cut his finger. 'Damn it' he exclaimed. Then, noticing that this was not an expression for a man of the cloth, he quickly mumbled something like 'Sorry brother', looking at the abbot.

'Is it deep?' the abbot wondered.

'Not really, I just need to get a bandage', and he left the room.

'It is good that you get this out, Steve', the abbot said, his arm still around me, 'You are very brave but I have a hunch that there is more to it'.

I nodded. The worst was still to come. But first, I had to come to my senses.

Our host returned and lit the new candles.

'So, this is better', he said casually. His presence somehow made me feel safe.

'We went to university', I went on, 'in different cities. When we came home for the weekend, it seemed she wanted to spend more time with her family than with me. I ignored that, hoping for better times. It would all come together when we would be married and she had agreed to do that right after earning our degrees. When the moment came however, she told me she wanted to break the relationship. 'I love you but not enough' was her expression. And 'Let us stay friends'.

'Oof, that is the worst', our host could not help himself, 'You must have been living in different worlds'.

'I later thought she might have used me to keep other boys at bay', I guessed.

Then the abbot stepped in:

'Steve, it is good that you have told me your story at last', he said. 'But I think there is more to it. How did you meet while you were students?'

'We would go home every three or four weeks and see each other in the evenings', I said.

'What else did you do while studying?' the abbot enquired further.

'Oh, I was very busy. Classes in the exact sciences occupied most of the daytime and in addition I was editor of a student journal, chairman of the fencing club and a scoutmaster in the weekends'.

'Did you call her often?'

'There was hardly time for that'.

'Doesn't sound she was a priority to you'.

The hit of a hammer could not have been more painful. She had always been on my mind but I had to admit, I had ignored her desire to go and see her during weekends, I was simply too busy.

'Perhaps you used her as a source of energy while you were doing your own things. Perhaps you were not ready yet for such a relationship while you did need the illusion. What happened to her anyway?'

'She married a pharmacist soon after we broke up, four years ago'.

'A pharmacist!' our host exclaimed. The abbot gestured him to stay quiet.

'And then?'

'She has got two children and I guess there are more to come but I don't know, we lost touch'.

'And you?'

While talking I could again feel the intense pain of her betrayal. The abbot may have referred to her as an illusion but to me my love for her had been very real, actually, it was still very real. And here I was talking about her, my dear Clara, for the first time, to those two fathers.

'I promised myself never to go out with girls anymore', I whispered. 'One experience like this is enough'.

Our host gestured that he did not believe this but the abbot ignored him.

'Perhaps it is', he said, 'Perhaps not. Let me tell you something, There is this girl waiting for you out there. You don't know her and she doesn't know you, yet when you meet, you will know'.

I had nothing to say to that and there was a long silence.

Our host decided to change the subject and come back to the Lesson.

'How do you feel about your own age', he asked the abbot, 'We must be about the same vintage'.

'That's right', the abbot responded, 'As I am still leading the monastery – albeit with much delegation – I am still in the Production stage. You might say I am overdue'.

'If you allow me to ask a personal question', our host went on, 'How do you reconcile your work with your unorthodox teaching?'

The abbot was hesitant – the first time since I met him.

'The truth is I love what I do at the monastery and my contacts with the people seeking my help. And though I do not like to confess it', he said after a while, 'being an abbot makes my position stronger for the messages I want to deliver'.

'You said people of our age want to produce their masterpiece. Why don't you do that?'

'Isn't that exactly what he is doing?' I interrupted.

'Oh, you smart aleck, stop it please', the abbot exclaimed jokingly, relieved to change the subject.

We helped our host clear the table. Then we decided to retire. After all, it was well past midnight and the abbot had to be well rested for the meeting in the morning.

8. Perm – Matrioshka

The next morning we took it easy. We skipped Prime, attended Terce, had a quiet breakfast, then met the congregation at 10 a.m. The abbot more or less repeated the Lesson he had given privately to our host the previous evening.

There was a lively discussion, mostly on the abbot's classification of birth and death as transition phases, in essence no different from the other transitions. Someone remarked that such a view hinted at reincarnation. The abbot said that sometimes he believed in it and at other times he did not. He admitted it was not logical but then emotions rarely are. The people were very surprised at his words that flew in the face of the Church doctrine but when they saw their own abbot taking it calmly, they seemed to set aside the dogma and try to understand the core of the idea.

We rounded off at about 1 p.m. and still had some time before departure. We walked along the vast river Kama, admiring the old steel bridge and viewing the many hills on which Perm is built. Perm is at the crossing point of roads as well as waterways. The river Kama is part of an important route that connects Perm not only to the Northern seas – the White Sea, the Baltic Sea and the Kara Sea – but also to the Southern seas: the Black Sea, the Sea of Azov and, as the Kama feeds into the Volga, the Caspian Sea. Tsar Peter I decided to develop Yegoshikha, the old name of the village that was to become Perm, together with Yekaterinburg. It became a major trade centre and the town – later city – has been expanding rapidly since that time. We visited the main church named after Mary Magdalene – a remarkable name for a church. I felt we were at a crossroads ourselves as I was wondering what direction the next Lesson would take.

At 5.42 p.m. it was time to board the train. After we had left the railway yards – Perm is also a major railway hub – a friendly guard came in. Though we had not ordered anything she was carrying a dinner tray with two glasses of vodka, sausages, cheese and pieces of tomato and cucumber. 'Compliments of the Trans Siberian Express' ', she said seeing our embarrassment. That was nice and we invited her to join us. She declined, saying it was not allowed for staff to sit with passengers, but the abbot saw her hesitation and asked her whether she wanted to talk to him. It turned out that she had attended the meeting in Perm – it so happened that she served on the same train with which we had arrived. Indeed, she wanted to talk about something that was on her mind and it became obvious she was a sharp observer and a good analyst of herself.

Parallel stages

'I liked the way you described the stages of life', she started. 'But I have this weird feeling that I don't fit in any of them. Sometimes I feel I am in one stage and the next moment it is like I am in quite another. I don't seem to fit your description.'

'Does that mean you feel at an earlier stage than the one you are in now?' the abbot inquired.

'No, and that is why it is so strange', she blushed a little. 'Sometimes when I talk to people my age, I feel I am talking like an old woman'.

'So, it is in relation to others that you feel like being in a stage different from the one you are in?' the abbot explored further.

'That is exactly how it is. It is not related to the age of the person I am with, it is just that I sometimes feel older or younger than what I really am', she concluded.

The abbot had to give this some thought. His answer came after a while:

'The stages of life represent layers around you. Underneath your appearance of a powerful adult, there is still the child, the adolescent, the young apprentice, like the layers of clothing you wear on your body. You can peel off these layers like the puppets of a Matrioshka that some of our brothers make for the tourists in our country. If you make the effort, you can approach someone at his former layers. You can communicate with the child in someone of advanced age. This explains why even very old people can fall in love like children, perhaps to the embarrassment of those around them. Similarly, at a young age, you can communicate at levels you have not yet reached but that are present in *statu nascendi* – in a state of becoming. This explains why young people can sometimes act remarkably mature for their years, they use the virtual layers of older age they carry. We live consciously in one stage of life but subconsciously we live all phases simultaneously'.

The guard had to think about this. Then she continued:

'I see what you mean and it makes sense to me. It is confusing because sometimes I relate to the same person as if I am in a different stage of life. For instance, when I do the dishes with the younger girls, I feel I am one of them, their age, we chat like teenagers. At another time, when I have to supervise them, because the women in the first class compartments are senior guards and they are in charge of junior staff, I speak from the position of someone considerably older'.

The abbot nodded. He told her it happened to him as well. Like all monks, he had to take turns working in the vegetable garden and when doing so, he would take instructions from the main gardener who was much younger than he but more experienced in gardening. In doing so, he would act as an apprentice rather than the head of the monastery.

'Wasn't there this theory that, when communicating with other people, we are either at the same age level, or a generation older or younger than the other person?' I remembered.

'It is much more complicated', the abbot answered, 'We can also be the younger or elder brother, in fact we can be any age. This applies to the person you communicate with as well. It can even change in the course of a conversation'.

Then, addressing the guard:

'What you experience is nothing uncommon, it is just that most people don't realise that communication is so complex. All is well as long as you are aware of what happens. And you are very much aware of this mechanism so I must compliment you on your insight, your knowledge of yourself'.

The circle of confidence

She blushed again and started cleaning the table. When she had left, I asked the abbot:

'When you have these very private conversations, how do you keep them confidential?'

'OK, let me show you', he replied smilingly. 'Let us both get up and stand next to each other'.

We did and I was curious what would follow.

'Now you stretch out your right hand and I my left hand.' I was on his left so our hands touched.

'Now we point our hands to the floor, say one metre away, and we both turn around 180 degrees until we face the other side of the room and our hands meet again. This way we draw an imaginary circle around us. Imagine that this circle is like a wall, sound proof, making a secluded space just for you and me. The wall has teeth. The teeth are two-way: nothing can go out and nothing can get in. Nothing we say can be heard outside the circle and nothing that happens outside can be heard inside. All that is said within the circle will stay there. When one of us has no need of the circle anymore, he will clap his hands and the circle will disappear. But whatever was said would remain within the circle, unless one gives the other permission to communicate parts of the conversation to others'.

I thought that was beautiful.

We prepared for a nap, as we would arrive at Yekaterinburg close to midnight. The abbot went to sleep quickly and I watched the mountains disappear into the moonlight, a sight of majesty and beauty. It was still cold, the sky was clear and there was no more snow or rain. Then, suddenly, a feeling of intense happiness came over me. I felt in higher realms, lifted up into an unreal world, surrounded by angels and it felt as if another veil had been lifted from my eyes. I could clearly see the situation I was in, as if I was looking at myself from higher up. All the abbot's Lessons, all our conversations, raced in my head. Then I came back to earth, the feeling subsided. It felt as if I had crossed a borderline. I got up, went into the bathroom and, as I had done at other turning points in my life, looked into the mirror.

'Hey boy, what is happening to you?' my reflection said.

'I don't know, I have learned so many things, it is so confusing and at the same time it gives me such a deep feeling of wellbeing'.

'You can be satisfied with yourself. You have gained much insight but remember the abbot said that getting to know yourself is a lifelong process, it never ends'.

I turned away from the mirror and standing again by the window, behind which the cold and crisp panorama unfolded, I realised that I would always be a student of myself. At the same time I felt I had entered a new phase of my development, one that had nothing to do with the stages of life, but something else and I did not know what it was, I could not even guess. I only felt a strong urge to get away from my computer and into the real world I had just a glimpse of, the world of real people. Although I never realised it, I had always been frightened of this world. To my surprise, I now found it fascinating and more interesting than my familiar world of physics.

Love

9. Yekatarinburg – Universal love

It was six hours to Yekaterinburg, Boris Yeltsin's birthplace, six hours of ploughing through the Urals, the time zone still two hours ahead of Moscow. We arrived an hour before midnight at the Sverdlovsk Passagiri Station, like Gorki-Most Vokzal still called by the communist name of the city. Although it is the first city in Asian Russia, at the very border between Europe and Asia, we did not notice any difference with the European cities, we would first see it in Irkutsk. Still, we entered another world. We had made it to Siberia, this land of endless wilderness, now polluted and corrupt but once pure and mysterious. The name 'Siberia' originates from the Mongolian word 'siber', meaning 'beautiful' and 'pure', or the Tartar word 'sibir', meaning 'sleeping land'. It is Russia's 'Wild East', similar to America's 'Wild West' with as many indigenous tribes – the Dolgan, Ket, Yakut, Buryat, Samoyed, Dauria, Entsy and so many others. Like the North-American Indians, they have their shaman beliefs, mixed sometimes with Mongolian Buddhism. These tribes were overpowered by the Cossacks, the cowboys of the East, who were followed by vagabonds, gold diggers and seekers of the 'soft gold' (furs), traders, river pirates, exiled religious and political dissidents and most of all by millions of convicts and prisoners of war who were forced into slave labour in the numerous mines of the Gulag – which only few survived. Larger in area than the moon, home to some of the world's biggest rivers – the Ob, Yenisei, Lena and Amur – endless forests and the deepest, oldest and largest lake of the world – Lake Baikal – Siberia is the site of immeasurable beauty and cruelty. And of love, as I was soon to discover.

For a change, the train was early and we ordered a cup of tea in the waiting room where we could not help overhearing the conversation of a young couple, sitting at the next table.

'Still half an hour left, how do we kill the time', the woman said. Apparently, they were heading towards the East on the train we had come with.

'Let us give each other a riddle,' he suggested.

She agreed, thought, then said: 'Tell me the difference between friendship and love'.

This was more a question than a riddle and we were quite curious how the conversation would develop.

He answered: 'They are very important yet very different'.

'That is not good enough'.

'Friendship has something conditional about it. With most people, you have contractual relations, implicit or explicit. When the contract expires or when it is no longer useful, the relationship comes to an end. Love is unconditional, if I love you, it means I will always be there for you, I will always back you up'.

'I don't agree', she replied. 'I have friends from the days I grew up. Some of them I haven't seen for years, yet when we meet, we pick up from where we left off as if no time has passed. If I can, I would certainly help them and vice versa. On the other hand, look at all these divorces, it seems it is love rather than friendship that is conditional'.

'Yes, but friends can be very critical'.

'That would only mean they are good friends. Friends can criticise or pass judgement on each other, even be quite blunt, but it is always understood that their advice is offered in good faith, unselfishly'.

'Are friends intimate?'

'Not in the physical sense of course, but otherwise, yes. A friend is someone you can trust, someone you can share your intimate thoughts with. A friend is always there for you'.

'Yes, but that is the same with someone you love. So, we are back to square one. What is the difference?'

She had to think a little and then said:

'It is not like love is friendship plus the physical thing. You also love your parents, your cat, perhaps your country'.

'Do you really love all of them?'

'Of course I do. And I definitely can say I love my friends'

'OK, you love your cat, your friends, your parents, perhaps your city and I hope you still love me. Not a very selective lover you are.'

He waited, then smiled:

'Why don't you tell me the difference between friendship and love, then that is my riddle for you?'

She thought a little, then put her arm on the table and asked him to place his next to hers.

'What do you see', she asked.

'I see two arms, lying parallel on the table'. The smile was gone.

'Can you see which is yours and which is mine?'

'Of course I can see that. This is your arm, here are your fingers, here it goes into the elbow'.

She then put her arm behind his, twisting the arms around and interlocking the fingers.

'What do you see now?' she asked.

'It is now basically one thing, you have to look carefully to see which fingers are yours and which are mine'.

'That is the essence of love, you merge, there is no longer a clear distinction between you and me, we become one. It is like two communicating vessels: you see the two vessels but underneath they are linked, they have a common base. You know that the Bible says: 'They become one flesh'. That is usually understood in the physical sense but it means much more. Now let us sit like this for a moment and be silent. Then you tell me how it feels'.

They sat silently with interlocked arms and fingers. It was a very intimate moment and we felt embarrassed to be eavesdropping but they did not seem to notice.

At first, there was nothing out of the ordinary. Then, looking each other in the eyes, their grips tightened. They held each other for several minutes, then loosened their hands and sat apart again. She looked at him with a questioning look.

'Well', he searched for words. 'It was as if a stream of energy was flowing from your body into mine. It was just too strong for words. And you?'

We could not hear her answer. Then his smile came back again:

'Does that mean we are in love?' he asked.

'Oh, you men can be so stupid'.

He started tickling her and she laughed:

'Stop that, we have a train to catch!'

At that moment, the abbot of the Ganina Yama (Ganya's Pit) Monastery entered the waiting room. He was young for an abbot and he had a calm, friendly face.

'At last I found you', he said. 'We didn't know the train was early and we searched all the platforms'.

The abbot apologised for the inconvenience but our host would not hear of it.

'Let us get in the car, it is only a short drive – fifteen kilometres', and he led the way. As we passed Kirovgrad, Nizhny Tagil and Verchnaya Tura, he was kind enough to explain to me that the area was an important mining region, reason for Yekaterina the Great to expand the city that by coincidence bore her name, Yekaterinburg.

'In one of the mines, the Four Brothers mine in Koptyaki, our city, is the Ganina Yama pit where the communists threw the bodies of Tsar Nicholas II and his family after they had murdered them in Yekaterinburg. How they must have hated them. When they learned the White Army had found out the location, they moved the remains a day later to Porosenkov Ravine, eight kilometres away. The bodies were only found in the 1970s and later buried in Saints Peter and Paul in St. Petersburg. The Ganina Yama area was declared holy ground and our monastery was founded there in 2001'.

Although this was nothing new to him, the abbot listened to our host and then, for his part, told him what we overheard at the railway station about love and friendship.

'Very interesting', our host said pensively. 'I can also say I love my brothers. Oh, please, don't get me wrong', he added.

'Perhaps we should make this tomorrow's subject. What do you think?' the abbot suggested, as we were approaching our destination. Our host smiled at him:

'I am sure tomorrow our friends would love that'.

At that, we arrived at our destination. Instead of the usual buildings coated with plaster, the monastery consisted of a number of small, wooden cottages, built amongst the trees on grassland, lamps fitted to the branches. The monastery sheds were surrounded by chapels, one for each member of the imperial family. It was a sober arrangement, yet very impressive. We stood silently, thinking of the murdered.

Our host broke the silence saying that the monastery was charged with the maintenance of the chapels.

'It is not just the physical maintenance', he said. 'We also have to protect the spirit of this sacred place. All the time people want to use the premises for fancy ceremonies but we won't have any of that. This monastery has to remain a sanctuary where people can pray for the souls of the deceased'.

'You must be proud of being its custodian', the abbot ventured.

He hit the nail on the head, as our host beamed into a big smile:

'With the personal intervention of the Patriarch. He considered me the only person capable of preserving this place and I was delighted to oblige'.

He then offered refreshments but the abbot waved them away. We just wanted to go to sleep and went to bed in the early hours of the morning.

Forms of love

After Terce, we had a late breakfast and were shown into the auditorium, the largest building on the site, where our host, dignified now, took the floor:

'Today, we are honoured to have Abbot Yevgeni Nikolayevich Rostov as our distinguished guest. He will speak to us about love'.

I was wondering how the Lesson would proceed. After all, love is such a common subject even though I understand little of it. What is there to say? The initial uneasiness was overcome by an elderly man with a matter-of-fact face and long, grey hair.

'Let me say, first of all, how grateful we are that you are here, father Rostov, and especially that you are willing to discuss such a delicate subject with us. We all know what it is but it is so difficult to put words to it. I have been thinking much about love but I must confess that I find the subject confusing. It seems to me that the word 'love' can have a variety of meanings as there are so many different kinds of love'.

The abbot took the floor and after thanking his young counterpart for his hospitality and greeting the congregation, said:

'I tend to agree with the brother who just spoke. Love is a complex issue as there are many kinds of love and strangely enough, our language has only one word for them all. The ancient Greeks did better, they had four words for love. *Agape*, the word used by St Paul in his letters, stood for deeper or 'true' love. *Philia* meant friendship, loyalty to friends, family, and community. It implied virtue, equality and familiarity and was used in the name of the city of Philadelphia – City of Brotherly Love. *Eros*, the third word for love in ancient Greek, was about passionate love, with sensual desire and longing. *Storge* stood for a natural affection, for instance the love felt by parents for their children. Now, all this is rather confusing. The meanings overlap and the words have no equivalent in our modern language. Therefore, I suggest that we make a fresh start, beginning with first of all universal love and then its different manifestations.

Universal love is the vital force for all that lives, unconditional, all-embracing and omnipotent. This love is present in every bit of the world and in every day of our life. We just have to learn how to recognise it. People whom the gift of recognition has been granted experience universal love directly; they often call it God's love. The less endowed experience universal love in one of its manifestations: romantic and eventually total love between a man and a woman, partial love, friendship, love for one's parents, love for one's children, one's cat and many other forms. If you think of it, all forms of love have something in common – the emotional attachment between you and the object of your love. You feel happy when something good happens to the objects of your love and you are sad when they experience hardship. To love means you are emotionally attached, even if your love is one-sided. We can love regardless whether the other responds to our feelings. But love can only lead to a relationship if it is mutual'.

A young man, nervous and fidgety, got up:
'It is terrible when love is not mutual. I was very much in love with a girl from our town but she did not love me back, however much I tried'.
'Alas, this happens often. Yet, if it is not mutual, your love will not develop into the relationship you yearn for. You simply fell in love with the wrong person. It is a situation that you have to analyse, despite the overwhelming emotions'.
'How do I analyse something like that?'
'Does it occur to you more often?'
He hesitated, then went on:
'As a matter of fact, yes, it happened a few times and it makes me wonder whether I am at all attractive to the opposite sex'.
The abbot had to think about this, then continued:
'You should never have doubts in yourself. Everyone can find true love if one is sincere, and I think you are very sincere. Deep in ourselves we have images of, in your case, women, who played an important role in your early childhood, for instance your mother, an aunt, a teacher. These women are familiar to you, your memory of them is imprinted on your inner cylinder. What happens is that we tend to fall in love with someone who resembles one of the images. That explains why we can fall in love with such different people. But the fact that we fall in love with a woman, who we subconsciously feel familiar with, does not mean that we also feel familiar to her. You have to analyse the situation, as you always have to when something goes wrong in your life. In this case, you may find that you fooled yourself by expecting that love would automatically be mutual which it isn't. Try to turn these sad events into a learning experience. Think about it, see other women and try to analyse your feelings'.

The meaning of love
The young man did not know how to react but a straightforward woman who asked a simple question broke the impasse:
'Yevgeni Nikolayevich, what is the meaning of love?'

The abbot's expression became concentrated. I could see he was connecting to his deeper layers. He took off his glasses and stared into the distance, quite unlike him as he usually looked at the audience. His words came slowly, with long intervals:

> 'Love is the essence of human life. Man's ultimate destiny is to give and receive love.
>
> Without love, we live in a mechanical world.
>
> Without love we are like a hollow vessel, we have no substance.
>
> Love turns the black-and-white picture of our life into a riot of colours, drum beat – into fine music.
>
> Love makes us humble, full of gratitude.
>
> Love is not selfish, it seeks the happiness of the loved one more than one's own.
>
> Love is patient, it bides its time.
>
> Love is understanding and forgiving.
>
> Initially, love will focus on those who are dear to you but eventually you may come to love all creatures as well as nature. This is true universal love. If you reach that stage, you become like Jesus, Gautama or St Francis and you can do miracles.
>
> Giving love and receiving love go hand in hand and together they are our central talent that every human being instinctively wishes to develop.
>
> Love in all its forms gives us security and the opportunity to grow.
>
> Indeed, to love is the purpose of every human being'.

This lecture was followed by silence, some people crossed themselves. Even the radio reporters were quiet. While speaking, the abbot looked for a moment like a holy man, transcending. Then I saw he was exhausted. I signalled to our host but he wanted to ask a question himself:

'Yevgeni Nikolayevich, you mentioned only briefly God's love for this world. Could you say something more about it?'

The abbot pulled himself together and answered:

'God is inside ourselves, a divine spark that is in each of us. So when you say: 'I love God', or 'God loves me', it means you are at peace with yourself'.

Our host then ended the meeting, saying we would resume after Sext. We were given a cell in which the abbot could rest. While bringing us there, our host whispered in my ear 'What he said about God's love is pure heresy.' I did not know what to say, and blurted out 'Well, it is close to how I feel about it'. He looked at me with disdain, but then we reached the cell. They brought us refreshments. I am not sure whether the abbot slept but I could not, despite the short night we had had before the meeting started, a new world had opened up indeed.

He must have felt my stare. He lifted himself up a little to say:

'Steve, don't look so worried. All I need is a moment to come to myself. But I can see there is something on your mind again. What are you thinking about?'

I hated myself for not being able to hide my anxiety. I hesitated. Mustering courage, I said:

'You may find it weird but ever since I read the Prologue of St John's gospel in your study room, it has been bothering me'.

'How come?' he asked.

'Well, it goes something like this:

'In the beginning was the Word, and the Word was with God, and the Word was God. He was in the beginning with God. All things were made by him and without him nothing was made that was made. In him was life, and that life was the light of men. And the light shines in the darkness, but the darkness has not understood it'.

'What about it? the abbot asked.

I had been thinking about it so much that my answer came in a flash:

'When I read it first, it seemed abracadabra to me. Then I found on the Internet that 'Word', 'Logos' in the original Greek, has a much wider meaning than 'word'. It can mean universal truth. I guess it can also mean love. I found that the Talmud answers the question 'Why did God create heaven and earth?' with 'Out of love'. And then we should not forget that it was God's Word that created the universe. The Bible says 'Thou seeest no other image of me than my Voice'. So, Word and Love are closely linked. Now when you were talking, I thought that, if you replace 'Word' by 'Love' and allow yourself some liberties, the text begins to make sense to me.

'In the beginning there was Love, and the Love was with God, indeed, it was God. All things have been made through Love and nothing that exists was not made by Love. In Love was life and that life is the light of men. This light shines in the darkness but the darkness has not understood its meaning'.

The abbot had to think about this.

'It just came up', I said.

Then he said:

'Apparently you have done your homework, I didn't know you studied the Bible. I am not sure whether you may make this replacement. But you are right, it does make sense this way and perhaps that is what John meant in the first place. At least, it is a good description of universal love'.

Hate

He paused but then he saw I had another question and he invited me to continue.

'You talked so beautifully about love and I was wondering whether you could say something about hate. Is it the opposite of love?'

'Ah, you got me there', he said, 'Indeed I don't like to speak about it, I guess, I wish it wasn't there. But you may be right calling hate the opposite of love. If you really hate someone, you feel good when something evil happens to this person. Hate comes when someone stands in the way of your happiness – either security or development. Unrequited love can turn into hate, as the other person blocks the development of one's talent for love. Envy, jealousy can turn into hate. In sport for instance, there are elaborate rituals to prevent this from happening: a 'good sport' congratulates the winner, though not always whole-heartedly. Oppression invokes hate, especially towards those who are the symbol of it, like the Romanovs. Hate is a deep emotion; like love, it rests in the inner cylinder like a negative talent. It can give rise to more hatred but it can also turn into forgiveness if you understand the reasons for it. Our Lord has taught us to love those who hate us and that is perhaps the most difficult thing to do'.

Another silence. Then I ventured:

'Humiliation also leads to hatred'.

'Indeed, it affects our self-respect and therefore our sense of security', the abbot answered. 'Then it is difficult not to nurture hate. If we jeopardise someone's security, this person will certainly develop feelings of hatred and that may lead to unforeseen actions'.

Unfortunately, these words would turn out to be quite prophetic.

10. Yekatarinburg – Friendship

We resumed after Sext and again there was some hesitation in the audience. Should they ask further questions about universal love or focus on one of its manifestations? If so, which one? The abbot encouraged his followers to ask anything that was on their mind. At last a young man got up, a student perhaps, a bit frivolous as he smiled when taking a lighter turn.

'You mentioned love between friends. I have some very good friends but I would not describe my feelings as love, that is reserved for women, I am afraid'.

He looked a bit macho and was visibly proud of his remark.

Deep friendship

The abbot shook his head slightly as though he was speaking to himself. He had to consider his answer but then it came, bit by bit:

'A friend is someone you can confide in without shame or hesitation. With a friend, you can safely talk about yourself and everything you are interested in. With a friend, you feel at ease.

A friend is always there for you. You may not have seen him for years but when you call him, he will be there.

A friend plays the violin for you at your initiation.

A friend loves you for what you are. He could criticise you but in a conflict, he will support you, without reservation. Friendship means also taking care of each other.

Friends wish each other the very best and are willing to contribute to each other's wellbeing. A friend is involved, not casual or indifferent.

A friend warns and encourages. A friend is critical, holds the mirror in front of you. He will do so for your benefit, he does not have an agenda of his own.

In this sense, a friend kneads your middle cylinder, he opens it up when it has hardened, revealing new horizons. He ruthlessly exposes the stumbling blocks inside you – your false ambitions and your emotional inhibitions – painful as this sometimes may be. Friends give each other security, feedback and support and they keep each other on the right track.

Friends influence each other, you can say that they write in each other's books, the books of life.

Friends are not envious, a woman will gladly help a friend get new clothes even if the friend will look prettier than she. A man will be proud if his friend achieves more than he does.

Friendship does not come easy, it has to be learned and cultivated. Only when you have enough self-respect, can you accept and reciprocate friendship.

Friendship is mutual, if one only takes and the other only gives, it does not work. Friendship is, therefore, also the art of giving and taking'.

The young man looked at the abbot in surprise.

'Wow'. This exclamation was a bit out of place but it seemed to escape him and nobody minded, 'I have dozens of friends but I never realised all this'.

Acquaintances
The abbot reacted critically:

'If you have dozens I wonder whether they are real friends. Perhaps you have a thousand friends on Facebook but you probably don't know half of them. You have of course a lot of acquaintances with whom you have social contacts but these relationships are often conditional: you know them from your work, a club, as a neighbour. When conditions change, the relationship with an acquaintance ends while friendship endures. Acquaintances may help you and you may help them but this cannot be taken for granted. The help has to fit your or their agenda, you cannot rely on it. Young people can form groups, even gangs, with strong codes of loyalty and conduct 'one for all and all for one'. This feels like friendship but like all acquaintances, it only involves the outer cylinder while true friendship involves the middle cylinder and love the inner cylinder. You may mistake an acquaintance for a friend and then be disillusioned if he lets you down. In this case, don't pity yourself, it is you who made the mistake'.

'How many real friends can you have then?' the man asked.

'Only a few, four or five at most, I would say. Like good wine, friendship needs time to mature. You have to spend a lot of time with someone before you become friends. That is why friendships formed at school can be so strong', was the abbot's reaction.

The man looked around to see whether other people wanted to ask a question, but then he addressed the abbot again and said:

'I am sorry for taking so much time, but may I ask you two more questions. Can people with different backgrounds be friends? Can you have groups of friends?'

'Hardly', the abbot answered. 'Most friends share a common background, common ideals, lifestyle, education but nothing is impossible as Kipling said in his 'Ballad of East and West':

> 'Oh, East is East, and West is West, and never the twain shall meet
> Till Earth and Sky stand presently at God's great Judgment Seat
> But there is neither East nor West, Border, nor Breed, nor Birth
> When two strong men stand face to face, though they come from the ends of the earth'.

To answer your second question: friendship is usually a relationship between two individuals. If you have several friends, they do not necessarily have to be friends too. However, there are groups of friends, often going back to the time you went to school or university'.

'Still, I have the feeling I have many more friends than say four, as you mentioned', the man responded.

The abbot: 'There is no clear distinction between a friend and an acquaintance. There are people whom you know better than an acquaintance but with whom you do not share your intimate experiences. Such acquaintances are people you have something in common with, whose company you enjoy, whom you love for what they are, whom you take an interest in, whom you would help or simply be there for if and when they need a shoulder to cry on, who would discuss certain thoughts and feelings with you. The saying goes that a good neighbour is worth more than a friend who is far away. However, in contrast with true friends, the range of subjects you discuss with these friends is restricted.

Then a woman asked the next question:

'Father Rostov, what is the difference between friendship and love, I mean love as in the sense of love between a man and a woman?'

'In the case of romantic love, say between a man and a woman, there is a merging of the inner cylinders, a merging of their deepest selves. In the case of what I shall call total love – of which I would prefer to speak later – there is in addition a common agenda, common objectives, a common home, common friends, common interests, in short, a common life. Friends do not share a life, they live their own lives'.

Sex

A young woman got up. She was not all that attractive, perhaps a bit the simple girl the abbot had warned me against. Still, there was intensity in her. She was blushing down to her neck and stumbling as she struggled to ask her question, which in the end turned out to be quite simple:

'Abbot, can friends have sex?'

I hoped the abbot would inquire why she asked that, but he was more reserved than I and answered:

'Of course they can if they both like it. People can have sex with just about anyone, an acquaintance or even a person they don't know at all and whom they will never see again. But beware: sex is a strong binding agent. Sex with an acquaintance or a friend may turn into love but not necessarily so'.

'Are you saying that sex can be had at the level of each of your three cylinders', the young woman came back, 'Like in a love relationship, in friendship and superficially, with an acquaintance or just anyone. Isn't that strange?'

Well, she was not that simple after all.

'No, it is not', came the abbot's reply. 'Sex is a strong and primeval force, speaking in terms of evolution. Therefore, sex with a stranger does not have to be superficial, literature is full of examples'.

The woman still looked puzzled, the concept was obviously new to her. She then said:

'If it is so easy, how can it be so powerful?'

'Evolutionary speaking, we have divorced sex from reproduction for only a very short period of time. This means that we are still governed by our old instincts, even if we are not aware of them. All living beings are equipped with a strong urge to procreate. Mind you, nature is not interested in the individual but in the species. With the emphasis on procreation, species secure their enduring place in the world. Although a boy may say he is only in for a bit of fun, he follows a primeval and strong instinct, which is to seed a girl, any girl. If a girl hesitates, it is not because she does not like the boy enough but because she has to consider her most important choice in life: who to be the father of her child. This instinct works even when having children is not on the agenda at all. When partners choose each other nowadays, the layer of basic instincts is covered by a mantle of civilisation. But the subconscious prospects of creating a healthy offspring are paramount in deciding whether or not to mate'.

Friendship between men and women

Then an older woman got up and asked:

'Do friendships between women and men differ?'

The abbot had to think for a while and then said, regaining his normal posture:

'Men find it more difficult to confide in each other, as they have to overcome their natural instinct for competition, especially when they are young and their brains are marinated in testosterone. In addition, men relate differently than women. Men like to achieve, women like to communicate. Men communicate in order to achieve something – women do things together in order to communicate. If men can achieve something by working together, they will do so without hesitation. When they are old, they will say, brimming with pride 'Do you remember how we did that project? Wasn't it great?' Women will say 'Do you remember how we helped our friend X solve her problem? She was such a nice girl, wasn't she?' Women are less inhibited than men in discussing their most intimate thoughts. I pity the boy whose girl-friend has promised him to not to reveal his secrets. In fact, she will tell everything to her friends. But don't worry, my boy, they will not laugh at you, on the contrary, they will be concerned and offer help. And it is nice to know that, provided you get her in the right mood, she will tell you everything about her friends: what they look like, what they look for in men, how they tease men they don't like. That is how men communicate about their intimate lives, through women. This is how the world sticks together'.

Then a young woman got up, apparently a student, carefully presenting her problem:

'Father, at the university we are a mixed group of friends, I mean, boys and girls together. We meet to have fun and we sometimes go out together. But it is difficult to stay friends with the boys as they always try to court you. Is it possible for a man and a woman to be just friends or should it always escalate?'

The abbot looked surprised and said:

'Man-woman friendships can be very stable, at all ages. They can be quite productive as they are usually based on mutual support, support of a different kind. For instance, the boy will 'do' things for his friend, the girl will 'listen' to her male friend and advise. Friendships between members of the opposite sex are an ideal training ground for love. People who have had such experience at an early age tend to form more stable relationships than people who grow up in a more isolated way. A man-woman friendship does not necessarily turn into love although that may very well be possible. Friendship is one way to start a love relationship, passion is the other. Members of student groups such as yours, often choose their partners from outside the group. But of course, Cupid can shoot his arrows any time and this can put great strain on the group'.

The answer was not enough for her:

'How then shall I find the right one?'

The abbot responded:

'Your love may emerge from a mixed group of friends but in this case you have to be sceptical as you may be inclined to mistake your feelings of friendship for feelings of love. You may meet your love through a friend, a hobby or at work. Hobbies are good for finding your love, you are more relaxed than when you are at work and you share an interest while the hobby itself is a good subject over which to make a contact. Don't sit in front of your computer checking chat rooms, go out and meet people'.

Brotherly love

Time was getting on and the host abbot took the floor, speaking in the rather formal way we were by now used to:

'Yevgeni Nikolayevich, we are all very grateful for your words and advice. Yet before closing this meeting, I would like to ask a question myself. You have spoken of universal love and about various forms of friendship as some of its manifestations. Can you say something about another form, I mean, brotherly love such as we have in our monasteries?'

The abbot replied immediately:

'This question has been bothering me ever since I became a monk. Between brothers in an order, there is much friendship but more so between some than others. Brotherly love originates from a religious or philosophical source, a common pursuit of truth, learning and worship. 'Common' here means two things: the goal of our lives is similar and so is the way in which we pursue that goal, through rituals, rules, the shared lifestyle. All this means that brotherly love is at the borderline between the inner and middle cylinders: it has elements of friendship and elements of the pursuit of spirituality or divinity which is in the inner cylinder. With our goals and rituals we create and sustain our humble abode, this in turn creates a strong bond between us'.

The girl and I

At this point the meeting came to an end. We went outside. People were talking to each other, enjoying the first nice, sunny day, warm for the time of the year. Although I had become quite interested in the people of the audience, I stayed with the two abbots, perhaps I was too shy to join the others.

'Very unorthodox beliefs, I would say ', remarked the host bitingly.

The abbot looked at him questioningly.

'I see you wish to tackle issues in a fresh and modern way while you try to stay within the borders of our doctrines but I am not sure that will get the approval of our clergy'.

'We'll see', the abbot replied but I noticed a shadow falling over his face.

We started moving around and then the girl who had turned out to be not as simple as she looked came to my side and took me by the arm.

'Come, there is something I want to show you', she said mysteriously.

She led me into the forest until we could no longer be seen. Then she leaned against a tree, the sun shining on her hair, her face turned into a smile.

'What do you want to show me?' I asked clumsily.

'Me', she said, smiling even more broadly.

'Well, eh, I think you are very nice'. What else could I say?

'Oh Stephen, that's your name, right, don't be such a prick. Kiss me!'

And before I knew it she put her arms around my neck and kissed me passionately. I didn't know how to respond, it was an awkward situation although I started feeling a certain pleasure. She noticed that and took courage:

'Steve, you won't be missed for a while. Come with me and I will give you all the love I have'.

'But I hardly know you. I don't even know your name', I protested.

'Your abbot just said that it doesn't matter'.

The fact was that I had never made love in my life. I always wanted the first time to be with Clara and now that she was out of the way, more or less, I was saving it for the real love, the one 'who was waiting for me out there' as the abbot had said. I had no choice. I had to turn this girl down.

'I can't do it', I stumbled.

'Why not?' she asked, still smiling.

'It's against my principles'. I hated myself for that.

'Oh, you stupid Englishmen, you don't know how to live.'

Her face was angry now. She started crying and then ran away, leaving me paralysed.

I shook my head to come to myself and went back slowly. Then I paused and tried to calm my emotions. This morning had opened another window for me, the abbot's Lesson and the girl had thrown it wide open. It was not the crisp Siberian air I was breathing in but a warm stream of, yes, of what? I felt as if I had known the brothers and sisters in the audience for years, especially those who had asked questions. I felt an urge to come back here in a few years' time and see how they had managed.

Then I composed myself, after all we were on a tight schedule. We would have to board the train around midnight and arrive at 4 a.m. in Tyumen, our next stop.

11. Verkhoturye – Total love

We had hardly dozed off in the afternoon when a discreet knock on the door woke us up. It was our host who, apologising, said there was a phone call for the abbot from the Spaso-Nikolayevski Monastery (The holy Nikolai Monastery) in Verkhoturye. When Yevgeni Nikolayevich came back he told me that the congregation there had listened to the broadcast of the Yekaterinburg lectures and were eager to learn more about total love, the expression the abbot had used there. Verkhoturye was not on our itinerary, we would have to take a side trip from Yekaterinburg on a local train.

'I already called Tyumen and they would not mind postponing our visit by two days', he said and, seeing my hesitation, added: 'It is actually more convenient for us as we can take a train tomorrow morning and get a good night's sleep. You will enjoy Verkhoturye. Russia's third largest cathedral is there. Because of its many churches, it was once called 'the Jerusalem of the Urals'. However, it will take us most of the day to get there'.

The next day we travelled in a rather untidy train, arriving in the late afternoon at the Spaso-Nikolayevski Monastery. Its beautiful Krestovozdrizhenski Cathedral (Cathedral of Exaltation of the Holy Cross) is only five minutes' walk from the famous Svyato-Troytzkiy Church (Church of the Holy Trinity) at the bend of the river Tura, which offers magnificent views. I noticed the large number of cathedrals in a city of only seven thousand and indeed, Verkhoturye is rightly considered one of the centres of Russian Christianity, a city of love.

The next morning, the auditorium was packed. Our new host, middle-aged and enterprising, was delighted that the abbot had agreed to make the detour, even more so because he would speak about nothing less than total love. He held a long introductory speech in which he expressed his own views on the subject, much to the embarrassment of the audience, which had rather come for the abbot. He did not seem to notice and when he started drawing parallels between love and quantum mechanics, the abbot coughed discreetly and the host broke off in the middle of a sentence, saying:

'And now, the floor is all yours, Yevgeni Nikolayevich.'

Phase of total immersion

A sigh of relief went through the audience as the abbot took the floor. He started solemnly without waiting for questions, as the subject was clear to all.

'Total love between two people is the most profound form of love. Such a love overtakes you, you don't choose it, it chooses you, it seizes you, you 'fall' in love. Whether it takes you suddenly or gradually, it takes all of you, it absorbs you and you realise that from now on your life will revolve around this person you love, all other things becoming of secondary importance. You cannot concentrate anymore, you cannot think of anything else but your loved one, you want to be with him all the time and when this can't be, you send him secret notes or e-mails while making endless phone calls and counting the hours until you will be reunited. And then, when you see him again, it is as if lightning strikes and when he holds you, you feel you are going back to your inner self, his inner self, you feel the most direct connection between your inner selves, your inner cylinders. You love him more than you love yourself, you are prepared to do anything for him, to give him everything, your life if need be, new life if granted. When you unite with him, you feel you are one being, you don't know where he ends and where you begin. It feels like a reunion after you were separated in ancient times, before your souls were born, separated because the two of you together were too perfect, too close to God. Now that you are reunited you feel a perfect balance in yourself, a primeval strength and you are afraid that God or the devil will separate you again. You almost cease to exist as individuals, you become one body, one soul, an experience that will only return to you when your children are born. Or you experience intense, acrobatic, sensational, almost painful passion that takes you to the brink of fainting. Either way, you feel that you explore parts of your physical and spiritual self that have never been touched before. You feel in heaven, which is the place where only souls can dwell and where there is no material world. You feel a richer, more harmonious person, you begin to shine, you feel that everything is possible, that there are no limits to what you can achieve, that you can overpower all your enemies, you feel on top of the world. If you are overwhelmed by such emotions, my children, you are experiencing total love.

You cannot create this feeling by yourself. It is a gift from God and he, not you, decides whom you fall in love with. Yes, you love many persons: your parents, brothers, sisters, friends, and perhaps teachers, but although these loves can be very intense, they are of a different nature than the total love between a man and a woman. This is because in all the other forms of love, the two remain separate individuals while in total love the partners merge. Some people believe this is a continuation of a relationship they had in a previous life and this should explain why they feel so familiar to each other even though they only met recently. In this sense, 'total love' is 'eternal love', it cannot be destroyed. Even when you harm and hurt each other, there always remains a spark that can easily flare up again into a blazing fire. Total love transcends death. Like the love for your children, parents and perhaps some friends, you can feel the presence of your loved one long after he has passed away.

Now the devil is always ready to corrupt God's good works and there are a few snags about total love that I must warn you about. First of all, total love is only total if it is mutual. Unrequited love is one of the most painful experiences in life. If someone feels a love for you that you cannot return, you have great responsibility towards him or her. And if your love is unanswered, try to distinguish rejection from time lag and if it is rejection, then accept it, mourn, learn from it, find warm arms somewhere else and get on with your life. You will overcome it and when you have, you will be better prepared for the true love that will follow.

Development phase
Another snag is that your loved one may not be a good partner in life. I always ask my young brothers and sisters: 'Is your love going to make a home?' This will transpire in the second phase of your love, the *development phase*. It follows the first phase, the *phase of total immersion*. The second phase starts when your love, like an airplane, comes down to earth. You will come out of your seclusion and start introducing each other to mutual friends and family. All of them will want to 'test' and 'taste' your loved one and you will be tested and tasted by his friends and family: 'Is she good enough for our dear boy, brother, friend?' Gradually, the two of you will become accepted in each other's circles. You will start doing things together, developing common interests, living together. In this way, the love 'finds a home', you cannot stay forever in total immersion and seclusion. Total love now becomes enduring love. When your love develops do not rush, my children, enjoy this springtime, as yet without responsibilities. Take time for the love to become solidly integrated in both your lives. Create memories by doing something special, you will benefit from this groundwork later.

During this development phase, you want to enjoy life and be careless. If there are subtle signals that your loved one may not be the good partner in life, your first urge will be to suppress and ignore them. Such signals can be that he is selfish, he enjoys your sacrificing love but he does not live up to it, all the time you feel he takes more than he gives. But then, you say, is love not giving? – and you hate yourself for making these calculations. Or there is no passion in sex anymore. It may be worse, your friends may tell you that he makes jokes about you or says nasty things behind your back. Or he becomes violent to you. You do not wish your dream to be destroyed and you think: 'After a while, he will be different'. Now that is usually the wrong assumption as, on the contrary, it often gets worse and thousands of people waste their lives 'working' to improve their loved one. Or they try to figure out with friends why he did what he did, another trick to postpone the inevitable separation. Again, it is better to accept that this is not the true love of your life, that you should overcome the pain and learn from it. But don't be deterred by my warnings of the dark sides of love, most loves find a 'home' and become enduring love.

The development phase ends with marriage, which is the finalisation and formalisation of your commitment to love and support each other and the new life that may come of it. It is a public event, this wedding, because the whole world should know that these two people are now together, that what the one says binds the other. It is an expression of the need and hope to grow old together. Many religions consider the wedding 'sacred', 'made in heaven', 'bound by God', the ritual – a 'sacrament'. This is logical because you felt yourself you were re-united with your other half that you were separated from in times immemorial. It also means that God truly loves this world.

Mature phase
After the wedding, you settle down, the *mature phase* sets in. New elements creep up in your lives, you will react differently to them and you have to reconcile the differences. Someone said that the purpose of marriage is 'to overcome in unison the problems you would not have, had you not been married in the first place'. The mature phase again is a learning phase: you learn to go through life together. Each of you will have to adapt to the other's unalterable peculiarities. Though still closely united, each of you will again develop his or her own individuality. The perception of being one body and soul is pushed to the background and you may be no longer conscious of it. But it is always there, it is the rock on which your relationship is built, a holy temple you can always return to. When one of the partners dies, the other suddenly feels how strong this attachment has been, a feeling that has subsided under the dust of everyday life. By taking care of this holy temple, many couples stretch their total love over a lifetime. When old and very old, they again become dependent on each other, in a way different from the immersion phase. Total

love lasts until death brings it to an end, not when one partner has gone, but after both of you will have stepped into the other world. Love ends when life comes to an end because life and love are basically the same thing'.

Young love and intimacy

The abbot paused and while people were still considering his words, a young man jumped up, more an adolescent actually. He was blushing as he worded his question:

'Father, maybe I am asking a stupid question but can total love happen to a young person?'

I felt I could answer this question myself but fortunately I did not have to.

'Your question is not at all stupid'. The abbot responded, 'I have known boys and girls who had a total love experience when they were only twelve. It is a curse as well as a blessing because it is impossible for them to handle the emotions let alone to make a home and this causes much hardship. But why do you ask?'

The young man hesitated, then, gathering courage:

'You know, my girlfriend and I know each other well and we feel strongly attracted to each other. I want to be intimate with her but she doesn't, she says she is not ready for it. What am I to do?'

He seemed pretty desperate, the poor fellow. The abbot nodded understandingly. Apparently he knew what the young man was talking about. This is what he had to say:

'I like that you say 'intimate'. Let us first discuss intimacy and then I will answer your question.

Intimacy is based on trust. You abandon your controls, you let go in total confidence that what follows will be good. It is like dying, you can only die in peace if you have trust in what comes next. Then, you can resign and accept what happens. Intimacy is similar, this is why the climax of physical intimacy is often called *le petit mort*, 'the small death'. Oh, my child, do not force intimacy, let it come naturally, be patient until the time is ripe. But then, do not hesitate a moment'.

This answer did not make the young man happy. One could see that patience was not his strong suit. So, the abbot went on:

'Intimacy has two parents: trust and respect. You can only build the holy temple if you trust and respect each other, which means waiting until the other is ready for it. Do not ruin the temple before you even start building it. Once built, the temple sets you free, it will give you immeasurable energy, the energy to become who you are. Patience is often a virtue but beware of the fact that you may have fallen in love with the wrong person, a girl who has less temperament than you. For a stable relationship, it is essential that temperaments match. So, you will need time to decide whether she is the right one but is not quite ready, or whether you have fallen into a trap'.

The youth still did not look quite satisfied. Perhaps he had hoped the abbot would suggest a trick to get his girlfriend over. He may have had another question but an elderly woman was already getting up:

'Father, you describe it all so nicely but the reality is so different. Men are not intimate with women, they beat them up and many women die because of violence at home. There is so much anger at women and for no apparent reason. How do you explain this?'

'Men are physically stronger than women but women are more powerful in existential terms. A man can try to impress a woman by showing his muscles, intellect, humour or wisdom, but whatever he tries, it is she who decides who will father her child. Women are the guardians of the evolution, it is they who hold the ultimate power. When a woman accepts a man as the potential father of her child, she sends a powerful message. Many men have confessed to me that the moment the woman says 'Make me a baby, I want your baby', this is the most profound experience of their life'.

'Why is that?' the woman asked.

The abbot sought for words for a moment, then said:

'Do you know what a blender is, a mixer?'

The woman was rather surprised at this question.

'Of course I do' she said, 'You put different fruits in it, press the button, and you get a nice drink'.

'What does the drink taste like?' the abbot continued.

'Well, you can taste the ingredients but basically, it's a new taste'.

'You know you have a blender inside you', the abbot moved on, 'It is called the womb. It does not mix fruits but DNA. Your fruit, your DNA, goes in by itself. The question is: which other fruit, other DNA, will you choose? That is the woman's problem'.

'And what's the man's problem then?' she still looked puzzled.

'Every man thinks his DNA is the best in the world. The question is: how to get it into the blender. That's the man's problem'.

The audience started laughing and it took a while before the meeting could proceed. But it got the message that the woman is the more powerful person when it comes to ensuring the human species in the face of the evolution, which explains the hostility and aggression of men against women.

Unbalanced growth

Then a young woman, girlish in her appearance, seemingly cold, got up and told us that she could not find a partner. Through her work she met plenty of interesting men but somehow it would not 'click'. She had a responsible and demanding position as a contract manager in a bank, it was not the job that was in the way, there ought to be something else. The abbot asked how old she was and what she did at work. She turned out to be twenty-five, very clever and mature, closing large contracts between the bank and its clients. She talked more about herself and then the abbot commented:

'I see you as two sisters, walking hand in hand. The elder sister is called Reason. She is mature, responsible, controlled in a pleasant way, successful, and, say thirty-five years old. The younger sister – called Emotion – is still rather childish, say fifteen, and overwhelmed by her older sister. When someone addresses her, the elder sister pushes her away and answers instead. She always takes over. This way, the younger sister does not get a chance to develop. In contrast, the elder sister becomes stronger all the time'.

'Does that mean, I am schizophrenic, two persons in one body?' She was obviously shocked.

'Not at all', was the reassuring reply. 'It means that your rational side is overdeveloped for your age while your emotional side is underdeveloped. This makes you a very successful professional, doing things well ahead of your age, but it is at the expense of your emotional side. As a result you have problems establishing relationships in which emotions play a role'.

She was wondering what to do and the abbot advised her to slow down at work, make time for contacts and activities that would stimulate emotional talents that had nothing to do with her career or anything rational.

'That is where you will meet your future partner', the abbot concluded.

Again, there was deep silence. Many couples were holding hands as they were walking out to attend Sext and, after that, to have lunch. Some couples related memories of the phase of total immersion and how nervous they were when introducing each other to their families and friends. Others were anxious to go home and return to their holy temple but then, they also did not want to miss the afternoon session.

The school of love

Yevgeni Nikolayevich looked pensive and I asked him what he was thinking about.

'It is this poor woman I compared to two sisters', he answered. 'There are so many people like her. The more they develop their intelligence, the more rewarding it is to develop it further. The gap will widen as they will neglect their emotional side'.

'What should she do about it?' I asked, refilling our glasses.

'It would be nice to have a kind of training programme that would help people like her activate their emotional side. Thinking about it, such a course would be good in general as people get increasingly alienated. They become self-centred and should learn how to love'.

'Blimey! Now you want to start a school of love', I teased him, 'I am sure that will be a hit'.

'Come on, don't make fun of me', he smiled back, 'Of course I don't mean *that* kind of school of love. But it puzzles me. Just think how many hours we teach children math and geography and how little time we spend teaching them to get on with each other, to communicate. We are such a one-sided society'.

'Is the opposite also possible, I mean, people who have a strongly developed emotional side and an underdeveloped rational side? I wondered.

'Lots of people', was his immediate response. 'Especially the pioneer-type of people have this but others may have it as well. Like our host, they are warm, full of ideas and emotions but they don't know what to do with them, they cannot put them to practical use'.

'What should they do then?' I asked.

'Find a partner who is complementary, emotionally as well as rationally. They can learn from each other and together become fuller beings'.

12. Verkhoturye – Enduring love

When we resumed, a couple took the floor, each of them trying to speak up, finally stumbling it out between them and it came down to the following:

'We think we have what you call total love and we have only one desire: that it lasts forever. You said that the person you love might not be a good partner in life, that love has to find a home. What do you mean by that?'

Without hesitation, the abbot replied:

'Total love can turn into enduring love if there is a balance between commonality and complementarity. Let me explain. On the one hand, you have common ground: similar or compatible norms, principles, ethics, ideals, lifestyle, intelligence. On the other hand, fortunately, you have differences with which you can complement each other. You are shy, he is bold. You are introvert, she is extravert. You are focussed on the long term, he – on the short term. You can cook, she does the gardening. You come up with initiatives that he would never think of and he has experience that is invaluable to you. I said 'fortunately' because if the two of you are very much alike the relationship would be rather dull, without challenges. If you have different talents and interests, it is like each of you holding pieces of a jigsaw puzzle. The pieces of either one of you do not add up to much but when assembled, the picture becomes much more valuable. This is called synergy, the total is more than the sum of the parts. The couple together is stronger than the sum of the two individuals. If there is synergy, the relationship is exciting and fulfilling. But life without common ground will turn into conflicts on just about everything'.

Four dimensions

In order to illustrate his view, the abbot asked one of the local brothers to bring him a blackboard. They found one in the closets and after having dusted it off – obviously it had not been used for years – the abbot drew the following diagram:

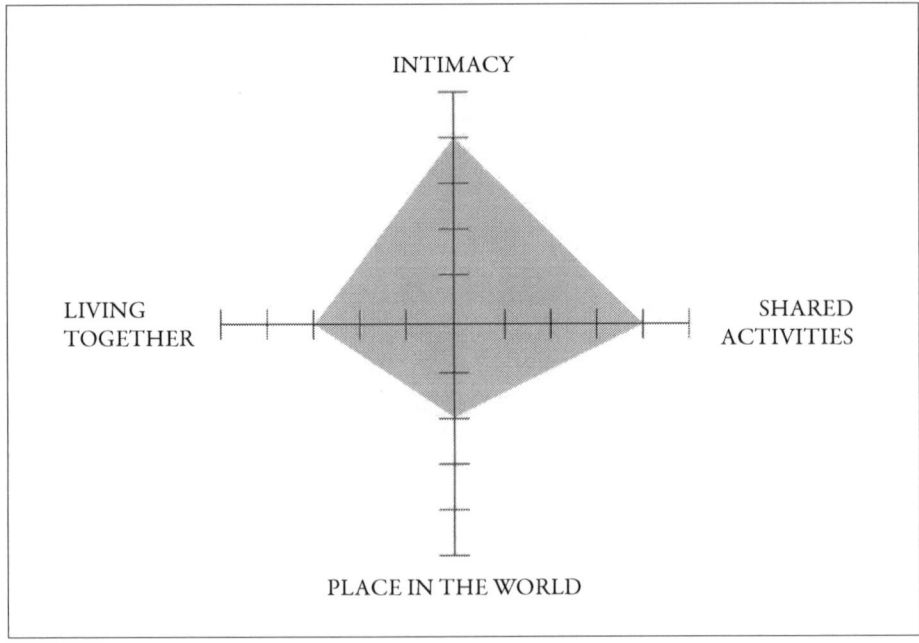

He then said:

'I see enduring love as comprised of four dimensions. The balance between commonality and complementarity applies to each of the dimensions.

The first dimension is *Intimacy*. Intimacy has two sides. *Social intimacy* evolves if there is trust and respect. These create an atmosphere in which you can share things that are sensitive to you or that you feel uncertain about. *Physical contact* is the other side of intimacy. Intimacy has to grow because you need to know each other closely, this is what the phase of total immersion is for.

Intimacy provides security. It also gives you immense energy, a fuel for the development of talents. Thus, intimacy becomes a basis for the development of talents as well as the source of security, the two dimensions of happiness.

The *Art of Living Together* is the second dimension of enduring love. Can you run a household together, raise children, meet friends and family, or are there arguments all the time? Family life, not only in your own family but including the parents and grandparents, brothers, sisters and their children are part of this. An uncle or aunt is a substitute parent and their role can be quite influential. When two people marry their families also marry.

Shared Activities form the third dimension of enduring love. If both partners pursue for instance the same sport, hobbies, literature, art, music, charities, religion, it strengthens their relationship. Sharing aspects of professional, cultural or religious life adds commonality as well as complementarity and it greatly enriches the relationship. If they have little to share, they can still take an interest in each other's activities. Working life, cultural life and religious life belong to this dimension.

Then, there is the wider world. Are you seen and accepted as belonging together? Do you behave as a couple? The fourth dimension, therefore, is how the partners manifest themselves in society, their *Place in the world*.

Now you can use this diagram as a test and rate each of the four dimensions on a scale of five. When at some point in time you are disappointed in your partner, you will find that the intensity of one or more of the dimensions has declined. Your analysis shows where the relationship is to be remedied. Know yourself and know your partner. Know and maintain your relationship, your most precious treasure'.

Somebody else got up and asked:
'How are the dimensions of enduring love related to the three cylinders we heard you talking about in Vladimir?'
'Good question', the abbot replied. 'To give a short answer: in total love all three cylinders merge. Intimacy is the merging of the inner cylinder. Family life and shared interests – the merging of the middle cylinder. Developing a common place in the world is the merging of the outer cylinder'.
He thought a little and then added:
'Actually, total love is called so because it is the merging of all three cylinders. Enduring love is total love that develops along all the four dimensions'.

Homosexual love
An older man had a quite different question:
'Can there be a love relationship between people of the same sex?'
'Of course there can be', the abbot responded, 'God has created man homosexual and heterosexual and God does not discriminate his creations. Some people call it unnatural because homosexual love does not lead to procreation but in our world sex and procreation have been disentangled long ago and many heterosexual couples choose not to have children. Homosexual partners go through the same phases of total love as heterosexuals, the four dimensions of enduring love are equally relevant and they often make good parents'.

This statement caused uproar. Our host was outraged and exclaimed emotionally:

'Dear Brother Rostov, with all respect, we should worship all of God's work but with this I think you are going way too far'.

The abbot was, however, certain of his case and replied:

'I know the Church condemns homosexuality but the dogma is wrong. Jesus never said anything against it. Even the Old Testament makes no explicit statement about it, only some references which can be explained by the fact that the security of the nomadic tribes of the early Israelites lay very much in the strength of their numbers and getting as many children as possible was their first priority'.

The older man had an unconventional view:

'Is it possible for people to be both?'

'I guess it is. The world is full of colour, things aren't just black or white. Likewise, sexual preferences are not just A or B. A woman may be attracted, say, eighty percent to men and twenty percent to women. One is hardly aware of this because of a cultural element. A generally heterosexual man may be attracted to a person of the same sex but he will repress those feelings because of the social reactions that may conjure up. This explains why happily married men or women turn homosexual later in life and vice versa and why numerous people have hidden intimate contacts with partners of both sexes'.

There was a general reluctance to explore this subject further and the meeting was adjourned. We spent the rest of the afternoon visiting the churches and at twilight we enjoyed the views of the river Tura, winding down from the intense session. Once we were on board the train, I wondered whether I could offer the abbot a glass of vodka – wine was not available on this train. As it would be twelve hours to Tyumen, via Yekaterinburg, I decided to try and to my relief the abbot accepted with pleasure.

We took a sip and after a while he said:

'What do you think of the lecture?' It was the first time he asked something like that.

'I liked a lot of it', I said. 'Much of it was very deep, very moving, for me also very confusing. I have never heard such stories before. But for the marriage to be sealed in heaven you need a priest and you always say: It is you who it comes down to. People could also get married by themselves'.

'You are right: when people get married they don't need an intermediary. You could design a ritual in which they exchange vows and then celebrate their union with family and friends who explicitly recognise them as a married couple. But that doesn't mean that spiritually their marriage is not sealed in heaven'.

For a while we were silent but I could see something else was bothering him. I made a wild guess:

'Are you still thinking about the negative reaction of our host after what you said about homosexuality?'

He hesitated and looked away. Then he confessed:

'Well, to tell you the truth, I am. Remember our host in Yekaterinburg when I talked about sex. Obviously he didn't like it. More seriously, it is against the official teaching of the Church and that may have consequences'.

'Well, we live in a free country' I tried. 'Why would it matter?'

'They can stop me talking to my flock', he answered. 'If that happens I would have failed to accomplish my mission'.

I did not know what to say. The last thing I wished was that the abbot would come to harm because of his integrity. Then the vodka started taking its toll and we turned in.

13. Tyumen – Partial love

We arrived in Tyumen, a rapidly expanding, cosmopolitan city with many rivers and reservoirs, centre of the West-Siberian oil production. We drove past the historic buildings – Tyumen is the oldest town in Siberia, founded in 1586 by Cossacks – and reached another Svyato-Troytzkiy Monastery, nicely located on the bank of the river Tura. This monastery houses the famous Svyato-Troytzkiy seminary, headed by the abbot who was our host for the day.

'How is the seminary going', asked Yevgeni Nikolayevich, addressing our host. 'Do you get enough students who follow the call?'

'In a way I cannot complain' our host answered. 'There are enough applicants but what bothers me is their disposition. Our seminary is the guardian of the faith. We need to educate seminarians to become priests who are completely loyal to the doctrines of our Church. Otherwise we open the door to heresy. Fortunately, most entrants are still pliable but some come with the oddest ideas that we have to root out'

This sounded rather tough. But then, had the Church not always fought against its archenemy – heresy – and claimed millions of lives? While we were walking to the auditorium, our host gave his last instructions and the abbot whispered in my ear:

'Although he is young, he is one of the old guard, you know'.

'Does it bother you?' I noticed I had asked him the same question the day before.

'We shall see' the abbot replied. 'I have seen worse'.

At that we entered the auditorium.

As could be expected, there were many seminary students in the audience but it was a middle-aged man who first took the floor. He looked upset, even angry, when he addressed the abbot:

'Yevgeni Nikolayevich, we listened to your Lessons on total love over the radio and what you say is all very nice and romantic but let me fill you in on the reality. I once had such a love, we got married and lived happily together. After our child left home to go to university last year, my wife took up piano lessons and now I discover she sleeps with the piano teacher. What am I to do? Should I divorce her?'

'Does she want to leave you?'

'No, on the contrary, she is nicer than ever. But it is obvious that what she is doing is wrong'.

'Wrong for you perhaps, but apparently not for her. *In all your dealings, consider the position of the other*. You therefore have to analyse the situation from her point of view, however difficult and painful that may be. Painful because you may discover shortfalls within yourself. You should not indulge in self-pity because it may be that your relationship has been deteriorating for some time and if that is the case, you are both to blame'.

The man looked perplexed but the abbot went on:

'There are several reasons why an apparently happily married person starts a relationship with someone else. The first reason is simply curiosity, adventure, an instant attraction. People with much vitality happen to meet others with whom they have short-lived relationships. I suggested in Kirov that certain archetypes are more prone to this than others. Although such events can be deeply disturbing to the permanent partner, they do not threaten the marriage as such. On the contrary, they often lead to more appreciation of the spouse. But I don't think your wife is like this?'

The man nodded 'no' and the abbot continued:

'The second reason is that, because love gives tremendous energy, people unconsciously seek such love in order to overcome difficult periods in their life. The transition from one phase of life to another or acceleration in the development of a talent can be greatly facilitated by love and the regular partner cannot always provide it. Such transitional love acts as a bridge between the old life and the new. It can be quite intense but it usually dissolves when the other side of the river has been reached. Or rather, the partner who has reached the other side will want to put an end to it. It may be that your wife wants to take up a new kind of life now that your child does not need her attention anymore. Did you ever discuss with her the consequences of your child leaving home?'

This idea had apparently never occurred to the man and he nodded 'no' again.

'Then I suggest you have a serious talk with her. Ask her how she feels about your child leaving home and what the consequences are for her, what she wants to do with her life now. Don't start blaming her for having an affair, that won't solve the problem, it will only make things worse'.

'Could you give an example of a love that serves as a bridge?', asked another man from the audience.

'The situation we discussed earlier could be an example', the abbot answered. 'In this case, the woman may have felt the urge to start another kind of life and subconsciously 'used' the relationship to give her the energy and inspiration to do so. It also happens at school, when children approach adolescence and get a crush on a teacher or another adult. Perhaps they feel safer to explore adult life with someone much older than a partner their own age where there are more risks and uncertainties. Literature is full of examples, O'Brien's Johnny, Schlink's Michael, Frisch's Sabeth or Pamuk's Füsun. Of course, the vast majority of first relationships start between people the same age'.

A second love

Now another man got up, he was clearly upset and said:

'You are very casual about it, you make it all sound easy and rational. But it is really painful, you know'.

'I realise very well it is painful. If you discover your partner has an affair with someone else, especially in the early days of a total love relationship, it is like finding an intruder in your holy temple, your most intimate world has been invaded. However, giving in to emotions is not the solution. Therefore, I want people to try to see the matter from the point of view of the other. When you try to understand the position of, in this case, the wife, the situation might become manageable. I am not condescending to the brother here, but there are far more threatening reasons for people to start an affair'.

'Such as?' the man came back.

'A more threatening reason is the deterioration of the marriage itself. If partners start to miss essential elements in an originally total love and if they are not used to talking to each other, this may cause them, consciously or subconsciously, to seek compensation elsewhere. Deterioration happens in almost any total love, usually with partners not noticing it. It often sorts itself out but having an affair with someone else may close the gap as it were. Let me draw this for you'.

Since Verkhoturye, there were always blackboards in the auditoria and so the abbot drew a diagram analogous to the one of his Verkhoturye lecture:

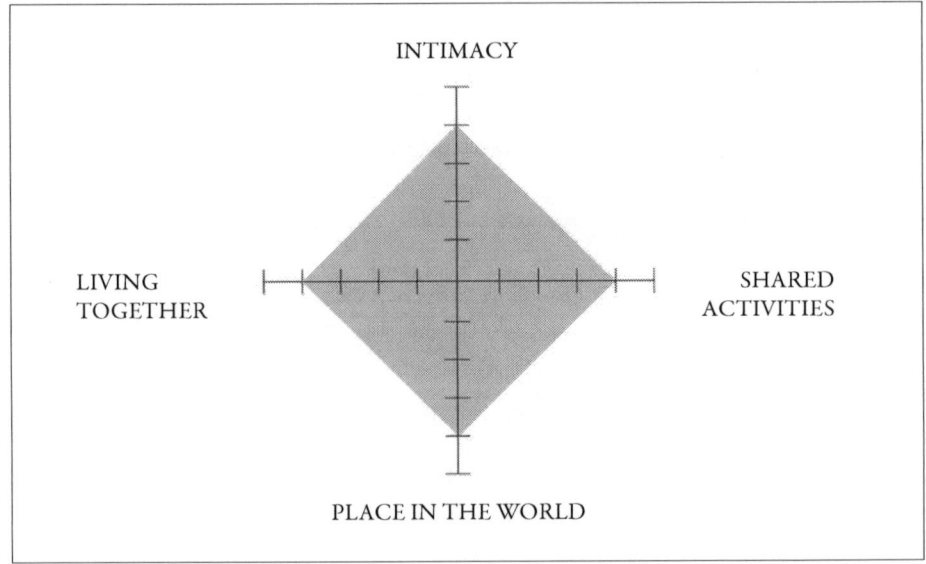

'With high ratings for all the dimensions this is an almost perfect total love. Now let us assume that the couple gets busy, the intimacy declines and they start developing different interests. At the same time, their living together goes on as usual and they still have a strong presence in the outside world. If this happens, you get a picture like this:

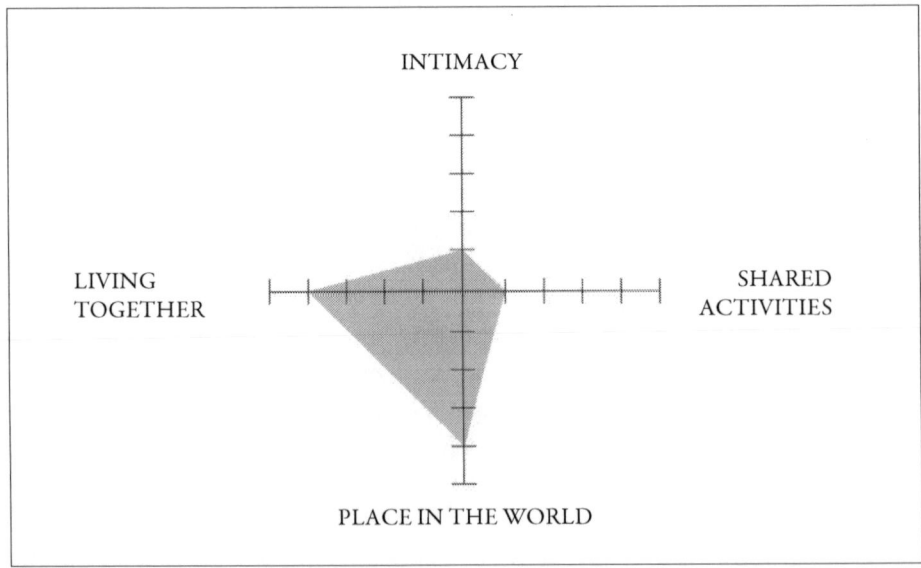

The total love has degenerated into partial love, which is love where only some of the characteristics are present. Suppose now that the wife meets another man who shares her new interests. They start a relationship with a high level of intimacy and their relationship will be like this:

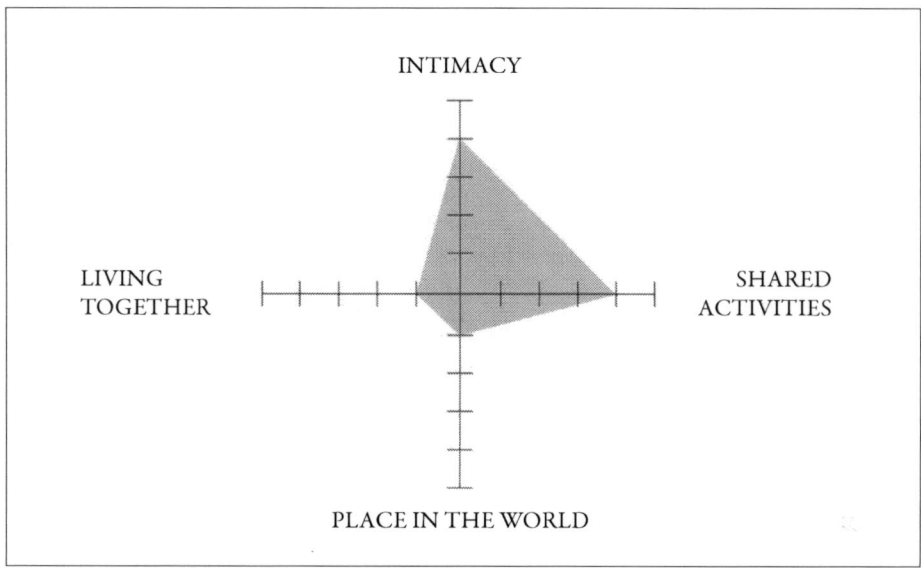

This is another partial love. As this relationship will be secret, there is no 'place in the world' for it, while they do not have a shared life. Now, if you add up the two relationships of the woman, they form an ideal combination for her:

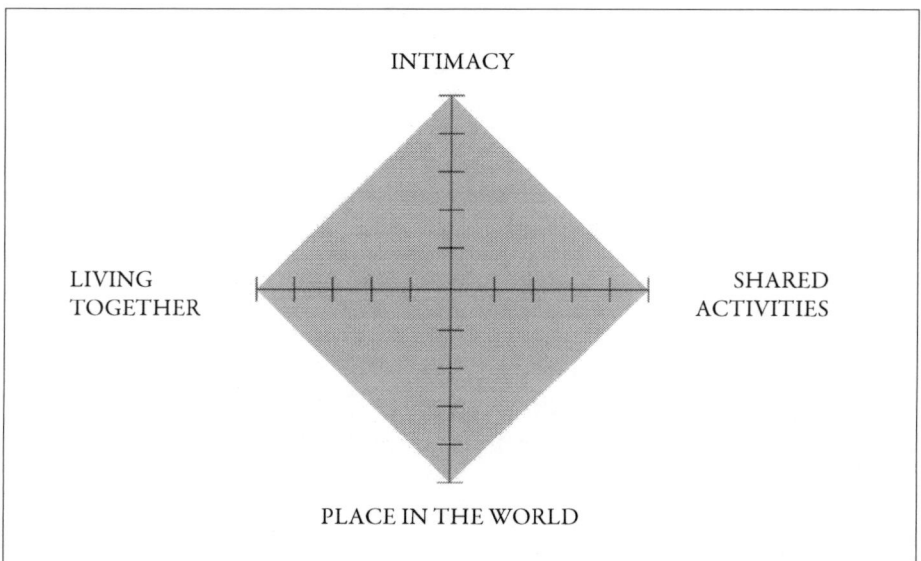

You could say, she shares with the other man what she no longer shares with her husband while continuing to share with her husband what she cannot or will not share with her lover. Another way of saying it is that two partial loves in this case add up to one total love.

Of course, this situation is not stable, although such combinations occur a lot and some of them can last quite long. Suppose the woman divorces her husband and marries the lover. She then trades one partial love for another and the new marriage will be even less fulfilling than the old one'.

'Certainly, the situation does not have to get this far if the original marriage can be revitalised', the student commented.

'It depends how strong the original relationship was', the abbot reacted, 'Marriages come around for the strangest reasons, say one partner being eager and the other giving in, thinking: 'Why not?''.

One of the seminary students got up and said in a rather formal stiffly manner:

'Father Rostov, your insights are very valuable to us students who will soon be called to help people in distress when we are ordained. May I therefore try to summarise your teachings on this important issue?'

The abbot nodded. As our host's frown got deeper, the student took a professional expression and went on:

'First, total love can only become enduring love if all four characteristics are shared from the very beginning. When total love deteriorates, as may happen over time, partners should analyse the situation, make time for each other and remedy the shortcomings. If they do not, the relationship will decline further and a conscious or subconscious desire for another partner, who can fill in the gap, will arise. This may be satisfactory for the partner who feels lonely but sooner or later, the situation will explode.

Secondly, if the marriage was weak from the beginning, based on only some of the characteristics, the weakness will become exposed if another partner enters the game and the marriage will then come to an end sooner or later.

Thirdly, if people form a partial love relationship that has a bridging function, this can be beneficial to both of them without necessarily harming another, total love relationship. Such relationships dissolve when their mission has been accomplished.

Then, fourthly, you have people with a high level of energy who seek short intimacies without forming any kind of relationship. So, in all these instances, partial loves are temporary and they do not find a home, to use your term'.

'Well done', came the reaction of a smiling abbot, 'Except that some partial loves, while not 'finding a home', can last a long time. They can also turn into friendship if the intimacy declines over time.'

Another student had a completely different comment:
'Father, you approach the matter of infidelity as a mathematical problem that can be solved easily when the partners put their mind to it. Of course we have limited experience in the dioceses where we serve helping the priests but so far I have seen only overwhelming emotions that require the patience and understanding of the pastor'.

'Matters of love threaten our inner cylinder, our very core, and they are therefore very emotional. The emotions become even stronger as partners feel helpless in this uncontrollable avalanche of threatening feelings. I hope that by analysing feelings, the underlying issues can be brought to light, simply getting carried away does rarely lead to satisfactory solutions. Under the layer of emotions, there is always a logical pattern of opportunistic behaviour, whether or not it is rational in the eyes of the observer. As a pastor, if you dig deeply enough, you may lay bare this pattern'.

Impossible love

Another student wanted to make a comment:
'In my internship I spent quite some time with a man who said he was unhappy in his marriage. He gave some examples of conflicts in his relationship and I could understand his feelings. To make it worse, he had developed a very intense and beautiful relationship with another woman. However, he did not want to divorce because this would affect his relationship with his children, whom he loved deeply and did not want to abandon. He said that if he had to choose between his new love and the love for his children, he would opt for the children. I deeply felt his dilemma and did not know what to say'.

The abbot sighed, then said:
'If the couple manages to divorce without too many scars, and if they continue sharing responsibility for the children, this can lead to a life that is satisfactory for the children as well as the parents. But if a sensible and peaceful separation is not an option the choice may really be devilish'.

'Devilish? You never use such a strong word', remarked the student.

The abbot was silent for a while and then he was hardly audible:
'An impossible love is even more difficult to bear than an unrequited love. After the bliss, there comes the black horror of the realisation that this love has no future, impressively put to music by Berlioz in *The Damnation of Faust*.

Those who survive it incur a deep wound on their soul that will cause pain as long as they live'.

'What do you mean with 'if they survive it'?' the student carefully continued.

'The theme of an impossible, strong and mutual love is found all over the world in novels, theatre, opera and dance. The letters of Abélard and Héloïse are immortal and so is the film about Elvira Madigan and Count Sixten. These are real life stories. In fiction, one can think of Pamuk's Kemal, Tolstoy's Anna Karenina and many others. In plays, you have not only Goethe's *Faust and Gretchen* and Shakespeare's *Romeo and Juliet* but also a number of Kabuki plays. In opera, there are Wagner's *Tristan and Isolde* and Verdi's *La Traviata*, in dance – *Giselle*. It is a universal theme that is at the centre of many Bollywood productions and Javanese Wayang plays. In all these cases, the partners love each other intensely but their love is impossible for social or other reasons. They end in suicide or in a deadly disease'.

The student was insistent:

'Surely, this doesn't apply to our world', the student objected. 'Would Anna Karenina live today, she would divorce on page two of the novel'.

'Impossible love occurs when there is a fault line between the partners. This is not necessarily class, clan or race, it can also be age or position. For instance, in the film *Noce Blanche* a fifty-year-old teacher is seduced by one of his pupils, leading to an intense love relationship. It ends with her suicide. Impossible loves occur when the partners are unable or unwilling to develop the dimensions of enduring love, other than intimacy. Their love is like a tree without roots, it is not rooted in life'.

Sin

'I would like to bring you back to the beginning of this lecture', said a man from the audience. 'You actually justified adultery, and in a previous Lesson you showed you didn't object against homosexuality as well. But we all know these are grave sins, severely judged by the Holy Church'.

'The Church evolved from groups of people who wanted to be followers of Jesus. As such, it is a human organisation with all the inherent shortcomings. Holy is only what is in heaven and heaven is in yourself, in your inner cylinder. So it is up to you to decide what is sin and what it is not'.

The seminary students started murmuring and whispering to each other but a glance of our host kept them in check – he was obviously very strict and did not tolerate poor discipline although he himself was seething inside.

'How can we form our own definition of sin?', a student asked.

'I can only answer that question for myself and then the answer is very simple. Jesus told us to do to others as you would have them do to you, or: not to do to others what you would not have them do to you. Well, for me, sin is the opposite, that you do unto someone something you would not like to have done to yourself'.

Unfortunately, or maybe, quite fortunately, it was time the students attended None. As our host would be the last to leave, we waited for him at the door. Many students paid their respect to the abbot and said this was the best lecture they had ever attended. But others did not hide their contempt – obviously in disagreement with the liberal attitude of the abbot. I felt the tension rising as our host was approaching us. When he was finally there, he burst out:

'Brother Rostov, I curse the day I invited you. Instead of giving a decent lecture as one might expect from someone of your position, you abuse our hospitality, instigate heresies and invite people to sin. I am deeply shocked by your teaching. What on earth are you doing in the Church with such misconceptions? In my view, you should be excommunicated at once'.

This was a rather shocking statement but the abbot took it casually.

'I realise these are difficult questions but all the more we do need to help our flock with their predicament. In this I just follow my conscience and use insights that have helped many people'.

'But surely, conscience must follow doctrine', was the incensed answer.

'I can think of someone who let conscience come first', the abbot said calmly.

Our host was perplexed – the abbot had obviously referred to Jesus' life and teaching – and he left indignantly as the Pharisees left Jesus after he had put them right.

One of the brothers showed us to our cell and we turned in, as we had to catch the 4.18 a.m. to Omsk the next morning.

Somehow we managed to get on the train. I tried to go to sleep but the hostile attitude of our host was still very much on my mind. It had been a great consolation that so many seminarians had welcomed the abbot's views and advice but I was really concerned about him. He pretended to take it all very casually but I knew he was deeply hurt by the mistrust of our host and the stupidity of putting doctrine above conscience and practical help. Yet I couldn't but agree with our host when he wondered why the abbot stayed within the Church if it was such a burden to him. He definitely could find another platform for his views. Obviously, no matter how much he insisted that people should look rationally at their problems, he himself was emotionally too attached both to the Church and his monastery.

LIFE

14. Omsk – Family life

It took us six hours through the black steppe land to get to Omsk, three time zones away from Moscow, and we arrived punctually at 11.17 a.m. We expected the abbot of the Svyato-Nikolskiy Monastery (Monastery of St. Nicholas) to meet us at the platform but instead, there was an excited group of people waving and greeting our abbot and we could hardly make our way out. When we finally managed to leave the station, we were met by a massive crowd that completely filled the vast Lobnova Square. After all, Omsk is a large city with over a million inhabitants and high unemployment as many of the military facilities and industry – the legendary T-80 tank was produced here – had closed down after the collapse of the Soviet Union.

There was heavy security around the square. As soon as the head of the police noticed the abbot, he sent his men to escort us. It was a very unruly gathering with people pressing forward and pushing against each other. I was afraid some might even be trampled in the stampede. Across the square, we could see cars waiting for us. There was a commotion. It turned out that a group of monks was arguing with the police officers who would not let them through. We recognised our hosts and the abbot hastened to tell the officer in charge the monks were there to meet us. Our host, an old man with silver hair and bright eyes, was panting heavily when he reached us at last and apologised for the mess.

It was around two o'clock when we finally arrived in Bolshekulachye, a little village with a well-known family resort. The monastery had only recently been reconstructed, on the site of the wooden original that was built there in 1751. A large audience had been waiting patiently so our host decided to proceed with the meeting immediately.

After the introductions and the inevitable apologies for the delay, a young woman, who was clearly going to have a baby, took the floor and put her question:

'Yevgeni Nikolayevich, we heard you talking on the radio about family life as an important part of the total and enduring love'.

She hesitated, carefully choosing her words. The congregation looked at her patiently and, in view of her condition, with a certain degree of tenderness. Then she resumed:

'We are a very happy family'.

There was an immediate laughter and even a little applause. When the woman realised why, she blushed but then pulled herself together and worded the question she wanted to ask in the first place:

'As you can probably see, we are expecting a baby pretty soon. My husband and I consider this an important moment, a holy moment as it were, and we would like to celebrate it. Now, you will probably say that baptism is the most appropriate ritual but we don't like it, as we cannot accept the idea of the original sin that has to be washed away by baptism and the intervention of the Church. Our child was conceived in love, not in sin, and this is what we wish to celebrate. The question is: how do we go about it?'

The abbot congratulated her, wished her all the best and then explained:

'The dogma that we are born in sin and therefore doomed unless we accept Jesus as our Saviour is a core concept of both the Roman Catholic Church and Orthodox Christianity, passed on to the reformed Churches of Luther and Calvin. The idea is that we are born in sin because of the act of our parents, all this going back to Adam and Eve who committed the original sin. It is a most peculiar philosophy because, if all is well, we are conceived in love. Jesus never mentioned the idea of original sin. It stems from St Augustine in the fourth century who could not control his sex drive; in his books he is quite open about it. He did not accept his weakness and invented the idea that sex is sin. His doctrine became the cornerstone of medieval theology. It was adopted by the Church which was then still united and Augustine was canonised'.

The abbot realised he had not answered the question, paused and then continued:

'Now let me come back to your question. The first duty of parents, family and friends is to welcome the newborn child into this world and give it security. You could do this at a ceremony where you invite your loved ones who could convey this message in their own words. In this way, all those present become the custodians of the child, giving it security by forming a circle of loving adults who will help it find its place in the world. You could record the ceremony to show it to the child when it grows up. This could be done when it reaches puberty when, in a second ceremony, the pledges could be repeated'.

Bringing up a child
This was a new idea for the woman and she said:
'Thank you for your advice, let us think about it. Perhaps I may ask another question' – she was a bit embarrassed as there was such a large gathering – but the abbot encouraged her and she went on:
'How should we educate our child? It is our firstborn and we feel quite uncertain about it as books and friends all have such different opinions.'

The abbot nodded understandingly and said:
'There are many ways to bring up a child and all have a lot of good in them but I think it is important that you follow your Inner Guide and distrust 'systems'. 'Systems' are rigid and rigidity, or orthodoxy if you like, paves the road to disaster. Deep inside, you know what is good for the baby, later the child. It is your responsibility until the child gradually takes over itself. Do not worry but beware of a few pitfalls.

It is perhaps a woman's most tender experience when it is confirmed that she expects a baby. The *annunciation* is a theme that has inspired all great artists. It is a moment between God and the woman with an angel – nowadays a doctor – as the intermediary. It is followed by a period of expectation and preparation. Then, all of a sudden, you can feel the child inside you – the father can feel it somewhat later– another milestone. The birth of a child, especially the first-born, is a mystery, a privilege granted by God the Creator. You have had quite some time to get used to the idea, now it becomes a reality. Although the child is now a separate being, you remain communicating vessels. Emotionally, it is like a total love relationship, you don't know where you end and where the child begins'.

The woman was not entirely satisfied:
'Thank you for these words, abbot, but can you be more specific about education?'

The abbot realised he had been carried away and tried to compose himself.
'Education starts by trying to understand your children, help them discover their talents and support their development. You should show your children what is dear to you in life and you should pass on the norms and values of our civilisation. In the Western world and increasingly also in ours, we have neglected this task, giving children too much freedom and not enough social structure. Violence and loneliness are the result. It is therefore good to teach children how to behave towards others but you should not burden them with

transferring your ideals or obsessions to them. Let them find their own way, do not push them into what you consider the best way. Give your children the opportunity to develop their talents and do not be disappointed if your efforts only help them to discover they were pursuing a dream, not a talent, and they need to explore in another direction. Remember a child is a child and not a friend. Discuss your problems with your friends, not with your children. Do not expose them to problems for which they are not yet ready.

The second duty of parents is to help and guide their children to find their place in the world. This starts with elementary things: walking, talking, hygiene, good manners. Next, coach them in the practical, social and emotional skills that are necessary for survival. Explain the constraints in life, mostly the borderlines between their space and the space of others. Tell your children to respect other people, however different they may be.

If all this works out well, let them gradually take responsibility for their own lives. In the beginning, when a child is small and vulnerable, you have to protect it and guide it in the ways of the world. This becomes a habit, you feel responsible, which is good, but the moment the child can take care of itself is always closer than you think. Those of you who have listened to my Lesson in Nizhny Novgorod will remember brother Sergei of my monastery. Now Sergei told me the following story: before entering the monastery he had a family. When his eldest boy grew up he got a bike and Sergei explicitly forbade his son to ride his bicycle when going to school, as there was a lot of rough driving in Novosibirsk. One day he was waiting at a traffic light and saw his son biking past. When he stopped him, the boy explained he had observed the dangers of traffic and found alternative routes. It was a very mature analysis and it dawned on Sergei that his little boy had grown up and could bear much more responsibility than he thought. Sergei apologised and from then on, once and a while he discussed traffic with him'.

Now a man around forty got up and said:
    'Yevgeni Nikolayevich, I have been trying to raise my children as you said, giving them, together with my wife and our extended family, lots of love. But it is to no avail. Yesterday my daughter called me an 'old sod' and she often uses expressions I would not like to repeat here. I told her she should show more respect but that only made it worse'.

The audience looked at him with a mixture of understanding and amusement but the abbot's face beamed into a big smile:
    'How old is your daughter?' he asked.

'Fifteen', the man answered.

'Ah', the abbot said, 'I thought so. Remember that when she was young, she wetted her nappies. You did not like it but you accepted it. It was something she would grow out of. Right?'

The man nodded, not understanding where the abbot was heading, so he continued:

'Now she is in puberty and she calls you stupid. It is a sign of her healthy development and it is typical of her age. Like the wetting of the nappies, she will grow out of it and you will establish a new relationship with her, more like adult friends than a child dependant on her father. The closer the family, the more of an effort children have to make to break out of it – and this they have to – so the paradox is that the more they shout at you, the better a father you have been'.

The larger family and the basic human deficit
This apparently had given him enough food for thought. Another man got up and asked:

'Yevgeni Nikolayevich, you said earlier that when two people get married, in a way the two families also marry. What is the role of the extended family in bringing up a child?'

This is what the abbot answered:

'Every human being needs a circle of security around him. This hull of a secure environment, includes the people who provide unconditional support, both mentally and physically. Family, the immediate as well as the extended family of aunts, uncles, grandparents and close friends, can be part of this circle of security. It is within such a relatively safe group that we develop our most important talent, the talent to love and be loved. This is important as loving one another is difficult because of what I call the *basic human deficit*. Let me explain this to you.

People are inclined to take themselves as a point of reference when dealing with others. This is what I call the basic human deficit, which means that it is most difficult for us to put ourselves into the position of the other, see the world from the other's point of view. It is like: 'I know all too well what I want, but it is nearly impossible for me to understand what *you* want. People then love *outside in*, 'I will do what I think is good for you'. True love starts with understanding the situation of the other, this is loving *inside out*, 'I will do what I know to be your desire'. Unfortunately, that is much more difficult. We are so busy with ourselves that we can't step into the other's shoes. Family life – or life within groups of good friends – is the training ground for rising above this conflict. If you do not manage it here, you will not manage elsewhere. But the extended family can also be suffocating if there are too many obligations, too much snugness. A balance must be struck between meeting often enough to be able to be involved in each other's development and giving a good deal of freedom to all family members to nurture their personal relationships.'

Growing up in a family

A young man got up. He had a simple question:
'Abbot, how should I treat my parents when they grow old?'
The abbot replied:
'One day you will realise that your parents are less powerful than you are, the relationship with your parents has turned upside down. You will feel proud as well as sad but this is the course of life and it will take time before you get used to this situation, as your parents were once so powerful. Always show your respect, even when they become childish in old age. They may be frail and in need of help, but they are invariably a source of security to you and you will miss them badly when they have passed away. Some say that when your parents are old, you have to return the love they gave you when you were small. Here we confuse love with care. Love always goes both ways, even the newly born baby gives as much love as it receives and a parent at old age who has become dependent on you does likewise. What matters then is that most precious feeling they can give you: 'I love you the way you are, you are good the way you are'. It can only be hoped that parents communicate this before it is too late'.

And addressing the pregnant woman who had spoken in the beginning of the session:
'My advice to you is to tread carefully. Give thanks to those around you for their good intentions even when you do not need them. Accept that you receive this baby in order to lose it. Enjoy the intimacy but allow the child to have contacts with others, do not smother it with your love. When the baby is there, everything will be different. Despite all our experience, each child is the firstborn human on earth'.

When the meeting came to an end I felt relieved: we had returned to the harmony of the earlier Lessons. I could see that the abbot too was relieved as no reference had been made to his Lesson – was it heresy? – in Tyumen. Amidst the sea of unrest and violence in Omsk, the monastery and the Lesson had seemed an island of harmony. Together with the congregation we moved to another room where our hosts had set up some refreshment – there were drinks and snacks. It was all very sophisticated. I felt in the best of spirits but I secretly longed to meet my friends at the next stop.

We spent the whole evening in the monastery and after a good night's sleep, we boarded the 11.32 a.m. to Novosibirsk.

15. Novosibirsk – Professional life

We were now deep into vast Siberia, travelling through the Barbara steppe, once a place of nomads and exiles, kept in check by Cossack fortresses. Although we were still within the same time zone, it took us close to eight hours to get to our next destination, Novosibirsk – New Siberia. We had ample time to go through my notes on the previous Lessons and the abbot was recollecting his childhood. He had been born and raised in St Petersburg – in those days Leningrad. He told me how he and his friends were showing tourists around the former imperial capital, earning a bit of hard currency that was difficult to come by in communist times.

'We organised a Dostoyevsky tour, visiting the places mentioned in his novels. We would also ask tourists for their preference in art and then offer a guided tour through the Hermitage. We would even take them to the Mariinski Theatre or the Oktiabrsky Concert Hall. That is how I learned a lot about art, ballet and music', he said. It appeared he had studied engineering in St Petersburg where he had made many friends, male and female, not only in his own department but also in others, notably the Department of Economics. 'There was one girl I liked very much but somehow I lost track of her', he said. He then talked about his life as an engineer and the problems he encountered while managing people.

'There is so much nonsense in the literature and what students learn at business schools', he said, 'while management is basically simple: you match people with jobs. I could write a book about it', he exclaimed.

'That would then be similar to the Lessons you are teaching now', I observed.

This took him by surprise. 'How come?' he smiled.

'Well, in the Lessons you very much go against doctrine and you seem to be equally critical of the doctrines of management', I ventured.

He sighed and the frown came back to his forehead. The train was already slowing down for we were approaching the railway station. The abbot's voice was hardly audible as the train was screeching over the shunting yards. 'Thanks for reminding me' he said sarcastically and looked out of the window. Just then the train came to a halt.

Founded as late as 1893 at a junction in the expanding railways, Novosibirsk is now Russia's third largest city. Summer temperatures go up to forty, winter lows – down to minus fifty. The city is well known for its university, Novosibirsk State University, where I had so many friends. The university also hosts a high-tech campus and is the cradle of many new enterprises. I was fond of this place.

The abbot preferred to speak in the monasteries he was so familiar with, but this time by means of an exception he had agreed, following a request from the rector, to speak on the university campus. The students had suggested the subject they would like to discuss: professional life, the third dimension of total love. As for myself, I hoped to meet my friends and catch up with them. After all, I had been away for quite a while.

We got off the train, facing the platform with the old steam locomotive kept as a reminder of the many transports that brought heavy industrial machinery from the European part of Russia to Siberia before and during World War II. We were greeted by the rector of the university, priests and local officials. The introductions were quite civilised, a sharp contrast to the messy reception in Omsk. The abbot was driven over Sovyetskoye Shose and crossed the dam to the eastern side of the river Ob. Apparently, they wanted to show him the dam – indeed, quite impressive – rather than taking the shorter route via Berdskoe Shose. I followed in an old car with my friends who had come to meet me. From the end of the dam, it was less than half an hour to Akademgorodok, the university campus, located outside the city, in the middle of dense birch forests. The rector had arranged for an intimate dinner with deans and some faculty members and the evening turned out to be rather pleasant. He told us that Akademgorodok was built on orders of Khrushchev with the aim of establishing a research community that was to solve the problems of science and outstrip the West. Construction started in 1958 and within seven years fifteen academies had been constructed that housed forty thousand scientists, together with a garden city, a beach on the Ob reservoir and night-time skiing facilities.

The following morning, we were led to the aula magna. The audience was noisy, messy, quite different from the congregations the abbot had spoken to before. I thought I sensed an air of scepticism, even amusement among the students who made up the larger part of the audience and who were not used to meeting a man of the faith. The rector, serving his last term, seemed to have everything under control and did not notice anything unusual. After introducing the abbot – and even greeting me – he invited the first question in a warm, welcoming way.

Finding physical security

A young woman rose to start the discussion:

'Father Rostov, I thoroughly enjoy my life as a student and, to be honest, I am frightened by the prospect of graduating and having to find a job. It seems much less interesting than what I am doing now. So, my question is simple: why should we work? Is it natural?'

There was laughter in the audience as she was clearly teasing him. The abbot also couldn't help laughing and when the noise subsided, he came back:

'Well, of course it is natural. Man has been working throughout his entire existence and the same goes for all animals. They do it for a simple reason: no work, no food – no food, no life. We have come a long way from the time of the hunter-gatherers to today's highly complex societies but the principle remains the same. Work provides for physical security, not only food but also shelter and other necessities, not only for tomorrow but also for the distant future as we save for our pensions. That is the first reason to work.'

A mocking student took the floor. I knew him well, he was always the sceptic and now he was clearly delighted by his performance:

'OK Mr Rostov, if that is the first reason, there must be a second. Or perhaps Dr Winderoy can answer that, after all, he has been with you for quite a while?'

Social skills

At this, the entire audience started laughing, wondering how the abbot would take this insult – calling someone 'mister' is highly impolite in Russia – and perhaps also curious what I would answer if I was given the chance. 'The bastard', I thought. But the abbot was not intimidated and, with a smile, made a broad gesture with his arms in my direction. He caught me off balance, I was not prepared. I stumbled and came up with the following:

'Much scientific work is multi-disciplinary which means we have to work with others. That is not easy because we have different backgrounds and we often have an individualistic inclination. Speaking for myself, I had to learn to match my insight and experience with that of my colleagues. We have to balance conflicting views and sometimes conflicting interests'.

The abbot nodded approvingly – apparently, I did not do too badly.

He took over:

'I fully agree. Working life, and especially professional work, is a social laboratory where people are trained in social skills'.

Professional development

The same man, perhaps a bit disappointed that the abbot had ignored his inappropriate interruption, pressed on:

'Sure, there must be more reasons'.

'Well, indeed, there are. Let us start from the beginning. Happiness is about security and growth. Security is comprised of physical security and emotional security, the kind we find in family life or within a group of trusted friends. Growth is personal growth – the growth you experience as you pass through the stages of life – and the development of talents. Talents come in many forms and their development materialises in different settings. Working life is by far the largest contributor to our 'professional capital' that is the sum total of the knowledge and experience we collect in the course of our life. At eighteen, we have obtained professional capital from our parents and our schooling. This capital is more than doubled after getting a degree. A few years later, it is doubled again by what we learn in working life. The working life component of our professional capital continues to increase until we are well over fifty years old. In contrast, the components of school and secondary education disappear quickly but the capital we owe our parents only diminishes slowly over time and is still substantial when we are old. Professional life, therefore, provides for the development of some of our talents'.

A somewhat older man got up, possibly a young lecturer. He hesitated as he was wording his question:

'Gospodin (Sir – also most impolite), perhaps I may introduce myself. I worked for a few years in industry and I do not subscribe to your idea of professional growth. The work I did was utterly boring, routine work, from which no doubt I developed social skills but it did not in any way contribute to my professional advancement. When I had the opportunity to join the faculty, I grabbed it with both hands although the pay is considerably lower than what I earned in industry'.

At last, this was a serious question I thought. The abbot had to think for a while, then answered:

'As in everything, in work there is a balance between gaining security and growth. Sometimes you work to earn a living and sometimes you work to develop a talent. In the ideal job, the two go hand in hand. If such a job is not available, you have to set your priorities: income or growth. May I ask you what you did with the money you earned while working in industry?'

'Sure', the man replied, 'I saved up to buy an apartment. It is not much but it is sufficient for me and eventually a small family'.

'This illustrates my case', the abbot took over, 'You chose to find physical security first and when you had achieved it to a certain extent, you chose to develop your talents'.

The man nodded and the abbot went on:

'The industrial revolution broke up the production process into individual components with workers specialising in one small segment. This has brought us a tremendous degree of prosperity but this type of work is unnatural. Man is degraded to become a machine and is nowadays often replaced by a machine. Now, in the past fifty years, and facilitated by the rise of information technology, workers are assigned integral duties rather than specialised tasks. This kind of work gives much more satisfaction and if you can find a job in this area, you should surely consider it, even if it pays less'.

Building the cathedral

There was some approving chatter in the audience and one could feel that the students were surprised by the abbot's answers. They had not expected such insight from a man who came from a secluded monastery in the wilderness. Little did they know about the abbot's almost twenty years experience in industry! All scepticism was gone and the youth who had asked the condescending questions got up saying:

'Thank you so much, Yevgeni Nikolayevich, for your answers. It will help us in deciding what to look for when we graduate and if we find the type of job you describe, perhaps work will not be as frightening as many of us fear. Still I wonder whether there are other aspects of work that you could touch upon'.

The abbot tried not to show how pleased he was with this change of attitude and continued:

'There is a fourth aspect to work. Look at the ants and the bees: they work together and thus achieve results that are far beyond what they could accomplish individually. It is the same with people. Teamwork is the great accelerator of human effort. Together you can build a cathedral, alone you cannot. Even people who are self-employed work in groups and take pride in what the team can achieve, whether it is scientific work, industrial production, running the state or the activities we pursue in a monastery.

Leadership

Finally, when people work together there is a need for coordination and direction. This creates the opportunity to develop talents of leadership. In the industrial age, leadership was very much provided from a position of power – top-down if you like. There was no need to motivate workers, they would do as they were told in order not to lose their income. In the post-industrial age, leadership no longer comes down to telling people what to do. The leaders need the talents of others to chart the direction and define the common goals. Therefore, leadership has become the talent to inspire others to work in the chosen direction. I hope you will bear this in mind when the time comes for you to be called to positions of leadership. Leadership means leading as much as serving'.

Choosing a profession

An older woman got up and asked:

'You have now mentioned five aspects of work: gaining physical security, learning social skills, development of crafts and other talents, contributing to something that goes beyond the limits of individual work and developing leadership talents. I have two questions. First, are these all the aspects or are there more? Second, it seems to me that the aspects can be conflicting and the question is, how do you reconcile such conflicts?'

The abbot smiled and said:

'May I compliment you on your excellent summary? Indeed, the elements I mentioned make up the five aspects of the work we do in the world. I agree that the different aspects may lead to conflicts among them, for instance between professional demands and the need to compromise. Decisions are not only the result of rational processes but also of social ones. People stick together in formal or informal groups, cover each other up and strengthen each other's positions – the best qualified person may therefore not get the job. Building a career is therefore not only a matter of suitability but also of connections and insight in the social structure'.

The same woman pursued the subject:

'So what are we to do?'

The abbot came back:

'First, escape slavery or dependence by mastering a profession: learning is the name of the game. Boost leadership qualities by observing others. If you work for a large organisation, find allies, link up with senior people who need your energy and originality and from whom you can learn and develop a network. Make no enemies, you may need your adversary on another occasion. It furthers to be on friendly terms with your colleagues but colleagues are not friends and they may turn into foes. Try to find a workplace that stimulates your development'.

At this, a young man got up, possibly a graduate student:

'I couldn't agree with you more Yevgeni Nikolayevich', he said, 'if only it was so simple. I am about to get my degree but I cannot choose a profession. All possibilities look exciting at first and then I start having doubts. I really don't know what to do when I graduate in the autumn'.

The abbot replied:

'If you don't know what to do you should talk to a lot of people. You will get all kinds of reactions that will lead to insight and possibly opportunities. In addition, you can ask each person to name three more and in doing so you will expand your network. See this as an exciting exploration, like studying a new subject. Since you do not yet belong to any organisation, applying for jobs will give you much information that will not be made available to you once you are settled. So, use the opportunity. Remember the two characters that make up the Chinese word for crisis: one meaning 'threat' and the other – 'opportunity'.'

Shared interest – the dimension of enduring love
It was getting late when a young woman said:

'We are both working here, albeit in different faculties. I mean, my husband and I both work here. In another Lesson we heard on the radio, you said that a common professional interest is an element of total love. I don't quite see what our work has to do with our love'.

The abbot had an immediate reply:

'What I was trying to say is that a couple's shared interests reinforce the bond between them. Now, 'shared interests' can mean a multitude of things: hobbies, culture, travelling, sports, and also work. There is, however, also the danger that at home you talk shop and you never stop working'.

The discussions had taken us well into the afternoon and the rector gestured we round up. The dam we had passed over the day before was built to create a large reservoir that feeds a hydro power station. The university had a boat on this Ob reservoir and we were offered refreshments as we went sailing. There were the inevitable academic speeches and toasts and I had a great time talking to and joking with my friends on board. Meanwhile, I kept an eye on the abbot but he looked content. Nevertheless, I guessed he was relieved when we boarded our 7.33 p.m. sleeper that would take us overnight to Krasnoyarsk.

'Did you take a little break from the Lessons, Steve?' he asked.

'I hope you don't mind', I answered.

'Of course I don't', he said, 'You have this powerful talent and you must follow the call to develop it. But you should not neglect the development of your emotional side. If I may say so, this is of equal if not greater importance to you at your stage of life. So it is good you spent time with your friends'.

My spirits fell. After all, I had gone through so much already and I felt I had really changed. Or was I deluding myself? The abbot sensed my anxiety and stroked me over the head.

'Don't you worry', he said. 'You are just doing fine'.

Then I looked at him and saw he was ash-grey, exhausted, more so than on any other occasion. I asked him how he felt and he confirmed that he was really very tired. I wondered whether it had to do with the frictions he had encountered in the previous locations. Then he looked even worse. I knew he did not like to admit it but I felt there was more to it than just a busy day, delightful as it had been. Suddenly I felt guilty. The day had been nice for me but not for him and while I was chatting away with my friends he had been choking on his anger and disappointment. How could I get him to talk about it? I took the liberty to put my arm around his shoulder and said:

'If it is bothering you, why not talk about it. It will all remain within the circle of confidence, I assure you'.

He nodded, it was not necessary to say so. Then he told me a long story about his clash with the Church earlier and how he always got away with it because the flock – as he called his followers – supported him and his advice was sound.

'I have a hunch that this time it is more serious. My brother in Tyumen was really aggressive, I have never encountered this before. And did you notice how much effort I had to put in today to win the trust of this audience? In the other sessions, there was opposition as well. It seems that the message of Jesus and the doctrine of the Church do not go well together. At times, I wonder what I am doing in the Church. On the other hand, I cannot imagine leaving it. It has been such a sanctuary for me after I lost my wife and I have grown so much into it. Besides, I wouldn't know what else to do. I want to serve people but I can't just go live somewhere and put up a signboard saying: 'Ye with problems, gather here''.

I saw his predicament but I could not offer solace, this was way beyond me.

'I am sorry that I cannot think of a solution', I ventured. 'I can only offer you my friendship, as you described it in Yekatarinburg'.

I felt he relaxed. He stared me in the eye for a while, then said:

'Thank you, Steve. That is what I need most'.

16. Krasnoyarsk – Cultural life

One of the older towns in Siberia, Krasnoyarsk was founded in 1628 as a trading post on the Yenisei – with its five thousand kilometres the world's sixth longest river, flowing from Mongolia to the Arctic Sea. The city grew rapidly when gold was found in the region, and eventually became a major river port, centre of mining and industry as well as a railway hub. All these activities created an affluent class in the city. The world's most famous classical orchestras and rock bands play frequently in Krasnoyarsk even when tickets are priced in the thousands of Euros. Outside the city is the Stolby Reservoir, a natural reserve, known for the odd, columnar cliffs that rise from the river edge. After passing over the Yenisei one leaves the treeless steppe and plunges into the taiga. The vast Siberian taiga, which extends over most of Russia, is the largest remaining primordial forest on the planet.

The train arrived at 7.25 a.m. We had spent eleven hours on the train and had to set our watches another hour forward; we were now four hours ahead of Moscow. The abbot looked refreshed, having made up for lost sleep, when we were greeted by our host of the Svyato Uzpenski Monastery (Monastery of the Holy Ascension). He whisked us off immediately to his car for the short ride to the monastery that was located outside the city in the middle of the forest, just like the monastery of Yevgeni Nikolayevich. After he offered us breakfast, he sat at a beautiful organ, and while we were eating, without any explanation, started playing.

'Music at breakfast, that is promising', the abbot whispered in my ear. And it was, indeed. The event had been announced as a Lesson on cultural life. Was this a coincidence or the deliberate choice of our music-loving host? As the meeting was not to start before the afternoon, we took a stroll around the premises. The monastery had been demolished completely after the revolution and rebuilt after 1978. The old monastery was known for its eighty-six thousand icons, most of them lost or burned by the communists, the remnants of the collection – still impressive. Indeed, Krasnoyarsk is a city of beauty, the most beautiful in Siberia according to Chekhov.

When we went back, the audience had already started to drift into the auditorium but we were called to a room on the side. Three monks were waiting for us there, they had just flown in from Moscow. Their expressions were grim and their manner arrogant, as they demanded to speak to the abbot at once in order to deliver a missive from the Patriarch.

I was shocked, this looked serious.

The abbot took the letter, read it and gave it to me. It was short, in plain language, saying that Yevgeni Nikolayevich had to vow that he would no longer express heretic thoughts on pain of defrocking.

'We must know your answer immediately', one of the fellows demanded.

The abbot pointed in the direction of the auditorium.

'My flock is waiting for me', he said. 'I am sorry'.

And he walked past them to our musical host and the congregation, who were unaware of the drama unfolding outside.

Three levels of art
The audience was excited, people were eager to start the discussion.

'Father, to begin with, I would like to ask you why people feel they need cultural life?' asked one of them.

The abbot sighed deeply before he replied, taking off his glasses:

'We all find art moving. It affects us at three levels: the aesthetic, emotional and religious level. If we want to appreciate art, we must understand how it resonates with the different layers within ourselves, with our three cylinders. A work of art may touch different people at different levels. What is religious to one person may be simply beautiful for another'.

The aesthetic level
The abbot paused to let the message sink in. Then he continued:

'Let us start with the aesthetic level. A work of art may appeal to us simply because it is beautiful. It impresses us and it stays with us because it resonates with the beauty within ourselves. If you look for example at Ivan Shishkin's paintings of our majestic nature you will be struck by their beauty and harmony'.

'It is not only paintings that can impress us with their beauty', our host stepped in. 'Music has an even stronger impact. Each time I hear, for instance, Mendelssohn's *Italian Symphony* it cheers me up. I think it is superbly elegant'.

The abbot was a bit confused by this intervention, but he continued:

'Indeed it is. Well, if we surround ourselves with beautiful objects or if we immerse in music, dance, opera, we feel invigorated, enriched. It gives us a sense of harmony. As Keats said 'A thing of beauty is a joy forever".

The emotional level

A woman who turned out to be a professor of art at the Institute of Arts and Sciences came up with the following:

'I do not entirely agree that a thing of beauty lasts forever. Much art is only appreciated when it first appears, loosing its appeal to the generations to follow. So, my question is, what makes certain works of art immortal?'

At this point, our host stepped in again, speaking in his own, convoluted way:

'I think that only art that addresses archetypal human conditions has a lasting appeal, provided it is also beautiful'.

'Please, go on', Yevgeni Nikolayevich invited him.

'First of all, the formative periods of our lives represent archetypal situations. Many formative moments in our life are linked to the passing of the stages of life of which you spoke earlier. Think of the birth of a child. In our culture we have the Madonnas but every culture honours mother-and-child renderings'.

The history professor responded:

'I see your point. I guess you might also consider the innocence of childhood an archetypal condition. It occurs in many myths and sagas that later become the theme of paintings. Sometimes innocence is contrasted by the presence of gazing old men, as in Rembrandt's *Suzanne and the Elders*'.

'Then also the loss of innocence is an archetypal moment, often depicted as Adam and Eve's expulsion from paradise', our host reacted. 'If you follow the path of life, first love also constitutes an archetypal situation. My favourites in that respect are *Le baiser* – the Kiss – by Auguste Rodin and Frida Kahlo's painting *The Love Embrace*'.

Then I asked our host:

'Since you are discussing the stages of life, would you consider death an archetypal situation?'

'I certainly would', was the immediate answer. 'Many ancient cultures had their psychopomps, those who took the souls to the world of the dead. The best known is probably the Greek God Hermes. Psychopomps appear in many pieces of art, including modern films like Ingmar Bergman's *The Seventh Seal* in which Death, presented as a monk, plays chess with a knight who returns from a crusade. Death wins the game by double-crossing and thus leads the knight to his death.'

The professor of art added:

'Many of us see the lady on horseback in Gauguin's painting *The Ford the Flight* as the psychopomp. Tomasi di Lampedusa, in his novel *The Leopard*, assigns this role to an attractive young woman. In Christopher Isherwood's novel *Single Man* the psychopomp appears as a young man. Thomas Mann's *Death in Venice* also uses a boy, Tadzio, to lead the protagonist, a German professor, to his death'.

'Then we should also mention the paintings of men facing death', one of the guests stepped in. 'Rembrandt's last self portrait, his *Portrait of an Elderly Man*, Pablo Picasso's *Self Portrait Facing Death* and Lucian Freud's last *Reflection* are good examples. Mourning a loved one is also an archetypal situation, hauntingly expressed in, for instance, Rossini's *Stabat Mater,* and Andrew Lloyd Webber's *Requiem*. Richard Strauss' *Im Abendrot* – At Sunset, one of his Last Songs, conveys the melancholy of a life that is about to be completed'.

It became clear that the audience had prepared itself quite well. Yevgeni Nikolayevich took the initiative again:

'Some paintings show us the 'way of man' as for instance the *Voyage of Life*, a sequence of four paintings by Thomas Cole. It depicts man's journey along the River of Life, innocent in *Childhood*, overconfident in *Youth*, troubled in *Manhood*, until in *Old Age* an angel guides him to a bright opening in the clouded sky. The idea of man's journey through life is also present in music. What immediately springs to mind is Bedrich Smetana's *Vltave* – Die Moldau, part of *Ma Vlast* – My Fatherland, one of the last pieces he wrote'.

Our host took over:

'Not only the formative moments of life are archetypal. Human interactions but also interactions with nature can be equally fundamental. Take, for instance, Rembrandt's painting *The Return of the Prodigal Son* and Sophocles' play *Oedipus the King*. *St. George and the Dragon*, the fight between good and evil, represents an archetypal conflict and so does Ernest Hemingway's *The Old Man and the Sea,* man versus nature'.

The religious level

A man, visibly moved, started speaking:

'Dear abbot. Every time I am in Moscow, I go to the Tretyakov to see the *Yavlenne Christa Narodu* – The Appearance of Christ before the People – by Alexandr Ivanov. Although the painting is not especially beautiful, it always stirs deep emotions in me while I remain cold when seeing other, superior pictures. How can this be explained?'

'Perhaps you could tell us what you find so compelling in *Yavlenne Christa Narodu?*', the abbot responded.

The man had not expected to be put in the spotlight but took up the challenge:
'As I said, the picture does not strike you as beautiful although the boys in the nude are very sensuous, as always with Ivanov. However, the composition is intriguing. The painting is huge – seven and a half by five and a half meters. The Tretyakov had to make special construction arrangements to be able to display it. The picture shows John the Baptist, interrupting his baptising as Jesus descends from a hill in the background. This, I understand, was a novelty as until then Jesus was always at the centre of a painting. In the foreground on the right, there is a queue of people waiting to be baptised, some of them undressing, getting ready for the great event. On the left some people climb out of the river, apparently they have just been baptised. There are also onlookers or those who still hesitate. At John's powerful gesture, some people look up at Jesus, no longer paying attention to what they are doing. The posture of John and his penetrating gaze almost force the spectator to look at Jesus, signalling that something extraordinary is happening there, something larger than us, something we cannot comprehend. Yet we realise, as the people in the foreground do, that it will have great impact on our lives. It induces strong emotions in me. I think this painting is deeply religious, at least, it resonates with my religious feelings. It took Ivanov twenty years to finish it. I think the painting is a reflection of his religious development'.

The audience had been listening in silence and the abbot concluded:
'Resonating with our religious talent comprises the third level of art. Many people just visit the Tretyakov to see *Yavlenne Christa Narodu*. Likewise, many people visit Glasgow just to see Salvador Dali's *Christ of St John of the Cross*, for many the most gripping religious painting of the twentieth century. It shows the crucified Christ floating in the darkened sky, drawn from a heavenly perspective at an extreme angle, which makes the viewer look down on the event; Christ's face is not visible. The lower end of the cross does not touch the earth. Below is the world, fishermen at work, perhaps a reference to the Lake of Galilee, painted from a horizontal perspective. Dali went to great lengths preparing for this work, he even went to Hollywood in order to find a suitable model'.

There was a silence. Most visitors probably knew the painting but had perhaps not recognised it as religious art, just a surrealistic painting by an extravagant artist.

Now another woman got up, she must have been in her forties, and asked a very direct question:

'Yevgeni Nikolayevich, which in your opinion is the most beautiful painting in the world?'

The abbot hesitated but our host answered immediately:

'If I may answer this, in my view, the most beautiful painting in the world is the *Adoration of the Lamb of God* by Jan van Eyck. It is on display in the St. Bavo Cathedral in Ghent. It consists of twelve panels in two rows – seven above and five below. I wish I could show it to you. The four panels to the left and the four to the right are on wings that can close. There are additional paintings on the back, uncoloured, amongst others a beautiful Annunciation with a tender angel and a frightened Maria.

The central panel at the bottom is the largest and most elaborate. In park-like settings with a Gothic New Jerusalem emerging in the background, it shows a bleeding lamb, looking us straight into the eye, on an altar in the middle, its blood caught in a chalice. The lamb is being watched intensely by groups of monks, knights, saints and common people, spanning on the panels to the left and right. The three upper central panels represent heaven, showing Jesus in the middle, Maria on his left and John the Baptist on his right, all seated and watching the lamb with great intensity. The group is flanked by angels making music and, at both ends, Adam and Eve, naked, Eve pregnant. The picture is totally static; all these people watch the lamb, apart from that nothing happens. Nature and the buildings in the background are painted with meticulous attention to detail, the work has been used to study medieval botany'.

'Why is this altar piece so important to you?' the abbot asked.

'Well, the entire work conveys that something divine is happening: the moment the world has come to a standstill, to its fulfilment. To me, the painting pictures the moment when the meaning of life and religion will be revealed to us'.

The silence was broken by the same woman:

'Can you give other examples of art that speaks to our religious talent?'

The abbot answered:

'When we talk about religious art the first thing coming to mind is the Old Testament's Psalms, especially the 23rd, the psalm of trust, the 130th, *de profundis*, – from the depths – and most of all the 90th, the song of eternity, in my view the world's most deeply moving poem. In the New Testament the teachings of Jesus are very powerful, especially the Sermon of the Mount. The icons made throughout the ages in our country are religious although it takes time and knowledge to appreciate them. Together with spiritual Jewish music, especially the various *Kaddish*, the music of our Orthodox Church is the most religiously inspiring music. For instance, the *Heirmi of the Canon* – The Exaltation of the Cross – from the *Kievo-Pecherskaya Lavra* monastery (the Kiev Monastery of the Caves) overwhelms me every time and puts me in direct contact with eternity. The *Pater Noster* (Our Father) of Bortniansky is similarly moving. Amongst others, Bach, Mozart and Schubert wrote music that has religious dimensions, Bach most of all in his zenith, the *Mattheus Passion*, Mozart in his divertimenti (especially KV 563), Schubert especially in his three last piano sonatas and string quintet'.

Our host exclaimed:

'Oh, certainly, Schubert's last compositions are heavenly, especially the slow parts. I think Mahler's third symphony also touches on the religious and even more so Debussy's *Syrinx*, a piece of music for flute solo that makes you imagine the soul of a deceased one fleeting to heaven'.

Then another woman spoke:

'I am an architect and have studied many buildings around the world. In some one can feel sanctity. Think of the Buddhist temples of Bangkok, the Samarkand mosque, the *Aya Sofia* and the *Sultan Ahmed Mosque* in Istanbul, the *Church of the Assumption* in Moscow and say, the *York Minster*. The Gothic cathedrals evoke feelings of mysticism, especially the churches of Chartres, Paris, Strasbourg and most of all the *Sainte-Chapelle* (Holy Chapel) in Paris, which to me is the most beautiful building in the world. However, not all religious buildings create feelings of sanctity. In contrast to Gothic cathedrals, the Baroque churches do not invoke religious feelings in me. Neither do the temples at Nikko in Japan. There are only few sculptures that have a religious impact on me. Michelangelo's *Pieta* in the St Peter's is an exception – his murals in the Sistene Chapel are likewise deeply religious. Bernini's *Transverberation of Saint Teresa* in the *Santa Maria della Vittoria*, though seen by many as religious, to me is simply an erotic sculpture, however well done'.

'I would say the Roman Catholic cathedrals would inspire even deeper religious feelings if the priests would follow Jesus' example and expel the merchants from the Temple', our host smiled and then, addressing the abbot: 'Perhaps you can tell us how your views on art relate to the rest of your teaching'.

Art and the three cylinders

'The three layers of art – aesthetic, emotional and religious – correspond to our three cylinders', answered the abbot. 'Art that is aesthetically beautiful resonates with our outer cylinder. If it stirs emotions it lingers in our middle cylinder. Some art is religious, it touches us deeply, it opens the gates to the other world, it links our soul, our inner cylinder, to eternity. Art that affects us most vibrates with all three cylinders'.

The meeting was coming to its end and the abbot once again addressed the man who had asked the question about Ivanov's painting:

'I can only advise you to go and see *Yavlenne Christa Narodu* as often as you can. See it at least every ten years and your appreciation and understanding of the painting will develop as your own soul develops, it will become part of yourself, it will enrich you forever'.

We had to prepare for our trip to the Yeniseysk monastery, our next destination, three hundred and forty kilometres or six hours away. And the three angry monks were still waiting. I looked at the abbot. He seemed very tired and I was getting increasingly worried. Then, all of a sudden, he said: 'Steve, I don't feel well, we must do something about it'. But he had a twinkle in his eye. With a monk and me supporting him and bypassing the angry monks, we managed to get into the car. Four hours later we reached the nearly inaccessible four-kilometre Kazachinskiy rapid, where the river Yenisey roars and foams through a gorge and then calms down. We also had calmed down after the narrow escape. We took a break to marvel at the view that has been painted by many artists. Then we continued. Dusk was falling and over the immense birch forest we silently saw the light go yellow, then red. We felt at one with nature, at one with God. At last, we came to the sacred place: the Spaso-Preobrazhenskiy Monastery, the Monastery of the Transfiguration of our Saviour.

I wondered what happened to the three angry monks who did not get the reassurance the Patriarch had asked for. Later I heard they were full of remorse, feeling responsible for the abbot's illness. Nobody knew where they went or what they did, they simply vanished.

But the threat of excommunication had not vanished with the disappearance of the monks.

17. Yeniseysk – Religious life

When we arrived, there was only a young monk to greet us and he urged us to hasten to Vespers where apparently everyone had gone already.

'Can't they wait a bit', I grumbled to the abbot, 'After all, we had quite a bumpy ride and you are not in good shape'.

'You don't understand', the abbot replied. 'Everything in and around Yeniseysk revolves around religion. To be late for prayers would be a great affront, almost a sin'.

I looked at him and saw how tense he was. We had been at many sacred places but this was surely the holiest one. I knew he had a lot to think about, after all, with the disappearance of the angry monks the bull of the Patriarch had all but vanished. I watched him during the Vesper prayers and saw how completely immersed in himself he was. It frightened me. After Vespers, we were invited to dinner but the abbot gestured that he would remain in the chapel. Dinner was sober and was served with water. Our host, a conservative man in his late fifties, behaved in a detached, formal way and I wondered whether he knew about the bull of the patriarch. If he did, he didn't show it, after all, he probably had a lot on his mind, this was no ordinary monastery. We moved back to the chapel for Compline. The abbot was still there, praying. His state made me uncomfortable and I wondered how this would end. I had never seen him so distant.

We rose early to attend Lauds after which we had an hour before the start of the meeting. Again, the abbot stayed in the chapel and I could not speak to him so I wandered around with a young monk to guide me. Yeniseysk is like an open-air museum. In this comparatively small town with a population of not even twenty thousand, there are close to a hundred architectural monuments. The monastery with its four churches, built around 1619 in early Baroque, is located outside the city in the middle of the taiga. Flowers were sprouting up between the birch trees, it was spring at last. Spring, I thought, the promise of new life.

This time the meeting would not take place in the monastery but at the Monastic Lake, thirty kilometres away. During the ride, I wanted to ask the abbot how he felt, but saw I should not disturb him. Upon arrival, the monk-guide, who had noticed my curiosity, told me that on this holy piece of Yeniseysk land, prayers are send uninterruptedly while many believers go there to get married and have their children christened. That's why they had chosen it for meeting the abbot.

Mysticism
There were no introductions or formalities. Once we were seated, outdoors, our host, cool, bordering on being unfriendly, quite different from the earlier hosts, simply nodded to the congregation by way of inviting questions. A woman in her mid-fifties got up, squeezing her hands, and slowly related her story:
  'When we were sixteen, my twin sister and I went out at twilight to stroll in the fields around the house in which we grew up. When darkness fell, I suddenly saw a light emerging at the horizon, a light that expanded over the sky. I felt that something larger than me was overtaking me. I was completely breathless, it felt like I was being lifted up, immersed in something sacred. There was no sound, no motion. I had no idea how long it lasted. Gradually, the light disappeared and I felt as if coming back, descending on this earth. My sister had not noticed anything out of the ordinary. This event has had a decisive influence on my life. I wonder whether you can explain its meaning and whether it has anything to do with God'.

One could see that recounting this experience still evoked strong emotions in her. It was so quiet that one could hear the proverbial pin drop. The abbot broke the silence, saying:
  'You had a mystical experience. Mysticism is to feel connected with God, eternity, the universe, the other world. You stepped out of yourself and felt this communion. For a moment, you were united with the Almighty. Mysticism is the connection of our inner cylinder, our soul, with the universe. We all came from somewhere where we shall return when we are called. On earth, we are lonely and we long for the reunion with this 'somewhere': God, the universe, the All, whatever you call it. We search for the *unio mystica*, the 'union with God', the union of our inner cylinder, our sacred soul, with the Almighty. The scarce moments when we are allowed to experience this union give us great harmony, divine inspiration, our life – a deeper meaning. The mystical revelation is the most profound experience in our lives'.

A monk got up, young, blond with a lively face, hesitating as he was wording his question:

'Father Rostov, isn't this experience, this *unio mystica*, what many of us are constantly searching for? Certainly we monks but possibly everyone? If so, how can we find it?'

I noticed our host frown, hardly visible, but the abbot did not see it when he answered:

'We can reach the *unio mystica* by prayer, meditation, solitary life, abstinence, a union with another person if you are in complete harmony. It can be triggered by music and other forms of art like Yayoi Kusama's *Infinity Net* paintings or the *Flow of Life* projects of Cécile Ex. But the *unio mystica* comes when we do not seek it, at a place where we do not expect it. It overtakes us, we feel uplifted, brought to higher spheres from where worldly matters seem unimportant. And you are right: the search for *unio mystica* is universal. Let's remember that the very word 'religion' comes from the Latin 're-ligare', 'to re-connect', with our beginning, with God. There have been mystic groups and sects at all times, all over the world and they are part of any religion. In the book of Genesis, God was still walking on earth and Adam and Eve could talk to him directly. This was paradise and it seems that now only small children can experience it. Jesus spent long periods in the desert, seeking the *unio mystica*. Many have followed him, but the *unio mystica* can also overwhelm you in a busy street. Certain environments help to connect with God. Gothic churches were designed to do that as the Middle Ages were the time for mysticism in the Western world. Mysticism is also the knowledge that you came to this world with a purpose, a mission, that you were sent, that you can have access to the One who sent you'.

While the abbot prepared to continue he was interrupted by an elder monk with long dark hair and a beard, who objected:

'Of course we are not searching for this. Mysticism is a heresy as it implies there can be a direct union between men and God while we all know that men can only find God through the Church, our mediator'.

I watched our host and now he nodded in an assenting way, again hardly visible.

The audience was confused by these contradicting views and I was curious how the abbot would respond.

'Well, in a nutshell, here you have the very conflict that has divided Christians from the beginning. It is the clash between those who maintain that man can be in direct contact with God and those who think that such contact requires an intermediary, the Church, a priest on its behalf. The Church has adopted the latter view as its official line and it has persecuted those who seek the direct communion'.

Then, addressing the young monk, he continued:
'Forms of mysticism have existed throughout history so far we know. The ancient Greeks had their mystical rites and so had the old Egyptians. Amongst the Israelites, a mystical sect called the Essenes emerged in the second century BC. It disappeared when the Romans conquered Israel in the first century AD. According to Roman historians, the Essenes lived in the desert but other sources claim they were all over Judea. The Essenes lived strictly according to the rules of the Torah, the Holy Book of the Jews. Many were celibate. The Essenes performed ritual ablutions. They lived an ascetic and communal life and had no money or personal property, the model for the later Christian monasteries. They elected their leaders. Although they were not persecuted, they were at odds with the other major sects at the time, the Pharisees and Sadducees, the same who often tried to trick Jesus with scholastic dilemmas. There are strong indications that Jesus and John the Baptist belonged to this group although this cannot be proven with any degree of certainty'.

The early Christians and the rise of dogmatism
A young man wondered:
'What happened to mysticism? It does not seem to play a role anymore'.
The abbot continued, addressing mainly the lay part of the audience:
'The early Christians tried to follow Jesus' example. They are believed to have lived in ways that resemble the life of the Essenes. They lived in scattered communities, often in secret as they were soon persecuted by the Romans. Emperor Nero used them as a scapegoat for all that went wrong in the empire, very much what the Nazis did with the Jews later. The pretext was that the Christians refused to accept the emperor's divinity. Following Jesus' teachings, they did not take up the sword to defend themselves. They baptised only adult followers, infant baptism came later, in the third century. Their groups were presided by elders, *presbyters*, who had no precisely defined functions. Only in the second century, bishops started being appointed as overseers. Even then, there was no central hierarchy in Christianity'.

Our host listened to this getting increasingly angry but he did not intervene. The abbot continued, now addressing the elder monk:

'Christians had different views on the nature of Jesus. The Gnostics saw him as a revolutionary prophet and his teachings as a breach with the Old Testament. Others saw him as the Messiah who according to the Old Testament was to reconcile God with man. These brothers and sisters interpreted Jesus' crucifixion not as a common murder but as part of God's plan for the salvation of humankind. Their argument was the following: It starts with Adam and Eve disobeying God's order not to eat from the tree of knowledge of good and evil. As a punishment they were expelled from the Garden of Eden and they henceforth lived in sin. This sin is transferred to the subsequent generations through the sexual act. As a consequence they believe that all mankind is born in sin. They found support for this belief in a line of Psalm 51:

'Behold, I was shapen in iniquity, and in sin did my mother conceive me'.

The next step in the argument of the brothers and sisters mentioned, is that the sacrifice of Jesus, who chose to die on the cross, was to exonerate mankind from the curse of original sin. Irenaeus, an influential Church father who lived from about 140 to 190, quoted John the Baptist who, on seeing Jesus, exclaimed:

'Behold the Lamb of God who takes away the sin of the world'.

Here Jesus became the Lamb of God. Irenaeus included the words of John the Baptist in his apostolic confession and the quote is still present in our mass today:

Agnus dei qui tollis peccata mundi, miserere nobis – Lamb of God, who takes away the sins of the world, have mercy on us.

Irenaeus also taught that priests are the direct successors of Jesus, a dogma known as the apostolic succession. This means that the Church can absolve the sins of man, but only of those who believe in its doctrine. The Gnostics rejected this view. Throughout the ages the Church has vigorously persecuted those who did not accept the doctrines of Irenaeus'.

Gnosticism – the first movement

'Why did the Gnostics reject this dogma?', asked a man from the audience.

The abbot answered:

'Originally, Gnosticism was an Israelite movement. It emerged in Alexandria in Egypt, then one of the world's most prosperous and influential cities, the second largest after Rome, a city of trade and different cultures, the New York of antiquity. The Gnostics put *gnosis*, 'inner knowledge of love', above analytical knowledge. They believed that after death, man would not be confronted by a divine judge but by himself. Every human being carries a spark of God and the purpose of life is the unification of the soul with the higher Self. You are right, this is pure mysticism.

Gnosticism was adopted by many early Christians. Christianity then was not a unified religion, each group had its own interpretations. Christian Gnosticism flourished in the second century AD. Valentinus, an influential Christian leader who lived from 100 to 160 in Egypt, put the original Jewish Gnosticism into a Christian form. Valentinus was a strong opponent of Irenaeus. Valentinus presumably was a follower of Theodas, who in turn was a pupil of Paul who taught him the secret wisdom of mysticism. Valentinus and the Gnostics viewed Jesus not as the son of God but as an angel-like messenger who came from celestial spheres to briefly touch the earth. This corresponds with the view of Islam, where Jesus is an important prophet, widely quoted in the Koran. The Gnostics attached little importance to the crucifixion or the role of priests and the institution of the Church.

Valentinus moved to Rome at a young age. Apparently there was quite a power struggle between what became the mainstream Christians and the Gnostics where the former benefited from their superior organisation. In 142, Valentinus was almost elected to become bishop of Rome, at the time one of the seven bishops of Christianity and not the all-powerful pope of today, but already the *primus inter pares* – the first among equals. When he lost to Pius, a martyr, the views of Irenaeus became mainstream, existing next to the Gnosticism.

Constantine and the establishment of the Church – the counter-movement
In the early fourth century the Roman Empire was severely weakened. Then a remarkable man became emperor – Constantine. He realised that Christianity had become too big to be destroyed so, in 313, with the Edict of Milan, he legalised Christian worship. Christians were now free to practise their religion, just after the worst persecutions earlier that century under Diocletian. Constantine did even more. In order to end the controversies in Christendom, that threatened the very existence of the Roman state, he convened the Council of Nicaea in 325. For this Church meeting, all bishops and other dignitaries of the Church were called to Nicaea (now called Iznik), a city near Constantinople (now Istanbul). This gathering should once and for all define the doctrine of Christianity. Constantine's soldiers stood at the doors with their swords drawn out, which no doubt helped reach consensus. The Council of Nicaea became the formative meeting of the Church. In forcing the bishops to get together, Constantine perhaps prevented the breakup of the Roman Empire for another hundred years; he had a political agenda. The paradox of this rescue was that much of the teachings of Jesus were sacrificed. The opulent Church with its imperial style and its dogmas, completely alien to what Jesus had brought, emerged from Nicaea. In 410 Rome was plundered by the

Visigoths resulting in a power vacuum. The Church then aimed at becoming the successor of the Roman Empire. It copied the authoritarian structures that kept the Romans in power for such a long time. The Pope in the Vatican still calls himself the *pontifex maximus*, supreme priest, like his predecessors in heathen Rome. Dignitaries of the Church dress like kings rather than in the simple clothes which Jesus must have been wearing as a carpenter's son. The popes in Rome have themselves carried around in a gilded throne as the Roman emperors did before him – Jesus went to Jerusalem on a donkey. Had Valentinus been elected, the Church would have developed quite differently, or rather, it might not have developed into a Church at all.

At the Council of Nicaea the vision of Irenaeus was accepted as the foundation of Christendom and Gnosticism was condemned as heresy. Mystic groups were vigorously persecuted because their claim to direct contact with God left no room for the Church as the sole mediator between man and God – which was and is the basis of its power. This mechanism, the dogmatic Church and the state joining efforts to deal with dissenters, has been repeated throughout history, for instance the extermination of Irish monasteries in Europe in the ninth century which ended the so-called Carolingian Renaissance. The persecution was also directed at individuals, for instance the influential Meister (Master) Eckhart, a thirteenth century mystic who wrote that thanks to a divine little spark, *ein Funkelein*, man can reach the 'Absolute', a profoundly Gnostic idea.

The elder monk who had objected to the abbot's view about mysticism, was quick with his opposition to the abbot:
'It is a good thing that Irenaeus established the dogma. The idea that ignorant people can address God directly is absurd. It is only natural that the Council of Nicaea would condemn it. Shortly afterwards, Augustine opposed it even more strongly. Later, the Cathars, another Gnostic group, were burned at the stake, up to the last man. They deserved it because they challenged the authority of the Church. Their idea that men and women are equal and that women can be priests was equally absurd. It is fortunate that the Church leaders did not hesitate and eradicated this heresy root and branch'.

Again a shiver went through the audience. Then another monk got up and asked:
'I can see why our Church prosecuted Gnosticism, mystics and the Cathars, but isn't it the role of the Church to bring man closer to God? What, if I may ask, is your personal view on that?'

This rather intimate question was met with silence. The abbot was deep in thought and I wondered whether he knew where he was. Then he spoke, or rather whispered:

'All my life, not only in meditation and prayer but also through the frivolities of secular life, I have done nothing but seek God and God and God alone. The Church has helped me in this quest, through the communion with others who were on the same journey, through its rituals, its martyrs who put obedience to principle above instincts of survival and comfort, through the divinity that descends in its churches and chapels, through the wisdom of its followers that comes to us in the written and spoken word. At the same time, my quest for God and truth felt like peeling an onion, as I had to sift the wheat from the chaff, removing doctrines that only serve the power of the Church as an institution and stand between God and me. I tried to find the original message of Jesus and his true followers. I was helped by my intuition and my slowly increasing wisdom. It took immense strength but from time to time, I was allowed to catch a glimpse of the beauty of God'.

Rituals and sacraments

A monk got up, rather agitated, and asked:
 'But surely, you believe in the holy sacrament?'

The abbot answered:
 'Facilitating the search for God is but only one task of the Church. Another is to bring the summits of our life to a higher, divine realm: birth, maturity, marriage, anniversaries, death. Churches and other religious organisations do so by offering rituals, the idea of which is that the event is placed in the hands of God: it is God who welcomes the child to this world, it is God who concludes the marriage, it is God who absolves us from our sins and thus prepares us for a safe take-off at death. In this way, the event becomes sanctified, it is taken out of the ordinary, it is brought to a level of higher meaning. People need such rituals. If they do not belong to a religious organisation, they will make rituals for themselves, especially to mark birth, marriage and death. Rituals also serve to create a bond between those who participate, they confirm that we belong to a certain group. Rituals are often repeated and that creates an even stronger bond between the participants. When attending the christening of a baby we remember how our own child was baptised; when attending a wedding ceremony we relive our own wedding.

In old times the passage of the seasons were also celebrated with rituals: the summer and winter solstices, the spring and autumn equinoxes. The Church has assimilated a number of these rituals: the winter solstice became Christmas, the spring equinox Easter.

In our Church, rituals take the form of sacraments, 'rites in which God is uniquely active'. Sacraments are useful because at the formative moments of our life we seek the proximity of the Almighty. All this is natural and good. The idea however that another man, however well ordained, can act on behalf of God is pretentious, worse, blasphemous. In the eyes of the Church, baptising a baby to deliver it from the original sin and thus save it for God, is a matter of urgency. In this line of thought, the soul would be lost if the child dies before being baptised. Therefore, the Church goes to great lengths to have a baby baptised as soon as possible. In the absence of water, as in the desert, the priest may also use sand. Most parents today use the ritual in order to celebrate the arrival of the child and bring it into the community. Some of them hold superstitious ideas, thinking baptism might give the child extra protection. And many just like the ceremony or do it for the sake of the grandparents'.

Baptism
The same young monk again took the floor:
'Now that you have explained what baptism is officially, can you tell us what you think it should be?'

The abbot acknowledged the question but more or less continued:
'Baptism, as practised by John the Baptist, was a purification rite. John, and also Jesus, believed that the Kingdom of Heaven would descend on earth, the Jewish people would be liberated from their oppressors and gain dominion of the world. Jesus was the Messiah, predicted in the Old Testament. John therefore said about Jesus: 'But after me will come one who is more powerful than I, whose sandals I am not fit to carry'. Only those who would repent their sins and be baptised would be part of this Kingdom. Later, baptism acquired the very different meaning we just discussed.

Coming back to your question Baptism, in my view, should be the conscious decision of a mature person, as practised by Menno Simonsz, a Frisian reformer of the sixteenth century, whose followers were persecuted by the Calvinist and Catholic Churches alike. Infant baptism is not in the Bible. Adult baptism is practised by many Churches today, notably the evangelical Churches in America, Korea and elsewhere'.

'I am sorry but I never heard of Menno Simonsz', the monk intervened.

'Menno practised adult baptism and he rejected the idea of sacraments. Unlike Luther and Calvin, he advocated full separation between Church and State. He did not form a Church but rather a brotherhood in which the pastor is a primus inter pares, first among equals, not a representative of Jesus. Mennonites don't have churches, they call their buildings 'admonitions'. Menno believed a Christian would be recognised by 'good works', not that a Christian is selected by predestination or that he is someone who obeys the rules of the Church'.

'What happened to his movement?' The monk asked a question that was probably on everyone's mind.

'As I said, the Mennonites were persecuted by all the mainstream reformers – Luther, Calvin, Zwingli. They fled to all corners of the world. Some of them fled deep into Russia where they welcomed the Nazis as liberators, but were persecuted when the Red Army pushed the Nazis back. Many then emigrated to Paraguay. They could not make a living there and were repatriated to Germany in the 1950s. Others fled to America, in particular to Pennsylvania, 'the heaven of Penn', William Penn being a Quaker who established this new state in 1681. The Quakers, Hernhutters and Mennonites are related although they have different organisations. The Mennonites split into many smaller denominations because of differences in the interpretation of the Bible. The Amish in Pennsylvania are descendents of the Mennonite movement and there are different small but active Mennonite brotherhoods in Germany, Switzerland and the Netherlands'.

Consolation
The monk was not satisfied with the answer, but rather than pursuing this line of thought, he opened a new subject:
'What, then, do you think of Mary, the holy mother of God?'

The exchange sounded more and more like an interrogation of the inquisition but the abbot remained calm:
'A third role of the Church is to offer consolation. We all feel the need of a loving mother who we can turn to when we are in pain, who offers help and who will reconcile us with God. The *Ave Maria* is a powerful and moving prayer:
Ave Maria, Mater Dei, ora pro nobis peccatoribus, nunc et in hora mortis nostrae – Hail Mary, mother of God, pray for us sinners, now and in the hour of our death.

The Maria worship does not stem from Judaism or the teachings of Jesus who gave us the *Pater Noster* – Our father. It crept in as an extension of the Egyptian worship of Isis, the mother of all gods, queen of all gods, often depicted with a baby at her breast. It has stayed because there was and is a deep human need for consolation. We need someone to turn to when we are utterly desperate: *Maria hilfe* – Mary, help. We establish a relationship with prayers like the *Ave Maria* and the *Pater Noster* and this relationship develops over time, just as our relationship with psalms and works of art develops along with us. When we are young, we tend to take an analytical view, we admire the content and the style of the prayer. When we grow old, it becomes part and parcel of our soul'.

Following Jesus
The monk argued:
'All this is not specifically Christian. Any religion, even the heathen ones, take up the three roles you described: mysticism, rituals and consolation'.
The abbot answered:
'I cannot agree with you more. There is nothing specifically Christian in it and therefore much of it was rejected by the reformed Churches: the veneration of Maria and the saints, the rich interiors of our churches that resemble the Egyptian temples. Yet, even if it is heathen, it provides for something we all need.

The specifically Christian task of the Church is to spread the gospel and help create a society which follows the teachings of Jesus. In this role, the Church is what it originally was: an *ecclesia* – community – of people who want to follow Jesus. The medieval book of Thomas à Kempis, *De imitatione Christi* – About the Imitation of Christ – was and is a real bestseller and today there are millions of people who want to follow the life and teachings of Jesus, as there are millions that follow Moses, Confucius, Buddha or Mohammed. The trouble is that we do not know exactly what Jesus' teachings were. The Church has canonised a number of books as the eternal and unalterable word of God. In reality, the choice of the books that were canonised was rather political – there are many books that were not accepted as the word of God for no other reason that they did not comply with the theological requirements of those in charge. After the establishment of the official Bible at the Council of Nicaea, all other books had to be burned and this order was followed rather strictly, only some books survived as the Apocrypha and others were hidden in the Egyptian desert'.

'I heard that there are not only more biblical books than the canonised ones but that there are more versions of each book as well'.

'The texts of all the books in the Bible have been transcribed continuously with different writers and copyists adding, editing and omitting sentences as they considered opportune. The oldest version of the Old Testament stemmed from the tenth century AD until, in the period between 1947 and 1956, much older versions were found in caves around the Dead Sea in what is now Israel, near the city of Qumran, the dwelling place of the Essenes. These so-called Dead Sea Scrolls stem from the second century BC and were probably left there by the Essenes. Older versions of New Testament books and hitherto unknown books were found in 1945 in Nag Hammadi in Egypt, in a sealed earthenware pot. These books shed some light on how the texts have developed over time. They date from the second century AD and were probably hidden by early Coptic monks when these books were banned. Finally, Jesus' time is well documented by Flavius Josephus, a Roman-Jewish historian with exceptional connections, in his *Bellum Judaicum* – the Jewish War – and *Jewish Antiquities* and by other Roman historians. Many people hope that all this will bring us closer to 'the historic Jesus".

The Bible
'How then do you view the Bible?', the monk asked.

'The Bible is an inspired book, in that sense, it is a holy book like the Upanishads, the Bhagavad-Gita and the Koran. The language is powerful and often beautiful, full of symbolic meanings and cross-references. The texts in it are multi-layered and give rich food for thought to anyone who touches them regardless of his beliefs. It introduces the concept of monotheism, taken from a contemporary of Moses, pharaoh Amenhotep IV (or Echnaton or Akhnaton IV). This pharaoh, who died in 1336 BC, drastically changed the Egyptian religion of his day by declaring Aton the only god. His revolution was reversed after his death by his son Tutankhamun and for over a thousand years the Jews were the only people to practice monotheism. The second part of the Bible gives four renderings of Jesus' life and teachings; other gospels – today we know of about thirty – were excommunicated'.

Jesus
The monk continued:
'How do you personally see the role of Jesus?'

'Jesus can be regarded as a renewer of the Jewish faith that at the time was being suffocated by too many rules, rules that were disputed by the various groups of scholars and religious leaders of the time. Jesus put the human being first and proclaimed that all humans are equal before God and that – likewise – humans should regard and treat each other as equals. He was the first humanist. A sober and factual but moving account of Jesus' life is given in Pasolini's film about the Gospel of Matthew. After Jesus' death, his pupils (disciples) became missionaries (apostles) and were assigned the task to spread his ideas. They were joined by a newcomer, Paul who very much reinvented Jesus' ideas and added the notion that Jesus was God's son and that he was sacrificed in order to appease God with man, to absolve man from his sins. Paradoxically, it is mainly thanks to Paul that we know about Jesus at all. The Church later added other doctrines. It is amazing that in medieval times, the one obsession of Christendom was to seek forgiveness in order to save one's soul. In this sense, the Church was very successful but it had little to do with Jesus' message. Remember how Dostoyevsky's Grand Inquisitor of Seville tells Jesus on his return that he will be imprisoned and sentenced to death because 'his return would interfere with the mission of the Church''.

Our host-abbot was becoming increasingly restless. Was it because of the severe deviations of doctrine the abbot had displayed or was he worried because the time for Sext was rapidly approaching?

The abbot seemed to wake up from his deep concentration and rounded off his Lesson:
'The role of the Church as an institution of power has always been in delicate balance with its calling to be the follower of Jesus. Its attitude towards mysticism and spirituality is ambivalent. Its position as sanctifier of our most important moments and as consoler of pain is powerful but to a large extent heathen or even downright weird as in the meaning of baptism. Therefore, you have to decide for yourselves where to place the focus of your religious life. Open yourself to mystical experiences. Form your own opinion about the ethical aspects of life. Celebrate your most precious and vulnerable moments through the rituals of the Church or make your own if it suits you better. Accept the comfort the Church may give you. Try to be a follower of Jesus by studying his original teachings. Open your soul only to those who love you. Within the Church, you will find people who can be your guides. Learn to distinguish them from those who try to impose their will on you'.

I looked at the abbot as he stepped down from his lectern. His eyes were hollow, his forehead wrinkled. He looked much older than just a week ago. I was afraid our host would give him a severe reprimand – after all, the abbot had now directly challenged many of the doctrines of the Church and to our conservative host this must have been much more serious than the deviations in Verkhoturye and Tyumen. But the host abbot kept silent, he just looked at us with utter disdain. Perhaps because of the controversy, there was much interest from the media and I found it difficult to keep the radio reporters at bay. It was not the right time to interview the abbot as they wanted. So we took Sext in the open air, just where the Lesson had been conducted, and I hoped this would relax the abbot a little.

Death

18.   Irkutsk – Fear, impasse, depression

After the Lessons, we drove back to the Spaso-Preobrazhenskiy monastery to let the abbot take some rest. As he had given strict instructions that his itinerary was not to be altered, I arranged for us to leave after None so we could travel back to Krasnoyarsk while it was still light, stay at a hotel near the railway station and then board the 7.45 a.m. to Irkutsk. We got up early the following morning and had breakfast on the train. I had managed to get a sleeper all to ourselves, as we would be on the road for eleven hours. After breakfast, our travelling companions retired to their own compartment and at last I had a chance to talk to the abbot in private.

'What happened?' I asked. 'You were so distant in Yeniseysk. I have never seen you like this before and I am very worried'.

'Yeniseysk was my Gethsemane', the abbot replied. 'I prayed for a solution but I could not connect and nothing came forward'.

'So what are you, then, going to do?' I dared ask.

'It is basically quite simple. I have to drink my cup, resign my position in the monastery and leave the Church as soon as we complete our journey'.

The way he said it sounded like he was jotting down a shopping list and this worried me even more. But I couldn't help noticing that he seemed relieved, as if a stone had fallen from his heart. I decided not to interrogate him any further, he had been questioned enough already and, anyway, the abbot lapsed into a deep sleep. I felt that the inevitable had happened, but how would the abbot deal with it?

The abbot and the Church

'How are you now?' I asked the abbot when he woke up, well into the afternoon, still on board the train.

'Much better, thanks'. It appeared the doubt had subsided but I sensed fear in his eyes.

'Aren't you afraid?' I asked.

'What should I be afraid of?' came his reply. He turned down my plea to see a physician and, at the moment of writing this, I regret immensely that I was not more persistent. He suddenly looked so old and frail. But the abbot was not a man to argue with. I felt he was fit enough to ask him about his own religious life, avoiding the subject of him leaving the Church.

'May I ask you something about yesterday's Lesson', I tried.

'Most certainly', he said, looking at me with his old curiosity, his eyes staring above the rim of his glasses.

'Well then. There are certain contradictions. On the one hand, you are highly critical of the Church, on the other, you are – or should I say have been – its high ranking and loyal servant. On the one hand, you are deeply religious but on the other you say that much of religion is superstition and therefore, heathen. You speak of Valentinus and Gnosticism with so much affection, yet you are not linked to, or leading, a modern-day Gnostic movement'.

The abbot sighed. 'You see, Steve, it is not all as straightforward as you, with your background in science, try to make it. Being religious means, in essence, developing a talent for the *unio mystica*. Here the Church can help as I have said earlier but most of it has to come from oneself; again, *it is you who it comes down to*. Quite apart from this, there is an instinct to follow where Jesus led, not so much for religious as for humanistic reasons – every human being has a natural affinity to the teachings of Jesus. The Church does a good job in spreading the gospel but it is just one of its many activities, the others having nothing to do with Jesus. It seems a rule in history that great prophets are followed by people who try to undo their work by building dogmas and 'systems' of orthodox thought. When they cannot come to an agreement on the 'right' interpretation, they cause schisms and eventually wage wars. You see this in Judaism, with, in Jesus' time the Pharisees, Sadducees and Essenes and in our time the numerous orthodox and liberal groups that make up Christendom. You also see it in Islam with the Sunnis, Shia, Alevis, Baha'i. So, orthodoxy, the making of 'systems', does not unite people, it divides them, and that is why I oppose it. All the martyrs, who died because they did not want to renounce the 'wrong' faith, will agree with me'.

'But you also said somewhere that people have the need to celebrate or commemorate defining moments of their lives, for which the Church provides rituals. In this respect it plays a useful role although many people who participate in rituals do so for reasons of superstition'.

'And of course for social reasons. In the days of the tsars, it was simply impossible not to baptise your child or not to marry in church. Coming back to superstition, there are pictures of priests blessing tanks on either side of the front in World War I. This is pure superstition and Christian Churches should have stuck to the message of Jesus not to resort to violence, for instance, by excommunicating anyone who advocates war or takes part in it'.

'Now you condemn superstition but you also say people need it'.

'Of course they do but please realise that this is a weakness, forgivable as it may be. It is a legacy from the days of animism when people looked for help in their powerlessness against the forces of nature or because they wanted to secure good luck in the hunt. They tried to rally fate to their cause by spiritual rituals or by avoiding things that might bring upon them the fury of the gods. People will do anything to avert disaster and when they don't have the physical means they will use spiritual ones'.

'Isn't this heathen and shouldn't the Church oppose it?'

'You have to be careful. Jesus first of all denounced insincerity, double standards, and only in the second place – superstition. Enlightenment tells us that superstition does not work but if you tell this to simple people you deprive them of their only hope'.

'What about the struggle between Church and Gnosticism today?' I finally found the right moment to ask the crucial question.

'Gnosticism today does not exist as a movement, in fact, it never was a well-structured organisation', came his reply. 'There is however much interest in what people usually call spirituality and although that is not the same as Gnosticism, it is rooted into intrinsic knowledge. This spirituality is an expression of individuals, only sporadically organised, completely outside the Church. Modern science and the values of the Enlightenment have further diminished the power of the Church. In all civilised countries nowadays the Church is separated from the State. Priests are not above the law and men and women are equal. Gay marriage is becoming mainstream. While the Church may be on the decline, science and spirituality are gaining ground. However, by their very nature, they are at loggerheads. The challenge today is to reconcile science and spirituality'.

This discussion gave me much to think about but more importantly, I felt supremely happy, as I felt yet again close to the abbot.

At last we arrived at 1.03 a.m. the following morning and again we had to put our watches an hour forward. We were now over five thousand kilometres and five time zones away from Moscow. At the pompous late nineteenth century Irkutsk Passagiri railway station we were greeted by a small crowd and the enthusiastic abbot of another Spaso-Preobrazhenskiy Monastery. He took us to the local train that brought us to Selenginsk on the Southern bank of Lake Baikal. From there, we went by car to Posol'skoe, where the monastery, as it turned out the next morning, is beautifully located on the banks of the lake. Although we were driving in the middle of the night, neither the abbot nor I were sleepy and we tried to lock our host in conversation, something he found difficult at this hour.

'Did I make a mistake in calling this monastery Spaso-Preobrazhenskiy, the name of the monastery at Yeniseysk?' I asked him.

The question was grist to his mill and he started explaining that Spaso-Preobrazhenskiy – the transfiguration of our Saviour – was a critical event for the orthodox Church as this event showed without a margin of doubt that Jesus was not just a wise teacher, a virtuous reformer, a charismatic miracle-worker, not even a prophet or a saint, but that he is the son and the word of the Living God. Therefore, many monasteries and cathedrals in Russia are named after this event.

'So, it is just a coincidence', he said. 'And we are really proud to have this name'. He gave more explanations, then suggested: 'Tomorrow the Lessons will not start until after dinner, so you will have the whole day to yourself. Brother Abbot, you will hopefully sleep in late. If you permit, we can take Stephen to see the city. It is really worthwhile'.

Then, addressing me:

'No need to worry about your abbot. I shall get you a car and a guide to show you around'.

And that is what we did. I had to get up early, as it would be a four hours' drive to the city. After making sure the abbot was in good hands, I joined one of the monks and we drove back from Posol'skoe to Irkutsk. After Shelekhov, we approached the Angara, the only river to flow out of Lake Baikal. Lake Baikal is terrifyingly large in volume, the size of the five Great American Lakes together. If it were emptied, it would take all the rivers of the world more than a year to fill it up again.

We came to the point where the small river Irkut joins the Angara. The city is built on the banks of both rivers, with a multitude of bridges spanning its different parts. The first Westerners who came here were gold traders, arriving in 1652 and building a winter resort that soon expanded and was granted city rights thirty-four years later. It was then in the middle of the wilderness; the first road to Moscow was only completed a hundred years later. The place became infamous for the exiles. After the suppression of the December revolt of 1825, numerous members of the intelligentsia and officers were exiled to Irkutsk, the so-called Decembrists, joined later by Poles after their failed uprising of 1863. Many others followed and around 1900 there was one exile per two inhabitants. The exiles started a rich cultural life, which gave the city its nickname 'the Paris of Siberia'. The discovery of gold in the nineteenth century made Irkutsk a city of quick fortunes: easily gained and easily lost, the St Louis of Siberia. I found the name 'Paris' a bit exaggerated but there were grand boulevards and still many beautiful wooden mansions with their famous carvings – resembling the palaces of St Petersburg. We visited several theatres and Decembrists' museums. We also went to the market and for the first time, I felt I was in Asia, it smelled of Asia. After all, the border with Mongolia is only some two hundred kilometres away from Irkutsk and the Mongolian capital, Ulan Bator, another two hundred further. Irkutsk is now the hub of many trading routes and although it is in the middle of Asia, its climate is temperate, thanks to its proximity to Lake Baikal. This was the first day during our journey when I could go out without a jacket.

Fear
We were back in time for dinner and I was happy to see that the abbot was in good spirits. The congregation waited in the auditorium and after the introductions a man in his late thirties came up with a surprising question:

'Dear abbot. I am sure I speak on behalf of all gathered here when I say we are most grateful for your visit to Irkutsk and appreciate you took such a long journey. Perhaps I may present to you a problem that bothers me very much. You may consider it a problem of luxury as I have, I think, a challenging life in the professional services. All my life I worked hard to achieve my present position and I still put in much effort to make my career a success. Sometimes however, I wake up in the middle of the night and I feel scared to death, paralysed, sweating through all pores of my body. If I stay in bed, it passes with no damage done, but it is a terrifying experience. There seems to be no reason for these panic attacks and I wonder whether you can explain it, possibly even suggest a remedy.'

To my surprise, the abbot smiled, saying:
'Thank you for your kind words, but I don't think we have come that far. We still have to travel another four thousand kilometres to our destination, so we are just over halfway'.

Then his face became serious as he continued:
'Yours is a conflict between your rapid growth and your feeling of security

that apparently is lagging behind. All the time, you are entering new avenues of life, leaving former securities behind, not having the opportunity to form new ones. Let me tell you the story of Ilya, one of the brothers of my monastery, perhaps you heard me talking about him in Nizhny Novgorod. He once told me that at the age of seventeen he left his village for Krasnoyarsk to go to university. He hardly knew anyone there and the communication with his family was poor because there was no telephone at the time. Although he knew what to expect, having heard stories of older friends, university life and life in a big city was new to him. He went there two weeks before the term started in order to find his way around. He took a room in a new residential block for students and was the first to move in, there was nobody else'.

The man who had asked the question was no longer frowning and stared at the abbot who continued:

'Everything was running smoothly, Ilya was full of confidence and looking forward to the new challenges. During the day he explored the city and in the evenings, he cooked his meal in his residence, as the university canteen was not yet open. He had no one to talk to but he managed all right. One evening he became frightened, for no apparent reason. The feeling increased to a point where he could hardly move or breathe. He lay on his bed and stayed awake all night and morning. All the time he felt scared to death, just like you, immobilised, paralysed. Around noon the next day, the feeling subsided and in the evening, everything was back to normal. First, he thought some ghost had haunted him but later he thought: 'This is the fear of freedom, the shadow of living life to the full''.

'What happened next?' the man asked. 'Did the fear recur?'

'Well, Ilya never had a similar attack of anxiety again. He did have frightening dreams later in life, nightmares of terrorists shooting at his children from the rooftops of buildings in a narrow street, but for that there was a reason, as he felt deeply threatened by severe personal problems. They affected his inner cylinder, represented in the dream by his young children who were dearer to him than life itself. It was a different experience than the fear-without-reason at the start of his student life'.

Then, summarising:
   'At such *moments of change* we have to let go of everything familiar and this is threatening to our deeper layers. In the daytime, we are active and while

we are busy, we don't notice these uncertainties. They bounce up at night in dreams or as a paralysing sense of fear. Such fears can last for days, one cannot move, eat or sleep, one does not see frightening images, there is just a paralysis of mind and body'.

The man took some time, then responded:
'Thank you. I never heard of someone having a similar experience and that, in itself, is reassuring. Is it common?'

The abbot answered:
'We need to strike a balance between fear and confidence. This balance varies from person to person and it can change during our lifetime, it is connected with the way in which we work alternatively on growth or security. Although few can or will acknowledge this, many people are driven by fear rather than development. There are many ways to combat fear: gaining power, status and money is one of them, planning one's future and even intimacy with a loved person is another. However agreeable this can be, it does not give the desired confidence. True confidence comes from within. If this fear overtakes you, you have to start taking it easier, it is better to combat fear than to suppress it. Power, status and money are only drugs that make life temporarily bearable. People who have amassed great fortunes are therefore never satisfied, they always want more'.

'Can you say something about ways to get out of such a depression?' the man came back.
The abbot replied:
'The only way to grow out of a fear-driven life is to define a situation in which you know you will feel confident, then plan your way towards it. This often means that you have to take a different route in life, pursuing other interests than a career or studies. It takes courage to make such a turn and change direction, as you have to sacrifice many things, but do it, restore the balance in your life. If you know where you want to go, you may be confident that you will get there because *Faithful is he that calleth you, who also will do it.* By the way, the situation you described is one of fear, caused by an imbalance between growth and security. It is not a depression, which is something quite different'.

Impasse
Suddenly, our young and energetic host was intrigued:
'What then can you say about depression, Yevgeni Nikolayevich?', he said.

'Let us first talk about impasse and let me give you an example', the abbot proposed. After a sip of water, he continued:

'Ilya also told me that one time he felt not so much fear but a total impasse when a close friend fell seriously ill and died, just before they were taking their final exams at university. Ilya had been with his friend day and night, taking care of him and seeing him gradually fade away. After he died, Ilya felt an emptiness, a feeling of paralysis, a total lack of energy. He said it was not a depression, when you long to die. It was also not fear as he was not afraid, he was just deprived of energy. It was an impasse, he just got stuck. In the end, he passed his exams with all the energy he could muster and then took a holiday reading simple comic strips. He gradually overcame the feeling but at every point in his life when he was at an impasse, the images of his dying friend would return to him'.

Apparently, an elderly man was deeply moved by this:

'Can you tell us how you get out of an impasse, father', he suggested.

'To get out of an impasse you need time and contacts. Time to digest what caused the impasse in the first place and contacts with other people to bring you back to earth. Such contacts may lead to suggestions for new avenues in your life. In an impasse, we have to recognise the *weak signals of opportunity* and not say 'no' too easily to something new'.

Depression and suicide
'Thank you, Yevgeni Nikolayevich, but you have not yet talked about depression', our host reminded him with a smart look on his face.

I thought I noticed a slight sign of disapproval in the abbot, or just a hint of it, but he hardly showed it.

'If someone cannot find a way out of an impasse, it may deepen to a depression. Initially, you feel no appetite for life anymore, you have this feeling that nothing matters. If it worsens and you feel you have no options left, the black terror of depression brings you to the antechamber of death – ending your life would feel like giving in to seduction. To make it worse, in a state of depression, you tend to avoid people while they are exactly what you need as they can show you the way to options you never thought of. Depression easily enters into a cycle which reinforces itself. In Mozart's opera *Die Zauberflöte* – the Magic Flute, Papageno, one of the characters, feels at a certain moment his life has come to a dead end, as he wants love and cannot find a person to share it with. With the rope already round his neck, he remembers the magic

Glockenspiel, chimes, he was given earlier and he says: '*Ich Narr vergass das Zauberding* – I fool, forgot the magic thing'. He plays it, Papagena arrives and soon he is happily united with her. The other main character, Tamino, who is also in an impasse though not depressive, plays his magic flute and eventually finds his great love, Pamina'.

'It can't be that simple', our host objected, now serious.

'In reality, it is of course not so easy to get out of a depression but you should remember it is only a disease of the middle cylinder, there is no communication between your inner soul and the outer world. Only when you are absolutely sure that your life will never have any meaning anymore, may you submit to the desire to end it. In this case, you should consider the pain you will inflict on those who love you. You will be inclined to trivialise such pain ('nobody cares', 'life will go on as usual') but please be realistic. You have no idea how much you will make others suffer and you have no right to do that. And remember, there is always some *Zauberding* that can help you out. A depression is just an indication you are on the wrong path. You overlook options. You pursue something that is not in your true – and as yet unknown – path of development. You turn your energy against yourself. Depression is built into us by evolution in order to warn us against going into the wrong direction. Suicide would be the wrong reaction as there will be a fulfilling life in front of you once you have found or created the new road to fulfilment, the new phase in your life, a new life after the death of a loved one. Don't be trapped by a depression – go out, see people, make new acquaintances. Even when this does not make you feel better immediately, a solution will emerge when you continue to pursue the weak signals of opportunity'.

'Is there a common ground of impasse and depression?' our host inquired.

'Fear, impasse and depression are all members of the same family, they are not signs of death, they rather signal a need for change. You will have to contemplate, learn and explore new avenues. You can get help but in the end, like the Baron von Münchhausen, you have to pull yourself up by your own hair out of the swamp'.

A woman, in her thirties, perhaps a professional councillor, got up asking:
'I have the impression that depression is becoming a pandemic. Half the American population is on Prozac'.

'That may be exaggerated but indeed, it is frightening that in our society, so many people are depressed. They take flight into drugs, alcohol or violence – all signs that in the atomised world we live in the flow of love stagnates. Out of this world will develop a new one, a spiritual world in which love can be given and received. It will take time and suffering – this is the meaning of *the New Jerusalem*. In the meantime, the only recommendation I can give to anyone in a state of fear, impasse or depression is to give it time. Take your feelings seriously, contemplate what is happening, force yourself to discuss it with intimate friends or, better, professionals. Do not try to escape in alcohol, drugs, hedonism, consumerism, illusionary love affairs or high-risk adventures, as this only postpones the solution and makes the situation worse. And most of all: look out for the *weak signals of opportunity*, they will help you out'.

This seemed to be a natural moment to retire. We got up and walked back to the cell of our host where we took some refreshments.

I could not help thinking the abbot had spoken of himself. Impasse – a situation in which one has to find a new course in life – was exactly the feeling he must have. He had said that if one could not find a new route, an impasse would turn into depression. So it was my job to prevent that. But I was not the *Zauberding* he needed. And he had also said that a great love provides the energy to cross borders. But then, I could not go and find it for him.

I was also afraid I might end up in an impasse myself, as my life as a scientist seemed so far away and so unattractive that I could not imagine returning to it with pleasure. Surely, this journey was not just a distraction from my work but a bridge to something else. I did not want to think of it. Fortunately, we had to prepare for Chita. It would take us close to sixteen hours to get there.

19. Chita – The meaning of life

We had to cover over a thousand kilometres, leaving Irkutsk at 1.33 a.m. and arriving 6.14 p.m. in Chita. We saw the sun rise and set. We crossed a mountainous terrain with coniferous forests where the journey became very slow. On several occasions, we had to stop to allow the train crew clear the fallen trees off the rail track. The watches again had to be set an hour forward.

Chita turned out to be a rather small town of around 300 000 inhabitants, located on the banks of the river Selenge that flows from there into Lake Baikal. There were no high-rise buildings and traffic was thin. In front of the two-storey railway station, white with a red roof, a few people and two police officers were waiting for us. Then an old ambulance made a sharp turn at the roundabout in front of the station and screeched to a halt by the curve. An enormous monk, plump and tall, in the prime of his life and in good spirits, climbed out of it. He introduced himself as the abbot of the Troytzko Selengiskiy Monastery – the Trinity Monastery at the Selenge.

'I am afraid our monastery is desperately poor and we don't even have a proper car for our guests so we use this old ambulance', he explained. 'One of our brothers is a good mechanic and it is his responsibility to keep it going'.

Well, the car was old indeed, battered and rusty, the rattling sound of the engine reminiscent of the old sewing machines. So much as we did not like using it, we could not turn down the offer. Our hesitation was quite apparent but our host laughed it away, making a broad reassuring gesture in the direction of the car:

'It is still quite reliable and we fitted it with benches for you to sit comfortably'.

He opened the back doors and we climbed in, a monk bringing in our luggage. Our host sat himself next to the driver. We could not see anything outside because of the frosted windows and we talked to him through a hatch between the front section and the backside where the stretcher used to be, the rails still in place. He told us that Chita Oblast (district) borders on China, covering a span of a thousand kilometres and another eight hundred with

Mongolia. This is a mining area: just about every ore imaginable is found here, including gold and uranium. Founded by the inevitable Cossacks in 1653, Chita was originally a place for exiles until people started to flock in voluntarily after the completion of this part of the Trans Siberia Express in 1891. Some of the migrants were Muslim Tartars who settled next to the Jewish Quarter and built a small mosque, remarkable because of its Western style tower in the middle of the building instead of the usual minarets at the corners. The railway station was opened by Tsar Nicholas II, who gave the monastery a cross – still revered – and three hundred roubles, a large sum at the time. Chita became quite revolutionary in the early nineteenth century when an uprising was drowned in blood. At the same time the city was home to the Zionist movement. After the revolution, Jews were outlawed and their large synagogue – the largest in Asia – nationalised, only to be returned to the faithful in 2004. There are also quite a few buildings of Japanese style as Japanese prisoners of war were put to work in the city during World War II. In short, Chita is a multi-cultural city with a tolerant culture in the heart of Asia.

When we arrived, we saw an inscription above the porch that proudly read: 'First Monastery at the Baikal'. Well, it was certainly old. There was only a small community of monks in the dilapidated building, its walls and roofs crumbling down. Many brothers worked in the mental hospital that occupied most of the monastery. They were short of just about everything and the state of the patients was deplorable. Despite all this misery, we had to laugh when some of the patients started imitating our abbot and turned out to be doing it quite well.

Material and spiritual development

One of the hospital rooms had been turned into a meeting hall. When we entered, we saw it was packed and there were many young people – Chita is one of the few regions in Russia with a growing population. An elderly monk started the discussion with a penetrating question:

'Dear Father Rostov. As you can see, here we take care of mentally ill patients. Although we do all we can for them, we sometimes wonder about the purpose of their life. Can you shed some light on this issue?'

The abbot answered:

'There is no difference between the purpose of your life and the life of your patients. I believe that the purpose of our life is to develop our talents, especially the talent to love and to be loved. The question underlying this is: 'What is the purpose of developing our talents, given all the joy and pain that goes with it? What is its ultimate meaning?"

The monk, stroking his beard, asked the abbot for his opinion.

'The way I see it is as follows. Billions of years ago, about fourteen billion years, the current universe was created by the separation of the physical and the spiritual worlds. This is known as the Big Bang. Since then, both worlds have been subject to turbulent development. In the physical world, material started spreading out at incredible speed, creating the universe. Tiny bits of particles clustered to become the galaxies, solar systems and other substances. We can observe this development with increasingly sophisticated instruments and analyse it with ever more ingenious reasoning. However, we know little about the development of spiritual energy as only few people claim they can observe it and we cannot verify their experience the way we can check observations of the physical system. Yet many people have access to a spiritual world. If we accept their intuitive knowledge, we must take the existence of a spiritual world for granted. By analogy with the development of the physical world, we may assume that the spiritual world also develops'.

'I understand', the monk said, 'the question is: how does it do it?'

'Let me try to answer this', the abbot went on. 'Life is nothing but a temporary combination of spiritual and material energy. You and I are nothing but temporary combinations of different samples of physical and spiritual energy. When a new physical body is formed, it is charged with a small particle of the spiritual entity. While this combination lives – plant, animal or human being – it encounters many challenges, positive and negative. In doing so, the spiritual particle is enriched. When the combination is dissolved at death, the particle reunites with the universal body of spiritual energy, contributing in an infinitesimally small way to its development. This is how I see the development of the spiritual world. The purpose of our lives, as I see it, is to make a little contribution to this process'.

Memento mori

Another monk, younger than the one who asked the previous question, got up and asked:

'Why were all people of all times so engrossed in the question about the meaning of life?'

The abbot answered:

'You will eventually arrive at the final crossroads of your life. You will have had busier periods with many things to take care of but none so charged with emotions. If your time has come and you want to die in peace, you have to come to an understanding about the meaning of your life. You already have a glimpse of what the meaning of life is to me. To you, life may have a different meaning. This may escape you now, but it is vital to become aware of it if you are to go in peace'.

The young monk responded:
'Quite frankly, I don't give death much thought. It seems so far away. How should we consider death?'

The abbot smiled as he answered:
'Young people live like they will last forever. For them, death is far away. But your time may come at any moment and you should be prepared for it. *Memento mori*, the Romans said, remember you will die. That does not mean you should worry yourself to death. You ought to see also the other side of the coin: *Carpe diem*, seize the day, *Gather ye rosebuds while ye may* as Robert Herrick said in his poem and as Waterhouse painted it.

Death is nothing but the dissolution of physical and spiritual energies, these energies being recycled after their separation, dust-to-dust and spirit-to-spirit. All your toils and pains, all your joys and successes serve – in a modest way – the development of the spiritual world just as the burning of stars and the movement of the galaxies serve the development of the physical world. All our pleasures, suffering, learning, all the joy and pain in our lives are nothing but a contribution to this development. By living our life, we contribute to the development of the higher being, the *Weltgeist* – the Spirit of the world. That is all there is to it – that is, in my opinion, the meaning of life'.

The young monk was rather annoyed when he said:
'Although I can see the logic of what you are saying, it all sounds too scientific to me. What happened to the mother of God who will pray for us at the moment of our death?'

God
I saw the abbot got tired and I waved to suggest we close the meeting. But he looked the other way, his concentration intense, and replied:
'You probably find my teaching cold-hearted and you wonder whether there is something more emotionally gratifying. Our Church teaches that if you follow its rules, after death you will be received by God the Father on his throne and join the community of saints in everlasting glory. Yes, this is much warmer and cosier but is it also not a bit primitive? Energy, including spiritual energy, cannot be destroyed and it seems odd that our life should be the last stage of a development that ends in heaven. A thought that may help you accept the inevitable is the Darwinian observation that life of a species is

only sustainable if it can adapt itself to the changing circumstances of nature. As an individual can hardly adapt himself, we have to re-invent ourselves time and again by creating new versions of our species and die. Death is the price of life – the purpose of life in nature is the perpetuation of the species'.

Now the young monk was downright offended:

'If you reject the image of God the Father, sitting on his throne in heaven, how then do you see God? Not as a mass of spiritual energy, I hope?'

'Actually, God as I perceive him is close to that. Like God, the spiritual energy is the one and only, undivided yet omnipresent, present also in us. When we die, our *Funkelein* – little spark – returns to the mass of spiritual energy and this is the meaning of the saying: 'His soul has gone to heaven', or: 'He now sits with his maker''.

The elder monk who started the discussion came back with another question:

'It is of course clear to us all that we should, during our lifetime, develop a sense of the meaning our lives have for us. In a way, you might say, that is obvious. What I would like to ask is this: is there, for each individual, only one answer to the question about the meaning of life or are there more?'

'What matters is that you work towards a 'meaning of life' that satisfies you and that gives you peace', the abbot said. 'Your 'meaning of life' may not necessarily be mine. Indeed, one may even have several meanings of life that are complementary, even contradictory. Personally, I sometimes think that my deceased father and my stillborn son are waiting for me at the gate of heaven, making fun of me as they see me stumbling about. At the same time, I can think of a new life after death, like the Buddhists and Hindi do. And ultimately, I believe in what I just told you. So, I have three completely different and mutually excluding views of what will happen after I die'.

The monk continued:

'Why is the question of the meaning of life so important to you that you pay so much attention to it?'

'When your time comes, you will need to make up the balance of your life. You have to come to a conclusion about your contribution, the purpose of your life. In your ultimate hour, you have to accept yourself the way you are: if you love yourself, God will love you. If you forgive others what they have done to you, you will be forgiven for what you have done to them. There will be no reason to feel guilty or to be afraid of divine punishments that might await you. If you die a slow death, you may have the luxury of time to think your life over, to discuss it with others. Try to use this time to come to a conclusion. Take care of your loved ones. Then go in peace'.

This last intervention had drained the abbot of all his energy. While talking, his face had become ash-grey. He sank back into his chair, heaving and groaning, unable to speak. I felt I should no longer pay attention to his dismissals of care so I addressed the audience and asked whether there was a doctor in the room. A young woman came forward and immediately examined the abbot.
'We have to take him to hospital at once', she said. I could never have imagined what happened after this, in this remote and seemingly old-fashioned town. She made a few calls on her mobile and all of a sudden, an army helicopter materialised out of the blue. The next thing we knew we were at the university hospital with a cardiologist taking charge. 'I am afraid he has had a small heart attack, already some time ago. He will have to stay here for a few days', he said. 'I will give him Sintrom and I hope he will be all right after that. You have to postpone his trip'.

The abbot was rolled into a hospital room, followed by the lady doctor, who had come with us, and me. When he settled down, we had to go outside. Our host went to the guest telephone in the entrance hall to call our next destinations. This left me alone with the doctor in the corridor. She was very interested in our trip and enquired about our travel plans. I told her they were quite simple: one more stop in Khabarovsk and then the final one in Vladivostok. We also talked about the abbot's earlier health problems and I told her I felt I should have called in help sooner.
'You should have', she said, 'but I can see the abbot would not have accepted it. So, you should not blame yourself'.

That, of course, was nice of her and we continued our conversation, glancing now and then at the abbot in his room. The cardiologist paid a visit and when he came out he told us there was no need to stay with the abbot any longer. If we wanted we could use one of the waiting rooms where there was a samovar with tea. We walked down the corridor and ran into our host who said he had informed the remaining monasteries about the delay.

'I am sorry it took me so long, but they are all very concerned', he added.
He had to go back and I was about to leave with him when the lady doctor offered me a cup of tea and promised to give me a lift in her car afterwards. I was pleasantly surprised and when our host had gone, she told me that she had

listened to all the broadcasts and how excited she was to finally meet the abbot in the flesh.

'And meeting you, of course', she added, looking at me. 'You have become quite a celebrity. The media never miss an opportunity to mention how cool you are'.

I blushed. I had hardly listened to the broadcasts so I was not aware of how the Lessons were covered. She laughed at me and put her hand on my arm, teasing me:

'Oh, how sweet, you are shy!'

I noticed she was actually quite attractive.

'You don't seem to have that problem', I managed to answer.

'I guess not', she laughed, 'although probably more so than it shows'.

Then, shifting the subject: 'I like shy people because they are sincere. You are clearly very sincere and dedicated to your abbot. You must love him very much'.

Now I was lost. Tears welled up in my eyes. I had increasingly been enjoying the conversations with the abbot but I had not realised how much he had become to mean to me, how frightened I was to see him in this condition.

She sensed my concern and broke the silence:

'Listen Stephen, your abbot had a heart attack. But you should not worry. As long as he doesn't get another one, he should come out of it all right; after all, he is quite strong'.

'By the way, I am Anna', she added.

While I let this sink in, she continued:

'Thinking of it, I guess it would be better if I travel with you to Khabarovsk. It is a long journey and your abbot is more likely to listen to me being a doctor than to you, with all respect of course'.

She was teasing me again but I liked the idea that she would come with us. Actually, I liked the idea for two reasons.

'Are you sure you can make the time?' I wondered, trying to hide my excitement.

'Well, I'd better start making some phone calls. Let us go'.

While she was driving her old Lada, I wondered where the abbot had had his heart attack. Had it been in Krasnoyarsk, after speaking with the angry monks? In Yeniseysk, after his decision? I did not ask my doctor friend, as I was sure she would evade the answer for nobody could know it for sure.

20. Khabarovsk – Death of a loved one

We stayed two weeks in Chita. The abbot received physical therapy every day. At first, he could only walk a few steps around his bed with good brothers at either side of him. Gradually, his rounds became lengthier and it was celebrated as a victory when he could go by himself to the bathroom down the corridor. His condition was constantly monitored and fortunately, he had a strong heart. I don't want to think what could have happened otherwise. Already after a week he thought he could take up travelling again but we convinced him to stay longer as the trip to Khabarovsk, our next destination, was the longest of the whole tour: 2 327 kilometres. With the lowest average speed of the journey – less than sixty km/hour – it would take close to forty hours. In Khabarovsk, we would be one more time zone ahead of Moscow, seven altogether.

With a heavy heart we finally started the journey, taking the 6.39 p.m. sleeper. The abbot looked confused when we left, vaguely thanking all who had taken care of him. A special carriage had been arranged with the necessary medication and equipment in case he had another heart failure. Anna was travelling with us, and thanks to her cheerfulness, the journey even turned out to be quite pleasant. I chatted a lot with her and she said: 'You are just like my husband, so careful and well organised'. The compliment made me happy but when the fact that she was married sank in, to my own surprise, I felt immensely sad.

The train made short stops at small stations: twenty-five of them altogether. During this long trip we lost track of the time – day and night merged. Between our naps, we discussed every subject under the sun and we did so in different combinations. Sometimes I was alone with the abbot, sometimes all three of us sat together and when the abbot had to rest, it was just Anna and myself. Again, I learned much from the abbot: about life, about love and also about death. But perhaps I enjoyed the talks with Anna even more. She was my age and at first, we talked about our university days, how she felt about studying medicine and how I almost automatically enrolled into physics and then got this once-in-a-lifetime opportunity to work at CERN where I felt we would be changing our understanding of the universe. She set the alarm on her mobile phone in order to remind her to check on the abbot. I would wait until she was finished and we would have tea together or something to eat.

It was not only that being with Anna was such a profound pleasure that I was inclined to avoid the abbot. Not energised by an audience, he kept very much to himself and talked about the way death cannot destroy love and speculated what might happen if he would not make it. I was a bad friend, I simply was not up to this. Then he would fall asleep and I would sneak out and spend more time with Anna. It was like living in two different worlds. Anna cheered me up, she was not afraid that the condition of the abbot might deteriorate. She said she had always been very close to her grandmother who played a large role in her upbringing – as Russian grandmothers often do while the parents are at work. Anna told me the story of her grandmother's illness and how she eventually died when Anna was studying for her Master's. She must have pushed her memories away but in the solitude of the slowly moving railway carriage they all came back. She became quite distraught and wept – 'I don't know why I am telling you all this, I have never talked to anyone about it' – and I followed my instinct, sat next to her and put my arms around her, giving her little kisses on the head. She reacted by drawing closer to me. Then we sat silently until the alarm went off again. She also told me what it was like to be a girl growing up. All of this was new to me; I did not have sisters. At school, she was ever so popular with the boys and had to learn how to handle it. I registered she avoided talking about her husband. I told her about Clara and I noticed I was not so emotional about it any more. When the abbot was up to it, we would discuss my notes of the previous Lessons so I could post them on the web once we had arrived in Khabarovsk. He noticed I did not like to hear his concerns and he just said that all would be well, which frightened me even more. Anna and I grew even closer. For long stretches of time we would sit silently with our arms around each other. It made me immensely happy and she obviously enjoyed it as well. She was curious about my life in the West, so different from what she was used to. Alternating between my two worlds – the one with the abbot and the one with Anna – the trip gave me many new insights. Despite a certain distance it sealed my friendship with the abbot – united as we were in finding new directions in our lives. With Anna I had the feeling that for the first time in my life I had a real girl-friend.

Finally, at 11.00 a.m. two days later, we arrived in Khabarovsk, where the river Amur flows into the river Ussuri, thirty kilometres from the border with China. During the Qing dynasty, the city and the region were part of the Chinese empire. The city is named after Yerofei Khabarov, a Cossack strongman who in 1649 was lured to the Amur area by a shaman's promise of gold, gems and grain. The Cossacks encountered a harsh environment – there were even instances of cannibalism. The Qing Chinese called them 'man-devouring demons'. Khabarov had to retire when the Chinese drove the invaders away. Eventually, the territory was transferred to Russia in 1858 – the year is still inscribed on the city's coat of arms. For a long stretch the river Amur now forms the border with China. Japan is only five hundred kilometres away. Khabarovsk has a beautiful cathedral, built by French Jesuits.

The monastery was located in Obitel – an ancient word for monastery – forty-nine kilometres out of Khabarovsk. When the area became part of Russia the monastery was completely cut off in the long winters. Monks lived in wooden houses, half dugouts underground. In 1917, there were only twenty monks left and the premises were converted into a school and a seminary.

The abbot was very frail and I would have preferred the lecture to be held in Khabarovsk itself. However, he insisted on keeping up with the original plan. So we found ourselves once more driving along deserted, winding roads, until we arrived at Obitel. Despite the remoteness of the village, the seminarians were well prepared for the abbot's visit as they had followed the previous Lessons on the radio and discussed their contents in class. As ever, the reporters were present to cover the Lesson.

One of the seminarians opened the session with a question that immediately drew the attention of all present:
'Yevgeni Nikolayevich, there is no way to express our gratitude for you being here in good health. We followed your Lessons and the medical reports and I cannot help saying we were all very worried. My question is perhaps the most difficult to answer and I can tell you that it has been weighing down like a stone on my heart. At a farm not far from here, in a happy family, one of the children got seriously ill. He was diagnosed with cancer and although he received the best of care, at a certain point it became clear that his illness had reached the terminal stage. He died two weeks ago. During their agony, we stood by the family day and night, in shifts, but now it seems there is nothing we can do anymore. The family is devastated and we don't know how to help them.'

The abbot had observed the young seminarian closely while he spoke and he took his time to formulate his answer, his face turning away from the audience as he did so.

'Losing a child, through illness or accident, is the most devastating experience one can have. It is like losing a vital part of yourself. There is no way to describe the sorrow and agony it invokes. You feel a part of you has been amputated and this feeling will stay with you all your life'.

Taking time to collect his thoughts, he faced the congregation again and said, as if in recollection:

'The unborn child already invokes strong emotions and feelings of bondage and after birth you establish an immediate and deep relationship with your child. As in total love, you are like communicating vessels, there is no clear border between you and the other person, you don't know where you end and where he begins. Underneath the joy is the deadly fear that something might happen to him. The baby is wholly dependent on you and you care for him more than you care for yourself. Undernourished mothers produce healthy and well-fed babies and in case doctors have to choose between the lives of mother or child at birth, our Church prescribes that the life of the child takes priority. When the child grows up, making its way in life and becoming independent of you, this emotion subsides but it is always present in the background.

Life is like climbing a mountain. If your time has come, you topple over the cliff and slide down into a valley where a new climb will start. If someone close to you dies, it feels as if you also fall off an edge but it is not the top of a hill you tumble over but the opening of a cave. You fall into this cave, dark and cold, and you wish it had been you who had gone over the mountain edge and not your loved one. Rationally, you know you should crawl out of your hiding place, if only because you have other loved ones to take care of but emotionally, you don't want to go on, you want to stay there and mourn your child or loved one forever. Gradually, you learn to live with the loss although it will always stay with you – the event will alter your life profoundly. Contrary to what people say, time does not heal all wounds but it does make them manageable.

To answer your question, indeed, there is little you can do. Time has to do its work. It is essential that those who have lost their loved one be given this time and you may help protect them against those who become impatient or who consider it better not to talk about it as talking brings back the terrible feeling of loss. However well meant, this is wrong. They simply have to go through everything again and again until the sharp edges wear off. People who lost a loved one often feel embarrassed to talk about it, as it is such a deep emotion that it is difficult for others to listen or react to. You can help by listening to their story, many times, and by accommodating their feelings. You don't need to react, at least, not always. People will also need to be left alone and you can help by making this possible, they need your understanding and protection'.

An older man got up – I judged him to be in his fifties – and he had an experience to share:

'We lost our son ten years ago and I agree whole-heartedly with what you said. During his illness, we were quite busy taking care of him and every single event, however insignificant, is imprinted in my heart. In hindsight, this phase was relatively pleasurable as we could still communicate and we did so intensely. After he passed away, I kept seeing the sequence of events like a film, it was as if it all happened again: his last week, his illness, his life. Three movies were running in my head, day and night. I had to talk about all this although it did not bring me solace. Gradually, in the daytime, I managed to concentrate on other things while at night, the films kept rolling. It took years before my sleep got back to normal but even now, when I suddenly wake up because of, say, dogs barking in the night, I realise the movies are still running'.

Sin and death

A woman in the audience was visibly shocked hearing all this and she exclaimed:
 'Abbot, if God is almighty and good, how can he let such things happen? It is not fair, or is it a punishment for our sins?'

The abbot replied:
 'In Chita, I explained that the purpose of our life is to enrich the little spark of spiritual energy that we were given at birth and that we return at death. If someone dies prematurely, we have to accept that his task has been accomplished. If he dies in painful circumstances, we have to accept that doing so is part of his task. All this is between the deceased and his maker and we have to stay out of it, passing a judgement would be blasphemous'.

'Still, isn't the premature loss of a loved one a punishment for our own sins?' she was not convinced.

'Many people feel indeed that there is a connection between their loss and the wrongs they may have done in life. Or, to put it more directly: they feel that the death of a loved one is the punishment for their own sins. One of our monks told us that in his childhood his parents had a friend staying with them who suffered from a perforation of the stomach. There was no medication against it in those days, the patient either died or survived the attack. The boy happened to borrow a 'dirty book' just before the guest fell seriously ill, screaming with pain. The boy linked the two events. In the middle of the night, he packed the book and threw it out of the window in an attempt to avert the disaster. The friend passed away and after that terrible night, the boy felt awfully guilty as he thought that, if he had not had the book, the friend would have made it. Let me tell you this is an illusion and it shows, if I may say so, little respect for the deceased. It is *his* life and it has nothing to do with you. So, if ever someone near you dies, don't burden yourself with the thought that you are the cause of the death or accident because, however common this belief, it is utter nonsense'.

Guilt

The seminarian who had spoken first got up again and asked:

'I still have little experience but I have observed that people often feel guilty when someone near them dies. I mean guilty in a different sense – a feeling that they should have done more and if they had done so, it might have postponed or averted the disaster'.

The abbot replied:

'Indeed, those who stay behind often feel guilty although they know that in practical terms this is nonsense: 'What if we had called the doctor earlier?', 'What if we had not permitted him to go to this dangerous place?' All this is in vain, as a young person formulated it: 'Shit happens and the universe doesn't care'. But this is difficult to accept for those who stay behind. Therefore perhaps, there always remains the nagging question: 'Did I do the right thing, could I have prevented this?' And in the case of a child, you feel that you have failed to protect it, that you have neglected your most important duty in life. But it is the wrong feeling, as almost by definition, you could always have done more. And even if you did make mistakes, you still have to accept that it was his process and that your possible failure to do enough was part of it and you have to respect that'.

The seminarian came back:

'I knew a boy who lost his brother. He very much looked up to him and felt he was better in everything. When the brother died, the boy developed a feeling that it was unjust that it was not he but his brother who died, that God made a mistake, that he himself did not have the right to live'.

The answer came immediately:

'This must have been most difficult for you to handle. You can explain that the brother had to go through his own process and that had nothing to do with the younger boy. But a rational argument does not take away the emotion. The feeling should rather be: 'We are so happy you are still with us'. When people die in, say, an accident, we should not only mourn the deceased but also rejoice that the survivors are still alive. Doing so does not desecrate the dead. At funerals, underneath the overwhelming feeling of grief, you can often observe a feeling of gratitude that those who are left behind still have each other. In this way, the chain is restored after a link fell out.'

Resurrection and ascension
Another seminarian got up and asked:
'Some people say they would meet the deceased after death. Is that possible?'

Before the abbot could answer, the man who had lost his child got up and said:
'Perhaps I may relate my experience. After my son died, I felt he was still very much around. I kept talking to him, asking his advice like 'Is this the way you want your funeral?' and he kept answering every time. We had complete conversations and it was often quite as if he was still there. About a year after his death, I went on a pilgrimage to the Spaso-Preobrazhenskiy Monastery in Yeniseysk. Walking to towards it, I felt very tense, tears welling out of my eyes. It was almost a religious experience. The church was swarming with people and I was trying to make my way through the crowd, when suddenly I saw my son, pacing at great speed, a knapsack on a stick over his shoulder, obviously in a hurry, waving good-bye to me, not having time to stop and talk. I was simply paralysed. I could not go after him, which he would not have wanted anyway. Since then, I haven't heard of him anymore.'

The abbot now looked tired, nodded, then remarked:
'You may find comfort in the thought that his death was a process you went through together, as you went through the process of his illness together. Then you feel that his soul has moved to realms unknown to you, where he feels insecure meeting other souls and where he needs your help as much as you need his. If he is still close to the world of the living, you feel his presence, sometimes almost physically. Yes, he loves you and he needs you, he reaches out to you and you should not let your sorrow stand in the way. The stronger the soul, the more powerful its presence after death – that is the meaning of the resurrection of Jesus. Gradually, the deceased becomes more remote, finding his way in the other world. You 'see' him less often until he departs completely like Jesus at the ascension'.

'Indeed, now that you mention it. The gospels say that after his resurrection, Jesus again walked the earth and appeared, even spoke to the Marias and his disciples. After forty days, Jesus ascended to heaven and afterwards he isn't mentioned anymore'.

'I think we have to take this literally. All religions and spiritualists refer to a period between death and ascension and the question is what it looks like. You sit in your dark and cold cave and you project your feelings on to the deceased, thinking the other world is also dark and cold and you pity him. But you only pity yourself. Those who have had near-death experiences report that they were taken up in a strong light, that they felt a harmony they never experienced before and many are downright angry with their doctors for bringing them back to life. Death is like a miniature big bang as spiritual energy is separated from the physical one, the soul – from the body'.

After parting
Another seminarian got up, trying to find his words as he spoke.
'Father, we shall often be in a situation when people have to bid farewell. Can you guide us what to do?'

The abbot also had to find his words as he was speaking:
'If death comes suddenly, as in an accident, there is no opportunity to bid farewell. But if there is an opportunity to say goodbye it will be a profound experience for all concerned. Dying is not difficult, parting from loved ones is. For those who stay behind, what is said will be irrevocable, they will remember it throughout the rest of their lives: his last words, the last words of the others to him. If the dying person is capable to hear it, the people around him should thank him for what he has given to them, however difficult this may be. Commemorate the good things and forgive the bad ones and hope he would do likewise. All conflicts should be resolved in love, allowing the dying person to fly away on wings of love and make a strong entry into the other world. Those who stay behind should feel that all that needed to be said, has been said, and in the best possible way. As a guardian, you may prepare them for this. You cannot afford to make errors, there will be no chance to correct them'.

'What if the dying person is old and ready to go, perhaps even eager to do so?'

'Sometimes family members or friends have already distanced themselves from the loved one, for instance from parents in old age who have been ill for a longer period. They feel that death will be a relief. In merciful countries it is allowed to help people to end their life if it is their utmost wish and if death is unavoidable. Thus, the terminally ill person can finish what he has to finish and die in dignity'.

'What happens to those who are left behind?' asked the same monk.

'Losing parents, even when they are old, still comes as a shock although one understands the natural progression, one knows it is to be expected. The death of a parent when you are young, when you are emotionally still dependent on that parent, cripples you forever, it opens a wound in the inner cylinder. Children who lose their father or mother at a young age will look for a substitute their entire life. Even if they find it, the wound will never heal.

When you lose a partner, husband or wife, part of yourself is amputated. You miss the closeness, the familiarity, the way of doing things together, the way you tell him what happened during the day, the sweet nothings you exchange daily, and most of all you miss the love, the care, given and received, the togetherness. You stand with one foot in the other world and it takes time before you wish to come back to life. When you do, the sorrow ebbs and flows – you have good days and bad days. And even when you find a new partner, the sorrow will always hang around you.

The death of a loved one sets off a period of a standstill and you should grant yourself the time to think things over, eventually plan a life for yourself after this death. Pain that we suppress grows within us and one day we shall have to pay the price. People may make tactless remarks – *are you getting over it already?* – but do not blame them because they mean well and they simply lack the words to help you accommodate your feelings. The death of a loved one is often a turning point, not in the way of the crises between the stages of life, more the emergence of new talents to be developed. Watch out for the signs'.

The abbot now looked exhausted and I shifted in my seat. The rector of the seminary took the hint and closed the meeting. Anna gave the abbot a medical check-up and said there was no reason for extra concern. Then the abbot went to his cell. In the evening I was asked by the radio reporters about his position in the Church. 'With all respect, he is so much out of line with the doctrine that even we can see that. Does the Patriarch tolerate this? No doubt he listens to the broadcasts'. Here I had to be careful. On the one hand, it wouldn't be possible to ignore the problem, as the deviations from the official teachings were significant and obvious. On the other hand, the position of the abbot in the Church should not draw more media attention than the contents of the Lessons. So I answered that the abbot had always been a renewer of the faith and that I expected that his views would be debated, perhaps even in a Church Council. 'Do you really believe that?' they came back. I said I could not say but I certainly hoped so. They left, not convinced.

As it was still early, I had time to think. To me it was clear that the abbot would be leaving the Church. His Lessons had also been lessons to himself, a quest for his own self, leading to the – in hindsight – inevitable conclusion that he had outgrown the Church. Then I thought how much I had changed myself. I had acquired great interest in 'the human condition' and although I would never be a wise man like the abbot, I wondered whether I would still find satisfaction in theoretical physics. It suddenly felt all very cold and rational. I wished I could stay with the abbot and the issues he addressed but of course I could not spend my life as a secretary; what was good for a journey would not be enough for a lifetime. I sighed and decided to take this conclusion about physics seriously and look out for signals – as the abbot was teaching.

Anna was packing her bags and preparing to leave. She would not come with us to Vladivostok and had to make the long journey back all by herself. I went to her cell and pressed her against me. We started kissing. I pulled her jumper up – 'I want to feel your skin' – and gently stroked her back. I felt we were approaching a point of no return. Then Anna loosened the grip and stood back a little. She put her hand on my heart: 'Let us never forget this trip, Steve. It has changed a lot for me. You are a good man, a very good man. There is much love in you, you just have to discover it'. Then, taking her hand away: 'Now you must apply all your energy to your abbot. He needs you and he needs your love to make a full recovery'. We walked to the car that would bring her to the railway station. 'Let us mail', was the only thing I could bring out as the car pulled away.

I was alone again. The abbot had already retired for the night. I felt immensely sad and tried to control my tears. I worked till deep into the night on the texts of the Lessons – during the trip I had neglected this task and was lagging behind. I decided to upload the latest Lessons on the Internet without the formal consent of the abbot as I considered their timely publication more important than the need of his formal approval. After all, he had not changed much in my previous renditions.

In the morning, after Terce, we boarded the motorcade that brought us to the Khabarovsk railway station where we left at 11.30 a.m. on the last leg of our trip. We were off to Vladivostok – the end of the Trans Siberia Express though by no means the end of Russia. As it would turn out, it would not be the end of our adventure, either.

21. Vladivostok – Your own death and the balance of life

It was close to midnight when we at last arrived in Vladivostok, at the beautiful white nineteenth century railway station with its towers and black roofs. Although the journey had been long – eight hundred and twenty kilometres – it was short in comparison with the previous three trips. As we travelled mainly South from Khabarovsk, the time zone was still seven hours ahead of Moscow. Altogether, we had covered 9 259 kilometres, not counting the detours to Verkhoturye and Yeniseysk. Still, the eight and a half hour journey had a bad effect on the abbot. Little did I know that this last stop – meant to be short as we were to fly back to Moscow after the session in the evening – would become a long one.

We were met by the cheerful abbot of the Svyato-Troytzkiy Nikolaevskiy Monastery (Holy Trinity Monastery of St Nicholas). He was in the prime of his life, heading a community of twenty monks. It was an appropriate name for a monastery in such an important port – St Nicholas being the patron saint and protector of sailors. While we drove down Partizanski Prospekt, then into the hills where the monastery was located, our host told us about the recent visit of the Patriarch to celebrate the hundredth anniversary of the monastery. So we came within an ace of meeting him. Vladivostok reminded me of Istanbul – the bay is also called the Golden Horn – with its low hills and omnipresent views of the Bay. The Muravyov-Amursky Peninsula, on which Vladivostok is built, is only thirty kilometres long and twelve kilometres wide. The Bay offers ideal protection for ships – no wonder it was chosen to be the port of the Russian Pacific Fleet. In addition, there are many piers for fishing and pleasure boats. Although the city's name is often associated with the end of the world, it is quite nice with its winding, tree-lined streets and its attractive boulevard on the western side of the bay. The city is truly cosmopolitan – it is close to China and Korea and not far from Japan. I was not aware that Vladivostok was at the same latitude as Florence and Toronto and was surprised by its mild climate.

After another medical check-up – our host had taken care of everything and had brought his own doctor – we went to sleep. When I was getting dressed the next morning, our host knocked on my door. His cheerfulness had disappeared and he now looked extremely worried.

'You better come with me at once', he said. 'There is something badly wrong with your abbot'.

We rushed to the abbot's cell where the doctors were already doing tests.

'The abbot fainted when he tried to get up', one of them said. 'Fortunately, a brother was with him and he raised the alarm immediately. Now we are trying to see what needs to be done'.

I watched the abbot, who had become so dear to me. He slowly regained consciousness, then looked at me. He was crying and said *Nostre vite gaudia abstulisti omnia* – All my joyful life has been taken away. 'No!' I shouted at the top of my voice. 'Remember your own Lessons. You just have to change course as you teach yourself'. He fell back into sleep and woke up several hours later. He looked rested and tried a joke: 'You look so worried, what happened to you?' and we told him about his condition. 'Oh, come on', he said, trying but failing to look his old cheerful self. 'I must have dozed off, what do you expect from an old man after riding an antique train for nine thousand kilometres?'

He managed a late breakfast and that gave him some energy. He could not get up however, and we had to sit him up in a wheelchair, draping his habit loosely around him. It was a bit of a masquerade and he enjoyed it tremendously. We would say things like 'when you don't need it anymore, this wheelchair will go straight into the monastery museum', and 'you will be the first prophet to lecture from a wheelchair', upon which he said 'well, Jesus did not make it to my age therefore he never needed one'. Finally, he was strong enough to be rolled into the small hall which was packed with people. They had been waiting for four hours, all in dead silence. In this sombre atmosphere, one of the older monks made the opening:

'Yevgeni Nikolayevich, in your lectures up to now, you have frequently referred to death. First in Perm, where you called death the last crisis of transition, with severe threats and unseen opportunities. You then promised to come back to this crisis. I wonder whether the moment is opportune for you to teach us how we should prepare for death'.

Again I noticed how many people had listened to the radio broadcasts.

The abbot had been nodding while the monk spoke.

'You quoted me correctly and I must admit I have postponed the subject subconsciously as it is not a pleasant one. I live my life intensely, with joy and pain, and although I love life more than anything, I have always been aware of the transiency of life and the need to be prepared for the moment I will be called. With the ups and downs of my health this last month, I had reason and opportunity to give it extra attention. Death itself is not a big deal, you might say that everybody does it. In fact, it is easier than the other transitions in our life. Parting from your loved ones, some of whom may still be in your care, is what makes it so difficult. But let me start from the beginning'.

The nature of death
He settled down in a more comfortable position, took his time to drink some water – and perhaps prepare his answer – and when he was ready, he spoke in a low voice.

'Death is frightening. One does not know what to expect. There are many scary stories about the events after death, like the Last Judgment, so frighteningly depicted by Michelangelo in the Sistine Chapel.

Death, however, is nothing but the last crisis in our life, the last passage from one stage to the next. Like the other crises, it poses threats and offers opportunities. When you die, you will lose something – the older you are the less you lose – but it is important to know that you will also gain something. What you gain however is unknown until you get there. Unlike the other crises, you cannot observe how other people handle it, you have no role models. It will be like setting off on a journey. You pack your bags, say good-bye to those you leave behind and prepare for what is coming. You have to trust that, as all forms of energy, your soul will not be destroyed although you cannot be sure in which form it will re-emerge. You know that death is the source of life. Nevertheless, people have all kinds of fantasies about immortality. If you are tempted to think this way, read De Beauvoir's *Tous les hommes sont mortels* – All Men are Mortal, and discover how boring immortality would be'.

There was some commotion in the hall as people in the back seats moved forward to hear the abbot better. For some reason, people always fill up the back seats first, out of shyness I suppose. When the room was quiet again, you could hear a pin drop.

'Many think that after death, sooner or later, you will come back to this world as an older soul. Young souls can be identified by their ego and energy, older souls feel uncertain and very old souls have this indefinable modesty and wisdom, an insight that does not come from education and experience but right from their inner circle. You, too, will move along this axis'.

How to prepare your legacy
Here the abbot paused but nobody wanted to intervene. So he continued:

'Let us move to some practical things. Death falls heavy on those you leave behind, whether they love you, hate you or are indifferent. You can make it easier for them by leaving clear instructions about your funeral and estate. All your life you should have a well-registered will, changing it whenever the circumstances or your intentions change. In addition, leave a clear description of your possessions. Many children have no idea of their parents' possessions and much may get lost if they are not properly registered. Love your children equally – make sure what you own is fairly distributed among them. I have seen families where brothers do not talk to each other because each feels the other has been favoured. Let them value your possessions and divide them among them, offsetting the balance in money. If you have a large estate, consider giving a good part of it to charity. Leaving your children with fortunes is not good for them or their children, as each human being has to find his own way in life.

More importantly, do not leave open-ended relationships when you die. Try to solve problems as well as vagueness in relationships where the purpose or status of that relationship is not clear. As your moment may come anytime, you should avoid open-ended relationships every day of your life. Naturally, this does not depend on you only but you should do your best.

Don't think: 'All of this, I can do later'. Most people die at a moment when they least expect it, at a place they do not choose'.

The moment of your own death
At this point, a very old woman stumbled up, leaning on a stick. She could not stand up straight anymore and had difficulty speaking:

'Father, I am old, as you can see. I know many will regard this a blasphemy but I wish I could leave this world right now. Why are we not allowed to choose the moment of our death ourselves?'

The abbot had to think about this.

'If your death comes suddenly, as in an accident, there is no way to prepare yourself or your loved ones. You simply have to be prepared in general. If, however, you suffer from an incurable and unbearable illness, or if you have grown old and life offers no further prospects, you may choose to end your life yourself. You may and must take the responsibility for ending your own life if you foresee unbearable pain or indignity as you approach your end, or if, at an advanced age, you feel you have outlived your usefulness, that life has nothing more to offer. With birth control, we take responsibility for new life. Likewise, we should practice death control and bear the responsibility for our end. I realise this takes incredible courage and energy but remember: *it is you who it comes down to*. It is only human to choose yourself the moment you die. This is difficult because you are afraid, you may still nourish hope, you don't want to say farewell to your loved ones. Here the will should override the emotion and you should choose the moment ruthlessly: Tuesday two o'clock. In many countries euthanasia, painless assisted self-chosen death, is forbidden or very difficult. In those cases, you have to do it yourself by taking a certain poison or simply stop eating and drinking. Either way, death can be gentle. In civilised countries, you may be assisted by others. Helping those who wish to end their life is an act of mercy, provided strict conditions are met: the person who wishes to die should have stated this explicitly and repeatedly. It should not be an act of impulse. It should be clear beyond doubt that life has no value anymore for the person who wants to step out. Those who help should not in any way benefit from the death and help should be provided by professionals only. Though deeply human, euthanasia is still forbidden in most countries. It is also a matter of culture. In the Indian tribes of North America, old people would simply be left behind, to be eaten by jackals. Imamura's moving *The ballad of Narayama* recounts how old people in a poor part of Japan, when the food is insufficient to support new family members, are carried up the mountain to die there. In Kim Ki-duk's *Spring, summer, autumn, winter... and spring*, the Korean Buddhist monk ends his life when he thinks the time is ripe for his apprentice to take over his duties'.

The old lady came back, she was not as certain as she looked at the beginning.
  'How can we be sure that we really want to end it. It is such a difficult decision'.

'Sometimes people reach a point in life when they have no desire to live anymore while there is also no immediate need to end it. They feel satiated with life. If this is the case, you enter a grey phase of uncertainty and indecisiveness, you linger at the gate. Wait in these cases, don't take your life too soon, you never know to what challenges you may still be called'.

The abbot was now exhausted and for the first time he asked for a break in order to get some rest. I communicated this to our host and he announced it to the audience. Some people stayed in the auditorium, others took a stroll. Some discussed what the abbot had said. Others just remained silent, getting to grips with what they heard.

Three hours later, the abbot felt strong enough to resume. The audience was quietly waiting for him and he continued with what he wanted to say.

How to prepare yourself – the balance of life

'When preparing for death, consciously or subconsciously, you will make up the balance of your life. The unknown moment of death, the separation from your loved ones and the prospect of the unknown is what makes death deeply emotional and frightening, different from the other crises. You may fear the judgment. But it will not be God or another heavenly creature that will judge you. It will be *you* who will pass the judgment. It is *you* who will come to assess your life: what you did right, what you did wrong. What did you do with your life, with the talents that were entrusted to you, the neighbours that you were allowed to interact with? Specifically, what did you do with the talent to love and to be loved? If you were allowed to gain fortunes, did you use them to boost your own ego or did you use them to give opportunities to others? The rules of the judgement are simple – you know them deep down. Even if you had good intentions, you did evil to others. We all cause suffering, perhaps indirectly, by not loving enough, not considering the other's perspective. In this way, we are all sinners and death is the ultimate moment when we have to come to grips with our shortcomings.

The balance of life is not like the company accounts, where the assets balance the liabilities. In life, good does not compensate evil, the constructive – the destructive. However big your virtues, your sins remain and keep nagging at you. When making up the balance of your life, you have to forgive yourself, and doing so in integrity is the hardest part of your last undertakings. It is too easy to think that Jesus has sacrificed himself to redeem your sins or that, in Schiller's words: *Überm Sternenzelt, muß ein lieber Vater wohnen* – high above the starry sky, there is a loving Father, dwelling. More than ever, *it is you who it comes down to*; it is *you* who has to come to a conclusion about yourself. You have to solve the puzzle of your life and the better you do it, with the more energy you will depart and the stronger you will make your entry in the other world. The puzzle is this: your sins are caused by your shortcomings. If you have lived consciously, you have analysed the origins of your shortfalls by contemplating your nature and the way you were brought up, the role of formative people and experiences, and what you did with these influences. Some influential people were given to you – like your parents – others were chosen by you. You were put in certain physical situations, by birth, by events later in your life. All these people and events offered you opportunities but also constraints, and thinking about them can help you find explanations why you lived your life the way you did. If you make up the balance of your life every evening, or at least at certain moments, the assessment at the end will be easier, your judgment milder and in your last hours you can concentrate on your loved ones. It is good for them as well as for you. If you leave on waves of love, your entry into the other world will be more powerful, you will take off like a missile.'

Bidding farewell

There was an elderly priest in the audience. From his wrinkled face you could see that he had been through much, as a pastor I guessed, and perhaps in his own personal life. He took his time to get up, stroking his beard. He was not a man of many words:

'Father, I have a simple question. If we know our time has come, how should we depart?'

'When the moment to bid farewell is there, it furthers if you leave from a surrounding of love like a butterfly leaves a bed of flowers. Be careful who you choose to be with you. It is important to you and it will be of great importance to them for the rest of their lives. Make yourself comfortable – if you have it, take your time. Be careful how you bid your farewells – your last words will be remembered by everyone present. Then, say no more, just meet your fulfilment:

> *When it is my time to go*
> *Come ye all and sit around me.*
> *Make some coffee, get some cake.*
> *Be together one more time,*
> *Stay with me till I have gone.*
> *Sitting on my Father's lap,*
> *I will read the solemn book*
> *That tells it all.*

When my moment is there, I will want the love of my life to be with me. She will be sad but we shall not be separated for long. I will give my children a special kiss, a kiss on their foreheads. They will giggle. I have not kissed them since they were small – hugged, yes, kissed, no. I will ask them:

'Do you know what this means?'
They will say 'No'.
I will say 'It means, I bless you'.
They will look puzzled.

I will say 'It means you are good the way you are'.
They will smile and it will be good this way. Do ye likewise'.

The abbot had finished his Lessons. He got up and walked outside, kissing all who left on their forehead. I wanted to shout: 'Don't do that, you are not dying yet', but I held my tongue. Then the abbot fell on the floor, unconscious. It was a dramatic sight and a deadly fear clawed at my heart, I could hardly breathe, I felt every nerve and organ in my body, I moved into another stage of consciousness, everything inside me was at top alert. There was a murmur in the crowd as the doctors examined him and ordered him to hospital immediately. The cars that were waiting to take us to the airport brought us to the Vladivostok State Medical University instead. He went into surgery at once and we waited outside, in the corridor: our host, nothing like his cheerful self, some brothers and me. After eight long hours – it was already deep into the night and the doctors had worked in shifts – they rolled him into intensive care. When he was properly settled only one person was to be allowed in. Everybody looked at me, so I went inside. There he was, still unconscious, countless tubes and wires going into and out of his body, hooked to an impressive battery of electronics. I sat there all night – they brought me chocolate and coke. I watched his breath. After he exhaled, there was a long interval and each time I thought 'Will he breathe in again? Will he live?'

Epilogue and the School of Love

The morning after the operation, the abbot regained consciousness. I had kept vigil over him all night and although I dozed off now and then, I was exhausted and the doctor convinced me to take a rest. In the late afternoon, I woke up and called our host, who, together with the others, had been dismissed after the abbot had been moved to intensive care, as there was nothing they could do. When the night nurse came at 11 p.m., she greeted the abbot saying, in her straightforward way:

'Thank heavens you are still here. I didn't think I would see you again. Now the doctor is on his way'.

It turned out to be the medical director of the hospital who greeted the abbot cheerfully:

'How are you doing, father? You know we had to do a lot of work on you'.

He told us that at first two surgeons had operated the abbot but they had not managed to remove a particularly difficult clot of blood.

'I then decided to do it myself', he said. 'And I cannot tell you how happy I am I brought you back to life'.

The abbot muttered something inaudible.

'Sorry, what did you say?' asked the doctor.

'I said: perhaps a new life', whispered the abbot.

'Well, yes, perhaps', the surgeon did not know what to say. 'Actually, here is someone who would like to see you'.

He opened the door and a woman walked in. She must have been the same age as the abbot, blond, with an erect, powerful posture.

'Hello Yevgeni', she smiled. 'Bit sick are we?'

The abbot's eyes were suddenly wide open, he must have recognised her voice.

'It has been a long time', he uttered. 'How did you get here?'

'I can ask you the same question', she replied. 'It is a long way from St Petersburg. After graduation – remember I read economics – I moved to Vladivostok to take care of my mother and now I am head of the administration of the hospital. Actually, you don't have to tell me how you got here,

I heard it all on the radio. I planned to see you but I had no idea you would come to me'.

Before I could start wondering whether she was 'the girl I liked very much', he had talked about, the abbot gestured to me. 'Yevgeniya, meet Stephen, my young and trusted friend. Steve, meet Yevgeniya Vladimirovna, an old and very dear friend of mine. At university, they always made jokes about our names'.

'Please, do not talk anymore', the doctor intervened. 'Let the abbot have some rest'.

She sat on the bed, leaning against him and started stroking his head. Then her composure broke and she started crying:

'Sorry Yevgeni, I was so worried about you'.

The doctor and I looked each other in the eye, he with a matter-of-fact kind of face, me – relieved. We both felt the room had suddenly become too crowded and left.

While the abbot was in intensive care, we developed a schedule. I watched over him during the night, subsisting on chocolate and coke. Yevgeniya would replace me in the morning. After a week, he could be moved to a regular hospital room and although the tubes and wires were fewer, the equipment was still impressive. I was told there was no point in staying with him during the night anymore. Yevgeniya and I kept him company in alternating shifts during the day. After all, she had work to do and I had to write out the Lessons.

One day she told me there was a group of reporters at the door – radio, newspaper and television. The abbot's illness had caused quite a stir. Indeed, I had noticed the vans with satellite dishes outside.

'I think Yevgeni has to make a statement', she said.

'That is out of the question', I felt strongly protective. 'Let us ask him'.

He took it rather casually.

'First I have to resign, then I think Steve should give a press conference', he decided with a glimpse of his old self. 'I don't think I am up to it'.

'Let me help you', she said, and together they wrote a short letter of resignation.

'One of my people will bring it to Moscow on the evening flight', she concluded. 'It will arrive around midnight local time and the Patriarch will have it first thing in the morning'.

In order to give the Patriarch time to digest the resignation, the abbot decided the press conference was to be held in the evening, at noon Moscow time. On the news, I had often seen such events with lots of cameras and microphones and I felt too small to be at the centre of such a gathering. I made a sober statement, saying the abbot put conscience above doctrine, as he had taught his followers. To my surprise there were more questions about the abbot's health than about his actual leaving the Church. When it was over, I overheard a monk from the abbot's monastery whispering: 'Let us hope the next one will be less demanding'. *Sic transit gloria mundi*, I thought. The abbot had hardly left the monastery and the rot had already set in.

When I stayed at his bedside, the abbot corrected my notes where necessary. From his room there was a beautiful view over the Golden Horn. One day, he said:

'Let me show you Time'.

I nodded affirmatively, not understanding what he meant. The bright summer afternoon was coming to its end and the sun was setting behind the hills on the other side of the bay, decisively, unstoppably. Nothing can defy the laws of nature.

'Now look at the sun', he said, 'and see how it sets behind the hills. When the sun moves in the sky during the day, we hardly notice its movement but when you watch it going down, it is a mystery, it brings you at one with the universe. It is always remarkable how fast it sets, how quickly time passes, how well we should use it'.

After a pause he whispered:

'Now you can catch a glimpse of how God made the universe'.

And there we were, silent, in amazement watching the sun touch the horizon, then sink behind it, you could almost see it move. When more than half of the sun had disappeared, it seemed to go down even faster, the remaining part diminishing rapidly. After it had disappeared he sighed.

'Now you feel sad. You mourn that a glorious day has come to an end but you are not yet ready for the night'. I nodded and he continued:

'You shouldn't be sad though. We know that the sun will come back tomorrow. Its absence is only temporary, its movement cannot be stopped'.

I understood the meaning but did not know what to say. It sounded so alarming, as if he wanted to comfort me in advance. He shifted his pillows and switched to quite another subject, asking:

'Steve, why don't you read out to me the whole text as it is in your notebook, so I can see whether it still needs corrections or additions.'

And so I did. We spent the following weeks writing, reading and correcting. He often returned to his idea of a School of Love, a theme that was apparently on his mind all the time. He thought it would help combating what he had called *the central human deficit*, that is man's inability to step into the other person's shoes, see things through his eyes. To him this was the source of much of the evil in the world. He had mentioned it for the first time in Omsk, when he was talking about family life and how family and friends are good training grounds for learning to *love inside-out* – perceiving the desires of the other and acting accordingly – rather than *loving outside-in* – acting according to the wishes of the other as you see them. In the night train to Novosibirsk we had not had an opportunity to work it out, but now he came back to the subject:

'The more I think about it, the more I see we are losing a culture in which we develop the talent to love and to be loved. In what used to be known as the developing world, people are busy building up their economies and the focus is very much on material things. In the former developed world, ever larger numbers of people are becoming increasingly individualistic and this leads to an atomised society. The Arab world is now also in turmoil and you wonder what will happen to, for instance, the famed Arab hospitality'.

I asked him about his ideas of the School of Love.

'It would be a school in which adult people would stay say three months. The school would not have a religious or ideological basis and its purpose would be to equip its participants to have a more fulfilling personal and professional life through stimulation of the talent to love and to be loved. The motivation of potential trainees would have to be assessed beforehand as there is no learning without motivation. Ah, can you rearrange the pillows please, I wish I was out of here'. I did and I felt pity that he had to suffer so much.

'How would you go about it', I asked. 'Listening to lectures about love would be pretty boring after a few days'.

'You scientists always think in terms of lecturing. As love is the child of trust and respect, these would be topics participants would have to learn first. You learn by reading, hearing, seeing, saying, doing and reflecting. If you stagger the entry dates, students who have already been there for a while would instruct the newcomers and show them around, they would thus simultaneously internalise their experience themselves'.

'You mean, like a kind of Montessori system?', I asked, 'older students instructing younger ones and the teachers monitoring progress and filling the gaps?'

'Something like that', he answered, 'but I see a larger role for the trainers as they should help participants become aware of their shortcomings. Becoming aware of shortcomings that one was previously not concious of, is the first step in learning. When one understands his weaknesses, he or she can work on converting them into advantages. At first, these will be concious efforts, but when routine sets in, they become a habit, like when you drive a car, you don't concentrate on what you do, it goes all by itself and you don't think about it'.

'But sitting in groups to discuss one's shortcomings seems just as boring as listening to lectures', I ventured.

'Only learning that is based on experience is effective', the abbot went on. 'Participants should, for instance, first learn to grow flowers and fruit trees in, let us say, a municipal garden. You can only do that well if you love what you take care of. After that they could work in a shelter for pets, taking care of abandoned and mistreated dogs and cats. They could then help in a kindergarten and serve in a hospital or an orphanage. Eventually, they could spend time in a rescue center for disadvantaged or mistreated children. At last they could nurse terminally ill patients. In all activities, they would have to learn to gain trust and show respect, while trying to understand the needs of those in their care. If this practical work is well-instructed and accompanied by good coaching, reflection sessions, obligatory reading, playing music, dancing and seeing art and movies, it would be a powerful way to learn how to love and be loved. It would change them for life and make them more effective in everything they do.'

'All you need is a good environment, with trust and respect, without making it sentimental', I suggested.

'You also need a better name. If you call it *School of Love*, people will think it is a type of Kama Sutra course and that is not what I mean'.

At that point the physiotherapist entered the room. She was a short, proud lady with curly black hair, in her early twenties, always full of energy, dedication and humour and I had increasingly taken pleasure in helping her out.

'Ah, Steve, here we have your friend', the abbot joked.

I felt embarrassed, blushing all over. She took it graciously and I helped her put the abbot in the right position. Then she said cheerfully:

'Now you must leave the room'.

She must have felt my reluctance and said, just as I was closing the door:

'But you may come back in a few minutes'.

Our eyes met and it felt like a bolt of lightning. For a moment we both stood paralysed.

'Hey Maria Igorovna, what about my massage', the abbot joked.

After she had completed her work and left, the abbot finished reviewing the text. Then he said:

'Steve, I want you to go now and bring the Lessons to our monastery so they can get uploaded. They should also be published as a book in order to reach a wider audience. The sooner you do this, the better, as I don't want discussions on the unedited version'.

I strongly objected – I wanted to stay with him. But, as he had regained his usual posture, he kept insisting and in the end, I gave in.

It was a difficult farewell but fortunately he did not kiss me on the forehead – perhaps I had become superstitious. I packed my bags and booked the flight to Moscow and then back to Novosibirsk, as there is no direct flight from Vladivostok to this city.

Upon leaving I paid a last visit to the medical director.

'I can confirm there is no reason for you to stay here', he said, 'but don't take this as a reassurance that your abbot will be all right. He has a strong heart, people with a weaker heart would not have made it. But he is still in grave danger. If he gets another heart attack, well, the third one is almost always fatal. You should be prepared to receive a call from us at any time'.

The feeling of extreme anxiety that gripped me when the abbot collapsed and which had gradually subsided, overtook me again. I am still trembling as I am typing this, waiting at the gate.

I must finish now, they are calling us to board. I close my notebook and I am off.

Itinerary and prayers

Trans Siberia Express

This is a network of railways connecting Moscow and other West-European locations with cities in the Asian part of the Russian Federation, as well as Mongolia and China. The main line, the Trans-Siberian Line, extends from Moscow to Vladivostok. Its length of 9 259 kilometres makes it the longest railroad on earth.

Itinerary

Below is the timetable of the trains of the Trans Siberian Express the abbot took.

Chap	Stations	km trip	km total	arr.	dep.	travel time hours	time-zone	detour
1	Moskou		0		9.25 p.m.	0	0	
2	Vladimir	210	210	0.18 a.m.	0.36 p.m.	2.53	0	
3	NN	251	461	3.27 a.m.	3.39 p.m.	2.51	0	
6	Kirov	456	917	9.43 a.m.	9.58 p.m.	6.04	0	
7	Perm	480	1397	17.22 a.m.	17.42 p.m.	5.24	2	
9	Jekaterinenb	381	1778	23.20 a.m.	23.43 p.m.	5.38	2	Verkhoturye
13	Tjoemen	326	2104	3.58 a.m.	4.18 p.m.	3.15	2	
14	Omsk	572	2676	11.17 a.m.	11.32 p.m.	5.59	3	
15	Novosibirsk	627	3303	19.04 a.m.	19.33 p.m.	7.32	3	
16	Krasnojarsk	762	4065	7.25 a.m.	7.45 p.m.	10.52	4	Yeniseysk
18	Irkoetsk	1088	5153	1.03 a.m.	1.33 p.m.	16.18	5	
19	Chita	1013	6166	18.14 a.m.	18.39 p.m.	15.41	6	
20	Chabarovsk	2327	8493	11.00 a.m.	11.30 p.m.	39.21	7	
21	Vladivostok	766	9259	23.48 a.m.		12.18	7	

Timing of the prayers

In this account, the Latin names of the prayers are used; the prayer schedule of the Orthodox Church is very similar. Basically, there are prayers every three hours. In practice, not all prayers are held and a monastery may deviate from the standard schedule.

Latin name	Time	Russian name	Translation	Time
Matins	at night	Polunoshtnitsa	Midnight Prayer	midnight
Laude	03 a.m.	Utrenya	Morning Prayer	at 03 or 04 a.m.
Prime	06 a.m.	Pervij Chas	1ste hour	06 or 07 a.m.
Terce	09 a.m.	Tretij Chas	3rd hour	09 a.m.
Sext	12 a.m.	Shestoj Chas	6th hour	12 a.m.
None	03 p.m.	Devyatij Chas	9th hour	3 p.m.
Vespers	at dark	Vechernya	Evening Prayer	around 6 p.m.
Compline	before retiring	Povechere	Bedtime Prayer	around 9 p.m.

Notes

Introduction

CERN: The European Organisation for Nuclear Research (French: *Organisation Européenne pour la Recherche Nucléaire*), with 2 600 employees and 8 000 scientists and engineers, the world's largest particle physics laboratory, situated near Geneva. Today's Mecca of physics.

Dr Zhivago: Novel by Boris Pasternak, published in 1957. It tells the story of Yuri Zhivago, a physician and poet, and the impact of the Russian Revolution of 1917 and the subsequent Russian Civil War. Boris Leonidovich Pasternak (1890-1960) was a Russian poet, novelist, and literary translator. The book was made into a film by David Lean in 1965.

Darkness cannot extinguish it: John 1:5. There are two different translations of this text. The King James translation of 1611 says: 'And the light shineth in darkness; and the darkness comprehended it not'. Similarly, the New International Version of 1984 gives: 'The light shines in the darkness, but the darkness has not understood it' and the New American Standard Version of 2001: 'The Light shines in the darkness, and the darkness did not comprehend it'. In short: the Darkness does not understand the Light.

On the other hand, we have: 'The light shines in the dark, and the dark has never extinguished it' (God's Word Translation, 1995), 'The light shines in the darkness, and the darkness has not overcome it' (English Standard Translation, 2001), 'The light shines in the darkness, and the darkness can never extinguish it.' (New Living Translation, 2007) and 'And the light shines on in the darkness, and the darkness has never put it out.' (International Standard Version, 2007). Summarised: the Darkness has not extinguished the Light.

The abbot apparently chose the latter translation.

Chapter 1

Iljitsa Square: Named after Lenin's father.

Andrei Rublev (1360s-1427 or 1430): considered to be the greatest medieval Russian painter of Orthodox icons and frescoes.

Yaroslavska Railway Station: Starting point of the Trans Siberia Express.

Komsomol Square: named after the Communists' youth organisation. There are three railway stations at this square, including Yaroslavska.

Father: normal term to address a priest.

Good fruits: Matthew 7:17.
Know yourself: Inscription in the ancient Greek temple of Apollo at Delphi.
Provodnitsa: Lady guard, who also provides drinks and snacks on the train.
Samovar ('self-boiler'): metal pot with oil heater to prepare tea.
Whoever is without sins, casts the first stone: John 8:7.
Gnostics: see Chapter 17.
Cathari: a Christian religious sect with dualistic and gnostic elements that appeared in the Languedoc region of France and other parts of Europe in the 11th century and flourished in the 12th and 13th centuries. See Chapter 17.
Bogomils: a Gnostic religiopolitical sect founded in the First Bulgarian Empire by the priest Bogomil during the reign of Tsar Petar I in the 10th century.
Mennonites: followers of Menno Simonsz, see Chapter 17. *Lutherans, Calvinists*: followers of these reformers.

Chapter 2

Knyaz (Count) Vladimir: Vladimir I of Kiev or Saint Vladimir of Kiev, also named Vladimir Svyatoslavich the Great (958-1015): the grand prince of Kiev who converted to Christianity in 988 and christened large parts of the Russian population.
Alexander Nevski ('Alexander of the Neva'; the Neva is the river around which St Petersburg is built): Saint Alexander Nevsky (1220-1263), Grand Prince of Novgorod and Vladimir who rose to legendary status on account of his military victories over German and Swedish invaders.
Maslow's theory of the hierarchy of needs: In 1943 Abraham Maslow proposed a hierarchy of human needs, basic needs such as food, water and sleep at the bottom level and self-fulfilment at the top. According to this theory, a person will only work on the higher levels after the lower ones have been satisfied.

Chapter 3

The other world: The abbot refers to the world that houses our souls after death.
As a good man of the Church, I always stay close to Jesus: Matthew 25: 14-30.

Chapter 4

Look at the birds: Matthew 6:26.
The curse will pass on to future generations: Exodus 20:5 and 34:7.
The touchstone is action: Matthew 7:16-20.
John Chrysostom (347–407): Archbishop of Constantinople and important Early Church Father. Chrysostom comes from the Greek *chrysostomos*, meaning 'golden-mouthed', as he was known to be an eloquent speaker.

Chapter 5

Gorki-Mosk Vokzal: Gorki Railway Station.

Gorki: the communists renamed Nizhny Novgorod Gorky after Maxim Gorky (1868-1936), a Russian-Soviet author. It was renamed Nizhny Novgorod in 1992.

Kremlin: castle. In most cities, as in Moscow, it is a walled citadel.

Pechersky Ascension Monastery: The monastery was founded in 1328 by the *Kievo-Pecherskaya Lavra Monastery*, an old and important monastery in *Kiev (see note in Chapter 16). Pechery* means caves. Although there are no caves in Nizhny Novgorod, the name Pechery has been preserved as a link to the old Kiev Monastery.

Orthodoxy: Orthodox literally *'having the right opinion'*, adhering to the accepted or traditional and established faith. The opposite is heterodoxy, *'other teaching'*. The word orthodox can also mean fundamentalist or conservative. The Orthodox Church claims to be the original Christian Church, which became the second in size after the East-West schism in 1054 when what is now the Roman Catholic Church split off.

Shishkin, Repin and Lewitan: 19th century romantic Russian painters.

Ayvazovski: Ivan Konstantinovich Aivazovsky (1817-1900), a Ukrainian painter of Armenian descent, most famous for his seascapes, which constitute more than half of his 6 000 paintings.

Malevich, Kandinski and Goncharova: Avant-garde painters, early 20th century.

Chapter 6

Aleksandr Nikolayevich Ostrovsky: Russian playwright (1823-1886).

Snegurochka: Snow White. The play was later turned into an opera by Rimsky-Korsakov.

Vera Stepanovna Beljajeva: well-known Kirov theatre artist and ballet dancer.

Generation transfer: see Chapter 4.

William Congreve (1670-1729): English playwright and poet.

Chapter 7

Oymyakon: Village of 520 inhabitants in Eastern Yakutia in the Sakha Republic. In 1924, a temperature of -71.2 C was recorded there, making it the coldest inhabited place in the world.

Wandergeselle: Young craftsman who learns a trade by travelling and staying with different masters.

Adam and Eve's longing back for paradise: Genesis 3: 23.

Machine language: a system of instructions and data fed directly into a computer's central processing unit. It is the lowest-level way of programming a computer; the 'ones' and 'zeros' have to be put in one by one.

Autocode: the name of a family of 'simplified coding systems', later called programming languages, devised in the 1950s and 1960s. With languages like Fortran, Algol and Cobol there was no longer a need for the cumbersome programming in machine language.

My Damascus moment: the abbot refers to Paul's conversion on the road to Damascus, Acts of the Apostles 9:3-9.

Bob Dylan: Robert Allan Zimmerman (1941-), American singer, song writer, musician, poet, film director and painter. The line 'that he not busy born is busy dying' is from his song 'It's Alright Ma (I'm only bleeding) of 1965.

Oh Mensch, gibt acht (Oh man, beware!): poem by Friedrich Wilhelm Nietzsche (1844-1900), set to music by Gustav Mahler (1860-1911) in 'Zarathustras Mitternachtslied', part of his Symphony no. 3.

Tverskaya Prospekt: major boulevard and shopping street in central Moscow.

Chapter 8

Matrioshka: Wooden Russian doll, in which there is a smaller, similar doll, in which there is again a smaller doll and so on.

Chapter 9

Cossacks: originally members of military communities in Ukraine and southern Russia.

Gulag: the government agency that administered the penal labour camps of the Soviet Union. Also: short for Gulag Archipelago, the name given to the 476 camps in Aleksandr Solzhenitsyn's 1973 novel of the same name, which likened the scattered camps to 'a chain of islands'.

They become one flesh: Genesis 2:24.

Ganina Yama: a pit, three meters deep, in the Four Brothers Mine near the village of Koptyaki, 15 km north of Yekaterinburg.

Kirovgrad, Nizhny Tagil and Verchnaya Tura: Villages north of Yekaterinburg.

Yekaterina the Great (Ekaterina II): Tsarina of Russia, 1762-1796.

Yekaterinburg: the city was named after Yekaterina I, wife and successor of Tsar Peter the Great. Its name was changed into Sverdlovsk by the Bolsheviks in 1924, after Yakov Sverdlov, the Bolshevik commander who ordered the execution of the imperial family. It regained its original name in 1991.

Francis: Saint Francis of Assisi (1181-1226), a Catholic deacon and the founder of the Order of Friars Minor, more commonly known as the Franciscans.

In the beginning was the Word: John, 1: 1-5. See also the last note of the Introduction.

Thou seeest no other image of me than my Voice: Deuteronomy 4:12.

Our Lord has taught us to love those who hate us: Matthew 6:44.

Chapter 10

One for all and all for one: (Unus pro omnibus, omnes pro uno), motto of Alexandre Dumas' novel *The Three Musketeers* and also the traditional motto of Switzerland.

Kipling's poem: Joseph Rudyard Kipling (1865-1936), an English poet, short-story writer, novelist and 1907 Nobel Prize winner. The abbot quotes the refrain of the poem 'The Ballad of East and West' (1889).

Chapter 11
You were reunited with your other half: cf Plato: *Aristophanes in the Symposium Dialogue*.
Professional life, cultural life and religious life: See Chapters 15, 16 and 17.
Family life: See Chapter 14.

Chapter 12
Inner cylinder: See Chapter 4.

Chapter 13
Do unto others as you would have them do unto you: from Matthew 7.12: 'Therefore all things whatsoever ye would that man should do to you, do ye even so to them, for this is the law and the prophets'.
Johnny: Edna O'Brien: *Johnny, I hardly knew you*, Penguin, 1977.
Michael: Bernhard Schlink, *Der Vorleser* (The reader), Diogenes Taschenbuch, 1995. Later filmed.
Frisch's Sabeth: Max Frisch, *Homo Faber* (the man, the maker, as opposed to homo sapiens, the knowing man), Suhrkamp Verlag, 1957. The book was made into the film *Voyager* in 1961.
Füsun: Orhan Pamuk, *The Museum of Innocence*, Faber & Faber, 2010.
Berlioz: Hector Berlioz, *La damnation de Faust* (*The Damnation of Faust*), opera, 1846, based on Goethe's poem, which he took from an ancient German legend. The abbot refers to Scene XVIII.
Pierre Abélard (1079-1142): a prominent scholastic philosopher. The story of his love for Héloïse has become legendary. People still bring flowers daily to their grave at the Père Lachaise cemetery in Paris.
Elvira Madigan: film directed by Bo Widerberg (1967). The second part of Mozart's 21st piano concerto in C (KV467) contributed to no small extent to the success of the film.
Kemal: Orhan Pamuk, *The Museum of Innocence*, Faber & Faber, 2010.
Anna Karenina: Novel by Tolstoy, 1877.
Faust and Gretchen: main characters in the legend and Goethe's poem Faust.
Romeo and Juliet: play by Shakespeare, 1597.
Kabuki: genre of 17th century Japanese drama.
Tristan and Isolde: opera (1856-1859) by Richard Wagner, based on a story by Gottfried von Strassburg (around 1200).
La Traviata: opera by Verdi (1853), based on the novel *La dame aux Camélias* by Alexandre Dumas fils, 1848.
Giselle: ballet, music by Adolphe Adam. Based on a poem by Heinrich Heine.

Wayang plays: Shadow puppet theatre in Java.
Noce Blanche (White Wedding; 1989): French film, directed by Jean-Claude Brisseau.

Chapter 14

Born in sin: see also Chapter 17.

Luther: Martin Luther (1483-1546), priest and professor who initiated the church reformation in 1517.

Calvin: John Calvin (1509-1564), influential French/Swiss theologian who developed Calvinism.

Augustine: Augustine of Hippo (St. Augustine, 354-430), theologian influential in the development of Christianity. Propagated the concept of original sin.

Which was then still united: The abbot refers to the Great Schism between the Roman Catholic and Orthodox Christian Churches in 1054.

Annunciation: announcement, in this case the announcement by an angel to Mary that she was going to have a baby, Luke 1:26.

To love God and our fellow men as we love ourselves: Matthew 22:40.

Whatever you wish that others would do to you: Matthew 7:12.

I do not what I wish to do: Romans 7:14.

Chapter 15

Hermitage (literally 'retreat'): one of the oldest and largest museums in the world, located in Saint Petersburg in the former imperial Winter palace.

Mariinski: Mariinski Theatre, a well-known venue for ballet, the equivalent of the Bolshoi Theatre in Moscow.

Oktiabrsky Concert Hall: the largest and most prominent concert hall in St Petersburg.

Mister: In Russian, one never addresses someone as 'Mr'; this only creeps in at international meetings. The normal way to address a person is by using the given name and patronymic, as in 'Yevgeni Nikolayevich'. Contrary to Western habit, this does not suggest familiarity in Russian. The student here is most impolite by addressing the abbot as 'Mr'.

Gospodin: Russian for Sir. This is always followed by a surname. Leaving it out is also very impolite.

Chapter 16

Chekhov: Anton Pavlovich Chekhov (1860-1904), one of the greatest short-story writers and playwrights in world literature.

Tretyakov: The State Tretyakov Gallery in Moscow is the most important gallery of Russian art.

Alexandr Ivanov: Alexander Andreyevich Ivanov, Russian painter (1806-1858). Yavlenne Christa Narodu relates the story of Christ's baptism by John the Baptist, of Matthew 3: 13-17.

Shishkin: Ivan Ivanovich Shishkin (1832-1898), Russian landscape painter.

Mendelssohn Bartholdy: Jakob Ludwig Felix Mendelssohn Bartholdy, (1809-1847), German composer, pianist, organist and conductor of the early Romantic period. His fourth symphony, also known as 'the Italian'.

A thing of beauty is a joy forever: poem by John Keats (1795-1821).

Waterhouse: John William Waterhouse (1849-1917), an English painter who is best known for his paintings of female characters from Greek and Arthurian mythology.

Rembrandt: Rembrandt Harmenszoon van Rijn (1606-1669), a Dutch painter and etcher, generally considered one of the greatest painters in European art history. *Suzanne and the elders* was painted in 1647 and is on display in the Gemäldegalerie in Berlin. The theme is taken from the book of Daniel.

Rodin: François-Auguste-René Rodin (1840-1917), French sculptor. *Le Baiser*, the Kiss.

Kahlo: Frida Kahlo (1907-1954), Mexican painter.

Psychopompus: an escort for the dead to help them find their way to the afterlife (the Underworld in the Greek myths, Hermes being the pschychopomp).

Bergman: Ernst Ingmar Bergman (1918 –2007), Swedish director, writer and producer for film, stage and television. The host refers to his film *The Seventh Seal*.

Gauguin: Eugène Henri Paul Gauguin (1848-1903), a leading French Post-Impressionist artist. The professor refers to one of his last paintings, *The Ford The Flight*.

Tomasi di Lampedusa: the professor refers to Chapter VII, *Death of a Prince*, in the novel *The Leopard* by Giuseppe Tomasi di Lampedusa (1896-1957), according to many the most impressive dying scene in world literature. The novel was published in 1958 and filmed by Luchino Visconti in 1963.

Isherwood: the professor refers to Kenny in the novel *Single Man* (1964) by Christopher Isherwood, filmed by Tom Ford (2009).

Thomas Mann: (1875-1955), a German novelist, short story writer, social critic, philanthropist, essayist, and winner of the 1929 Nobel Prize for Literature. The professor refers to his novella *Death in Venice* (*Der Tod in Venedig*, 1912). The novella was filmed by Luchino Visconti (1971).

Portrait of an elderly man: painted by Rembrandt in 1667 and on display in the Mauritshuis in The Hague.

Picasso: Pablo Picasso (1881-1973): Spanish painter and sculptor. The guest refers to the *Self Portrait Facing Death* of 1972, now at Fuji Television Gallery, Tokyo.

Lucian Freud, Self-Portrait, Reflection, 2002 (in a private collection). Freud (1922-2011) painted a number of self-portraits, calling the later ones 'Reflection'. Although the Reflection of 2002 was his last self-portrait, the guest was not entirely correct in listing this painting as a 'portrait facing death'.

Stabat Mater: a thirteenth century hymn. Its title is an abbreviation of the first line, *Stabat mater dolorosa* ('The sorrowful mother stood'). The hymn, one of the most powerful medieval poems, meditates on the suffering of Mary, Jesus Christ's mother, during and after his crucifixion.

Rossini: Gioachino Antonio Rossini (1792-1868), Italian composer. He put the *Stabat Mater* to music in 1832 and 1841.

Requiem (Requiem or Requiem Mass): a liturgical service of the Roman Catholic Church for the repose of the soul of a deceased person.

Webber: Andrew Lloyd Webber (born 1948), English composer of musicals. He wrote his *Requiem* in 1982, dedicated to his father.

Im Abendrot (At sunset): poem by Joseph von Eichendorff, put to music by Richard Strauss in 1948. One of the *Four Last Songs*.

Thomas Cole: American painter (1801-1845). He painted *The Voyage of Life* in 1839-1840, now in the National Gallery of Art in Washington.

Bedrich Smetana: Czech composer (1824-1884). He composed *Má vlast* (My Fatherland), a cycle of six symphonic poems, between 1875 and 1882.

The return of the prodigal son: painted by Rembrandt between 1662 and 1669, now in the Hermitage Museum, St Petersburg.

Sophocles: Greek dramatist, 497-406 BC. *Oedipus the King* (Oedipus Rex in Latin) in which a son unknowingly kills his father and marries his mother, was first performed in 439 BC.

Hemingway: Ernest Miller Hemingway (1899-1961), American author and journalist who, won the Nobel Prize in Literature in 1954. He wrote the novella *The Old Man and the Sea* in 1952.

Christ of St John of the Cross: by Spanish painter Salvador Dali (1904-1989) in surrealistic style, completed in 1951, on display in Glasgow's Kelvingrove Art Gallery and Museum.

Jan van Eyck: (1395 –1441), Flemish painter active in Bruges and considered one of the best Northern European painters of the 15th century. The Ghent Altarpiece *The Adoration of the Mystic Lamb* was painted in 1432.

Kaddish: prayer in the Jewish prayer service. The central theme of the Kaddish is the magnification and sanctification of God's name. The term 'Kaddish' is often used to refer to 'The Mourners' Kaddish'.

Kievo-Pecherskaya Lavra: the Kiev monastery of the caves (Lavra is a large monastery). See also Chapter 5.

Bortniansky: Dmytro Stepanovych Bortniansky (1751-1825), Ukrainian composer, mainly active in Russia.

Debussy's Syrinx: A piece of music for flute solo, 1913.

Sermon of the Mount: Matthew 5-7.

Samarkand mosque: The *Bibi-Khanym Mosque* of Samarkand, Uzbekistan.

Aya Sofia, (Hagia Sofia, 'The holy wisdom'), Wisdom Church, built in 532-538 in Istanbul, later a mosque, now a museum.

Sultan Ahmed Mosque: popularly known as the Blue Mosque.

Assumption Cathedral in Moscow: Built in 1475-79 to underline Moscow's ambition of being 'the third Rome' (after Rome and Constantinople; Constantinople fell in 1453 to the Turks and the Russian tsars took over the role of leader of the Orthodox Church, including the emblem of the double-headed eagle).

York Minster: York Cathedral, York.

Gothic cathedrals etc: all in France.

Sainte-Chapelle: La Sainte-Chapelle (The Holy Chapel), in the centre of Paris, commissioned by King Louis IX of France, later Saint Louis, built between 1239 and 1248.

Transverberation of Saint Teresa (the ecstasy of Saint Theresa): sculpture by Bernini in the Santa Maria della Vittoria in Rome.

Bernini (1598-1680): leading Italian Baroque sculptor and architect in Rome.

Expel the merchants from the Temple: Matthew 21: 12-17.

Spaso-Preobrazhenskiy Monastery: Monastery of the Transfiguration of our Saviour, Matthew 17:1-13.

Chapter 17

Mysticism: the pursuit of communion with, or conscious awareness of an ultimate reality, divinity, spiritual truth, or God through direct experience, intuition, instinct or insight.

Unio mystica: the union with God, eternity, the other world, etc.

Yayoi Kusama (1929-), Japanese avant-garde artist and writer, one of the most creative talents of the twentieth century. Her 'Infinity Net' paintings, large canvasses in a few off-white colours, are made up of carefully repeated arcs of paint built up into large patterns.

Cécile Ex (1965-), Dutch visual artist.

He spent a great deal of his life in the desert: Matthew 4: 1-11.

The Essenes: a Jewish religious group (much smaller than the Pharisees and the Sadducees, the other two major sects at the time) that flourished from the 2nd century BC to the 1st century AD. The Essenes were dedicated to asceticism, voluntary poverty, and abstinence from worldly pleasures, including marriage, and daily baptisms. Both Jesus and John the Baptist are believed to have been members of the Essenes.

John the Baptist: a mission preacher and a major religious figure who led a movement of baptism at the River Jordan in expectation of a divine apocalypse that would restore occupied Israel. He was killed around the year 30.

Behold, I was shapen in iniquity: Psalm 51:5.

Behold the lamb of God: John 1:29.

Meister Eckhart: Eckhart von Hochheim (about 1260-1327), commonly known as Meister Eckhart, a German theologian, philosopher and mystic. Meister is German for 'Master', referring to the academic title Magister in Theology he obtained in Paris.

Rites in which God is uniquely active: quoted from Hexam's *Concise Dictionary of Religion*.

But after me will come one who is more powerful than I, whose sandals I am not fit to carry: Matthew 3:11.

Menno Simons (1496 –1561): a Dutch religious leader from the Friesland region. Simons was a contemporary of the Protestant Reformers and his followers became known as Mennonites.

Zwingli: Huldrych Zwingli (1484-1531), a Swiss church reformer.

Ave Maria: Hail Mary, Mother of God, pray for us sinners now and in the hour of our death: central prayer in the Roman Catholic and the Orthodox Churches.

Pater Noster: Our father, Matthew 6:9-15.

Isis: goddess of motherhood, magic and fertility in Ancient Egyptian, whose worship spread throughout the Greco-Roman world.

Thomas à Kempis (1380-1471): late Medieval Catholic monk and probable author of *The Imitation of Christ*, one of the best known Christian books on devotion.

Bellum Judaicum (The Jewish War): Flavius Josephus's book of the history of the Jewish War against the Romans, written in the year 75. Flavius Josephus was a very well informed Jewish-Roman historian.

Pier Paolo Pasolini (1922-1975): Italian poet, film director, and writer. The film *Sopralluoghi in Palestina per il vangelo secondo Matteo* (Investigation of the events in Palestine according to the gospel according to St. Matthew) was made in 1965.

Apostels: Literally: messengers, here meaning missionaries.

Paul: The self-appointed apostle to the Gentiles (non-Jewish people).

Grand Inquisitor of Seville: from Fyodor Dostoyevsky's last novel: *The Brothers Karamazov*.

Chapter 18

Spaso-Preobrazhenskiy ('Transfiguration of our Saviour): Matthew 17:1-13.

Gethsemane (literary: oil press): a garden at the foot of the Mount of Olives in Jerusalem most famous as the place where Jesus and his disciples (students) prayed the night before Jesus' crucifixion. While his disciples had fallen asleep, Jesus prayed three times 'to take this cup away from me', the cup meaning the crucifixion. Matthew 26: 36-46.

Faithful is he that calleth you, who also will do it: Thessalonians 1:24.

Die Zauberflöte (The Magic Flute): last opera of Wolfgang Amadeus Mozart, 1791.

The new Jerusalem: Revelations, 3:12 and 21:2.

Chapter 19

Robert Herrick (1591-1674): 17th century English poet. The abbot quotes his poem: 'To the Virgins, to Make Much of Time'.

Waterhouse: John William Waterhouse (1849-1917), an English painter who is most famous for his paintings of female characters from Greek and Arthurian mythology.

Weltgeist (world spirit): a metaphysical principle that helps explain the world, especially used by the German philosopher Hegel.

Sintrom: (Acenocoumarol), anticoagulant, used to treat and prevent blood clots in the veins.

Chapter 20

In the Act of the Apostles 1:1-11 it is described that Jesus appeared and spoke to the apostles until forty days after his resurrection. He was then lifted up and disappeared in a cloud.

Chapter 21

Nostre vite gaudia abstulisti omnia (All my joyful life has been taken away): from a 13th century codex of 250 songs and poems of Benediktbeuern, Bavaria. Put to music by Carl Orff (1985-1982) as the Carmina Burana (Songs from Bayern).

Jesus after the ascension: see note Chapter 20.

Tous les homes sont mortels: (All Men are Mortal), novel by French writer and philosopher Simone de Beauvoir (1946).

The ballad of Narayama: a film by Shohei Imamura, 1983.

Spring, summer, autumn, winter... and spring: a film by Kim Ki-duk, 2003.

Überm Sternenzelt, muß ein lieber Vater wohnen (High above the starry sky, there is a loving Father, dwelling): line from Friedrich Schiller's poem *Ode an die Freude* (Ode to Joy), 1785. Put to music in Beethoven's ninth symphony.

Memento mori: Remember you will die.

Carpe diem: Seize the day. Live the life to the full.

Epliogue

The central human deficit: see Chapter 14.

Love is the child of trust and respect: see Chapters 4 and 12.

Montessori system: The Montessori method employs the natural curiosity of the child and the fact that a child learns by playing. Older children guide younger ones. Based on the work of Italian educator Maria Montessori (1870-1952).